THE DARK ARCHETYPE

Exploring the Shadow Side of the Divine

DENISE DUMARS
LORI NYX

NEW PAGE BOOKS
A division of The Career Press, Inc.
Franklin Lakes, NJ

This book is dedicated to the "Smart Beast" in us all.

THE DARK ARCHETYPE
EDITED BY LAUREN MANOY
TYPESET BY EILEEN DOW MUNSON
Cover illustration and design: Jean William Naumann
Printed in the U.S.A. by Book-mart Press

To order this title, please call toll-free 1-800-CAREER-1 (NJ and Canada: 201-848-0310) to order using VISA or MasterCard, or for further information on books from Career Press.

The Career Press, Inc., 3 Tice Road, PO Box 687,
Franklin Lakes, NJ 07417
www.careerpress.com
www.newpagebooks.com

Library of Congress Cataloging-in-Publication Data
Dumars, Denise.
  The dark archetype : exploring the shadow side of the divine / by Denise Dumars & Lori Nyx.
    p. cm.
  Includes bibliographical references and index.
  ISBN 1-56414-693-6 (pbk.)
    1. Magic. 2. Gods—Miscellanea. 3. Goddesses—Miscellanea. I. Nyx, Lori. II. Title.

BF1623.G63D86 2003
202'.112—dc22   2003059958

Contents

Part Three
Bad Boys, Bad Boys, Whatcha Gonna Do?
The Dark Gods
67

PART FOUR
RITUALS, SPELLS, TALISMANS, AND CORRESPONDENCES
117

Who's Afraid of the Dark?

What is it about the dark that frightens us? Why are so many of us unwilling or unable to acknowledge the power of the darkness? Power. Hmm, there's an interesting word. In Santeria and Vodou no one is afraid of power; it is a buzzword, in fact. You may have heard the word: Aché, Ashé, or Ase, depending upon the tradition. It's not for no reason that the seven principle orishas of Santería are often referred to as "The Seven African Powers."

What is it about this word that frightens us? We have all seen the misuse of power; maybe that's the problem. But can power be wielded wisely? Of course. It is done so every day, all around the world. So what we need, then, is empowerment. We seek to empower each other: for example, our sisters and brothers in the Craft. But when we want to wield power for ourselves—aye, there's the rub.

Perhaps it's because there's an aspect of magickal power that scares us. Like the dark side of the Force in the *Star Wars* mythology, power seems to come from a dark and scary place. We're afraid that somehow, as with the Force's dark side, it will seduce us and we will misuse it.

The genesis of this book came from our frustration at seeing all too many of our sisters and brothers in the Craft without power. I am upset when I see them walk through life afraid—afraid to succeed in the secular world; afraid to be proud of who they are; afraid of their own shadows, sometimes, it seems. And just what is so frightening about those shadows, anyway? It's good to stay in the shadows when there's a hole in the ozone layer!

First of all, to accept the Goddess—the feminine side of creation—is to accept her in all her guises. Yes, it is lovely to imagine her as the Maiden, the spirit of youth and new beginnings. Yes, it is lovely to imagine her as the Mother, giver of life and nurturer of each of us. And yes, it is lovely to see her as the Crone, the wise elder to whom we turn when in need of advice. But these archetypes are also much, much more, and in order to understand them and their full potential—and understand and access the full potential of each of us—we must look to the darkness as well as to the light.

For that maiden is also the student who must fight her way through gang wars and sexual harassment; she must fight for equality in the intellectual and athletic worlds; she must shield herself from deadly sexually transmitted diseases at the same time she is discovering her burgeoning sexuality.

The mother is also the woman who must try to break the glass ceiling without cutting her own wrists. She must often juggle parenting, household, and professional duties while being excoriated in the media for being a single or a working mother, or for preferring to remain childless—all this while trying to find fulfillment in her career, relationships, and family.

The crone is also the woman who must fight against ageism in her profession, who must find the truth about her own aging process while keeping doctors from unnecessarily mutilating her body, who must protect herself from predators in our society and rail against those who see seniors as invisible.

Many of us come from Dianic traditions where we felt that it was important to worship solely the female side of divinity in order to bring balance to an out-of-balance world that, by and large, sees deity as male-only. But now is the time to reclaim the God as well as the Goddess. We feel moved to extend our hands toward the male deities who so often were demonized for their masculine prowess and associations with death.

There are gods and goddesses who fit the archetypes we need most, who will bring us the power that many of us feel has been denied to us. But to access them we must not be afraid. They have always been with us—sometimes as our shadows, sometimes as that inner voice that we are taught in our youth to ignore.

In this book we will look at the archetypes of god and goddess power that have been demonized by patriarchy and which even some of today's Pagans find frightening. We will look at how and why these deities may be safely accessed.

Now ask yourself this question: Why are you afraid of the dark?

Let's try this exercise to explore the fear of darkness: Start just after dark, preferably on a Saturday. Turn on all the lights in your bedroom, close the door, and then walk from the doorway to the opposite wall and back, taking stock of your path and the placement of furniture and other objects in the room. Then turn out all the lights. Stand still with your eyes closed and take three deep breaths, exhaling completely between breaths. Now open your eyes and cross the room again. Trip over anything? Feel apprehensive? Now close your eyes again. This time visualize the layout of the room, the objects in your path. Take as long as you need until you feel centered. Now open your eyes and cross the room again. Got your "night vision" yet? I thought so! And we haven't even done any magick...well, not much anyway. Author H. P. Lovecraft's grandfather did this with his young grandson to cure him of his fear of the dark. It worked, and Lovecraft went on to write some of the most influential supernatural fiction of the 20th century. Coincidence?

You won't find political correctness in this book. Honesty is what you will find instead. Denise is a professor of English; Lori is an art historian. This book comes from a solid background in scholarship and from actual experience with these deities. So if you have courage, if you are willing to accept the darkness with the light, and if you have a rock-solid set of ethics that helps you to understand the difference between darkness and evil, then come with us. We have something very special to show you.

Honey, I am not all sweetness and light.

That was the New Age eighties.

Thank God, that phase is over.

> —quoted by Jennifer Louden in *The Comfort
> Queen's Guide to Life*

We have been taught that taking the Spiritual path means rising *above* pain. In fact, taking the Spiritual path allows the acceptance of *all that is*. It means embracing the darkness as much as the light. In the darkness, many seeds of greatness have been sown.

> —Susan Jeffers, Ph.D., *End the Struggle and
> Dance With Life*

Part One

Working With the Dark Archetypes

What Is the Dark Archetype?

The Dark Archetype basically deals with all of those things that we are taught to ignore, to sweep under the rug, to not think about; in other words, those things we keep in the dark: death, anger, fear, illness, and yes, even sex. It is no accident that the word *occult*, which simply means "hidden," is a pejorative nowadays. Instead we are expected to use terms such as "New Age" or "Metaphysics." Euphemisms are but one way our society seeks to cover up the topics it would rather not deal with.

The Dark Archetype is represented in our culture by those images in films, television, and popular literature that many in the Wiccan/Neo-Pagan community have tried so hard to dispel all these years—understandably so, mind you, in the face of criticism of our path by mainstream religions. So don't look at the Baba Yaga of Russian folktales as a typical Witch, they tell us: Witches are young and beautiful!

And heaven forbid you should look up to Maleficent, the magnificent Witch in Disney's *Sleeping Beauty*. Oh, really? Then why are her sister and brother villains and she so popular that Disneyland opened the Villain Shop, where you can buy tchotchkes of all your favorite evil Disney characters? Let's face it; some of us like the pointy-toothed, red-lipped, Dracula-caped, bustier-clad wicked witches of film and television. If you're reading this book, chances are you do, too!

The reality is that Witches come in all sizes, shapes, and ages, as do the Goddess and the God. The Dark Archetype has a necklace of human skulls like Kali; a wolf's head like Volos; a crone's face like Baba Yaga, and a black robe and a pointy hat like Hekate. Some wish these archetypes would just go away. But they won't. They can't because we need them.

Some of our Wiccan friends make a fetish out of hating horror films and stories. They're "too scary" for them. Explain to us, then, how they practice magick? There isn't anything scarier than trafficking in the unseen, dealing with entities that we perhaps have only the vaguest understanding of, and then trying to manipulate reality through one's own will. Holy cow, Hathor! Nothing's scarier than that, except perhaps brain surgery.

Think about the color of darkness, the enveloping blackness. What comes to mind? If we learned anything from the Civil Rights Movement of the 1960s, it was that "Black is Beautiful." Then why are we still calling negative magic "black"? Why are we still considering the cowboy in the black hat (or the Witch in the black robe) to be the bad guy?

The true Witch takes the darkness with the light, the good with the bad, and the end with the beginning. It is in darkness that we sleep; it is often in darkness that we make love, and in both cases we experience "petits morts." It is important that we acknowledge what happens in the dark and the power it unleashes for what it is: a reaffirmation of life and yes, the light.

Most of us also do rituals in the dark, without electric lights, usually with only candles or starlight for illumination. What is the outcome of such a ritual? Consider a recent ritual we attended that did not adequately deal with its own dark aspects or the power it called up:

The ritual took place in the dark backyard of a suburban dwelling. It was a Dark of the Moon ritual, and Hekate was invoked. A spiral dance was performed, and power arose—but it had nowhere to go. Rather than release the dark energy evoked, the ritual turned into an adventure in wimpiness, with "gifts from the goddess" being nothing more than fortune cookie platitudes. The corners that had been called were dismissed (another bad idea—deities should be thanked, not dismissed like schoolchildren), but the power raised was still there. Inside the home a surge of kundalini energy swept through the cocktail-party-like crowd. Many people were obviously feeling uncomfortable as the sexual energy spread around the room, and it was clear to us that the leaders of the ritual had no idea what they were calling upon. How interesting that a ritual featuring a death crone should end in a surge of sexual energy! There you have it: the life force coming from death—from the dark.

When you access darkness, you access power, and it is up to you what you do with it. It can consume you, like a black hole in space, or it can set you free.

How Is the Dark Archetype Accessed?

Uh, very carefully. Now that we've gotten that part over with, let's get real. In the Rituals, Spells, Talismans, and Correspondences section of this book you will find specific methods for taking you into the realm of the Dark Archetype. It is assumed that you are not a neophyte and have had proper training and experience in magickal rituals, and know how to cast a Circle and use elementary ritual tools. However, because when one "assumes," she makes an "ass" out of "u and me," we will go over the basics of accessing the power of the Dark Archetypes.

Always use protection! It's important to understand how to do so while attempting any kind of magickal working or trafficking with gods, spirits, and other discarnate entities. Bear in mind that instructions in the Rituals section may vary a bit from these basics depending upon the intention of the ritual or the pantheon accessed.

Magickal protection begins with what is called casting a Circle, calling the corners, or calling the Elements. Whenever you call the four Elements of magick—Earth, Air, Fire, and Water—you are also calling the Elementals that inhabit these spheres of influence. With Earth you get gnomes; with Air you get sylphs; with Fire you get salamanders; with Water you get undines; and with six you get eggroll. Traditionally there are four corners. Some just cast a Circle by walking the perimeter of those assembled with symbols of the four Elements. In calling the corners, some call the Elementals by name. We often add deities to the mix. Many Witches also add a fifth direction—the Center, which represents Spirit. The ancient and venerable Hindu rituals call ten directions, so every tradition has its own way of looking at such things.

Traditionally, in the United States we call Air in the East, Fire in the South, Water in the West, and Earth in the North. Other traditions and other places may do this differently; go with what works for you, and start deosil (clockwise) to cast the Circle. You will open (we dislike the practice of "dismissing," and believe the entities and gods do, too) the Circle widdershins (counterclockwise). Don't forget to open the Circle when you are done—

nobody likes hanging around wondering if it's okay to leave, even if She is a goddess.

Begin with your athame, wand, ankh, rolling pin, or whatever magickal tool you care to use, including your own hands. You will want to draw a pentagram in the air. You can also do this at the end, but because I cannot draw a widdershins pentagram to save my life (I leave the spatial relationships to Lori), I just do what feels right. In some rituals you may not want to draw a pentagram at all, or you may use ritual gestures such as mudras instead. Most traditional Wiccans and Neo-Pagans use a symbol on the altar for each Element: incense or ringing a bell for Air, a candle for Fire, a libation for Water, and salt or a crystal for Earth. Now, face the East and begin. Here is a suggestion for calling the five directions. Modify the lines as you please:

Elementals of the East
The sylphs that glide on air
The Element of intellect, creativity, flight, breath,
Attend us now!
Thoth, Athena, Borias
Be here now!

Elementals of the South
Salamanders engendered of fire
The Element of passion, of cleansing, of forging
Attend us now!
Sekhmet, Vulcan, Pele
Be here now!

Elementals of the West
Undines, children of the waves
The Element of water, of nurturing, of growing
Attend us now!
Yemaya, Tiamat, Neptune
Be here now!

Elementals of the North
Gnomes of the earth
The Element of germinating, endings, grounding
Attend us now!
Hekate, Kali, Osiris
Be here now!

(optional)
Elementals of the Center
The spirits within
The Element of the soul, the psyche, the voice
Attend us now!
Bastet, Kwan Yin, Obatala
Be here now!

Now you are ready to do your ritual. When you end your ritual, return to the corners beginning with the North (or Center, if you have called it), repeat the first three lines of each invocation, and end with a version of one of the following: "We thank you for blessing our ritual. Go if you must, but stay if you will. The circle is open, but unbroken. Merry Meet and Merry Part and Merry Meet again!" or, "You who have honored us with your presence, we salute you. Go in graciousness. Blessed be."

As additional protection you may enact an invisible shield. Remember how the starships on *Star Trek* shield themselves with an invisible force field? It's like that, only without cheesy special effects. This is where we get into a big fight with other trads in the Craft. Some say that you should only shield yourself when you are able to bolster the shields with conscious power, but many of us believe in shielding ourselves before going to sleep, if only to feel more safe and secure in our beds. It is up to you. Do as thou wilt shall be the whole of the law...oh, sorry, channeling Uncle Al there for a minute. Anyway, here's how to shield yourself. You can do this sitting or lying down, but because it's a better meditative position, let's do it sitting down.

First you need to feel grounded and in proper balance with the universe. Place your feet flat on the floor. Hold your hands palms up, comfortably, on your lap. Close your eyes. Take a deep breath in through your nose; let it all out through your mouth. As you inhale, feel roots from deep within the ground reaching up and connecting with the soles of your feet, connecting you with the Earth. As you exhale, feel the light from the stars come down into your head, illuminating your mind and connecting you with the universe. Take at least three of these "pranic" breaths or as many as you need in order to feel grounded.

Power to the shields, Scotty! Keep your eyes closed. Inhale again, but this time feel a column of white light (or whatever color works for you) rising up around you like a force field. Keep this process up, adding more "power" to the shield as necessary. Some see this shield as a nimbus of white light. I have sometimes seen it as a fountain of sparking light, like fireworks, spouting out of a blessed violet lotus suspended above my crown chakra. Some use pink light, especially before bed, as it comforts as well as protects and brings positive, loving vibes. Blue light is cooling and healing and should be used if you are ill or in pain.

Some extend the "force field" all around the room, while some "draw" it around doors and windows too. Shields should be self-supporting once put up and can be released by literally "grounding"—that is, by placing one's hands and feet on the floor, dissipating the energy into the Earth. It's a good idea to eat something after any ritual work to further ground oneself. A shield placed before sleep dissipates of its own accord when the sleeper awakes.

Are we there yet? When do we get to do our ritual? Soon, bubbelah. But there is yet more protection that one might wish to take. Depending upon your ritual, you may wish to wear a pentagram, a sigil of some type, a piece of jewelry representing a deity, or a medicine bag. Protective symbols can be placed around the room or the whole house. They need not be fancy or expensive. A cheap gargoyle statue is a fine household guardian. A horseshoe with the open end up, nailed over the front door, is also a good house protector. Around the peephole in my front door is a pentagram made of ocote wood from Mexico. Not one to traffic with fairies, I use the horseshoe to keep the "Good People" out and the pentagram to keep out the "bad people"!

On my computer keyboard is a Mardi Gras doubloon from the Krewe of Thoth. Because Thoth is the Egyptian god of writing and academics, and is therefore one of my patron deities, it makes the perfect amulet for my computer. Think about a symbol of protection that fits your lifestyle. Nearly any botanica, occult shop, or online magickal supply will sell some kind of Protection oil. These are fine if you wish to use them. Sandalwood or lotus oil works well, too.

Feel protected? Hope so. Now make sure you have your deities and magickal properties firmly understood before beginning. For example, you wouldn't want to chow down on filet mignon before calling on Kali (sacred cows and all that). In fact, the real protection is reading about, meditating on, and understanding the deity you are calling on. There is no substitute for doing your homework. Of course, the deities aren't grading you on your performance. The gods laugh at our mistakes, and we need to lighten up, too.

Now go and learn the truth by doing.

"Love is the law; love under will."
    —Aleister Crowley
      (sometimes referred to as Uncle Al)

Part Two ———————————————

Femmes Fatales:
The Dark
Goddesses

Baba Yaga: The Witch-Cult in Eastern Europe

By Denise Dumars

Margaret Murray was right. She just needed to venture a little further east to prove her point: The witch-cult did persist in Europe, primarily in Russia and other parts of Eastern Europe, into the modern age. One of the proofs of this pudding is the existence in most peoples' imaginations of Baba Yaga.

The stereotype of the Witch—old hag, dressed in black with a babuschka on her head—comes directly from fairy tales featuring Baba Yaga, folktales that made it literally all the way around the world from the taiga of Siberia to the redwoods of California. When I was a child, fairy tales were in great abundance in the local library, and I read all I could find. Baba Yaga was not only a fixture in collections of Russian fairy tales, she popped up in general collections as well. Echoes of her penchant for devouring youngsters were seen in Grimm; the Witch who caught Hansel and Gretel might as well be Baba Yaga's Bavarian cousin. This is no accident; Jacob Grimm is one of history's finest mythologists, and his multi-volume set *Teutonic Mythology* is an amazing overview of European folklore, Pagan religion, and myth.

But Baba Yaga did not start out as a Witch. Though her name translates to "old hag," she was originally a horse goddess, and even in modern stories she is said to have 40 mares as daughters. Her hut is in the deepest, most remote forest, and she is a primal Earth deity who can control weather, animals, and plants. Another of her names is *Khoziaka Lesa*, "Mistress of the Forest." Her earliest representations have her looking middle-aged, kindly, and wearing a married woman's headdress.

With her spinning wheel—a symbol of the cycle of life—she weaves the web of life from the bones of the dead. She is described as a chthonic Earth deity who, like Plouton, controls the riches of the Earth. Some see her house as marking the spot where the worlds of the living and the dead meet.

Later on in mythology, Baba Yaga, whose name can also mean "grandmother Witch," becomes more frightening and demonic. She not only has mares as children, but also reptiles and supernatural beings. She hangs around with vampires, werewolves, and the left-hand path magicians known as the Volkhvi (see Volos).

Although Baba Yaga has many children she has no consort. This is not unusual in Slavic mythology; there are many myths of parthenogenesis throughout Eastern Europe. But this does not mean that Baba Yaga doesn't like men. She often appears as a beautiful young woman to hunters or soldiers who stray off the beaten path and happen onto her hut. She often grants them boons, whereas she is not as kind to most women who come upon her dwelling.

Baba Yaga does embody a few unusual props that set her apart from other Witches of her ilk. The first is her flying machine: No broomstick for this aviatrix! Baba Yaga flies in a huge mortar and steers with a pestle. The symbolism is both obvious and unique. A mortar and pestle set is a typical Witch's tool—herbs and other ingredients for potions are ground in one. So she is literally flying in a symbol of her craft. Secondly, the mortar and pestle resembles the lingam and yoni set-up in Hindu mythology, which is so often associated with Shiva/Shakti. The pestle, being the symbol of the male organ, makes Baba Yaga's control over it part of her scariness—especially to men! For who were most feared in old Europe but the women who didn't need men—women alone, who had either never married and so could live to a ripe old age having sidestepped the dangers of childbearing, or widows, especially those with property and money. These "women alone," especially if they were elderly, were seen as quite threatening to the "natural order" of things (women as men's property). The mere fact that such a woman could live to an old age was sometimes considered proof of her sorcerous abilities. Her appearance—back bowed by osteoporosis, chin and nose seeming to almost meet as her teeth fell out, hairs bristling on her chin now that her estrogen had waned, and wispy white hair and milky, cataract-clouded eyes made her frightening in lands where old age was mostly just a rumor.

Baba Yaga's house had an interesting architectural detail—it stood on huge chicken legs, so that when she wanted to see above the treetops, all she had to do was have the legs stretch out and raise the house. Ah, chickens in religion! They're not just for Vodou anymore. Her property also boasts a fence made of human bones, and each fence post is crowned with a human skull whose eye sockets flash red at night. Baba Yaga sweeps her house with the traditional birch broom, a symbol of the sacred sauna. In some stories—again, in striking similarity to details in "Hansel and Gretel"—Baba Yaga's house is made of pierogies, blinis, and other Russian treats. So much the better to lure in young people for the soup pot! Stray Urchin Stroganoff, anyone?

But what was the purpose of the continuing myth of Baba Yaga, other than using her as a bogeywoman to frighten children into being good? Most of her tales have to do with capturing and con-spiring to devour young people. She often fails at her evil task, primarily because her familiars, usually a cat, a dog, and a rooster (sometimes also a horse), are so abused by their mistress that they aid the captive in making his or her escape. Sometimes these ani-mals embody the spirit of Baba Yaga herself, as in Russian myth where a person's astral form can travel around in the body of a cat, dog, bird, or other animal while the person's body is asleep. This is how she sometimes catches her young prey conspiring with her pets.

Are you scared yet? No? Well then consider, for example, the following: Ibn Fadlan, the ancient Arabic anthropologist, wit-nessed a funeral among the Viking Rus. During this funeral the dead chieftain was not only set aboard his ship and then burned, but his young mistress was sacrificed so that she could go with him into the afterlife. The person appointed to carry out such tasks was an old woman, whom the assembled funeral attendees called the Angel of Death. She slit the young woman's throat, and then the dead girl was placed on the boat with her lord and burned.

Is that scary enough for you? Undoubtedly. The story of a scary old woman killing young folks is not just a myth, it was a practice. Even into the Christian era, the power of the crone was acknowledged. Russians and other Slavs honor their ancestors.

Some believe in the *Stopen*, a protective house spirit that is also an ancestor. To honor the *Stopen*, the crone in the family performs a house blessing ritual. She sacrifices a black hen, sprinkling its blood on the coals in the hearth. She then roasts the chicken, and makes a special cake. She pours three cups of wine and places them in the loft, attic, or top floor of the house, in three corners of the room, along with the left leg of the chicken and pieces of the cake. She pours more wine on the fire, and then she and the family feast and sing the praises of the *Stopen*. If some of the wine or food is later found missing, it is considered a sign that the *Stopen* is in residence and appreciates the offering.

The Russians also celebrate a holiday very much like the more familiar Mexican holiday, the Day of the Dead. On St. Demetrius's Day (Oct. 26), the family visits the cemetery and brings offerings to departed loved ones. Men may leave vodka for the dead and brandish swords to frighten away evil spirits. Back at home, a "dumb supper" takes place. A place is set at the table for the departed. The family sits down to eat and prayers are said to bless the ancestors . Any sudden sound such as a gust of wind, branches scraping on the window, or a moth flying into the room is taken as a sign that the spirits of the dead have arrived. The departed are then served food and drink along with the rest of the family.

Clearly, Baba Yaga is both a frightening and an essential part of Slavic mythology. She is the crone in the triple goddess form of Russia—Rusalka being the maiden, Mokosh "Mother Moist Earth" being the mother. But watch out—that beautiful girl by the river might sing the siren song of the Rusalki, who are also water sprites. She might sing you to your death, especially if you're a handsome young man (or maybe that's Baba Yaga in Rusalka's diaphanous gown, throwing a glamour on you). Whereas Mokosh is wholly good—she is the mother of all the Russian gods, is considered literally to be Mother Russia, and is the Earth itself, like Gaia—she does not exist alone. She needs Baba Yaga to do her dirty work, to play the role of the evil Witch, and to bring death—which, although feared, is a necessary part of life.

The Black Virgin: She Is Black Because She Is Goddess

By Lori Nyx

Tonight is a holy night, a night when a divine child's birth is venerated by millions. Being a modern Pagan, my thoughts are not of this sacred child, symbol of light, renewal, and hope. Rather they dwell upon his mother—the Blessed Virgin and her miraculous and mysterious nature.

In mid-December, devout Mexican-Americans celebrate the feast day of Our Lady of Guadalupe. Too busy and cross with mundane activities and pre-Yule preparations, I only realized it was her feast day when I happened to catch the late late news on a local Spanish TV station. As I watched Angelenos offering flowers and lighting votives at a host of local churches, I was filled with regret that I hadn't remembered to honor her myself, this dark-skinned Madonna of the Americas

It has taken me until Christmas Eve to remember the Holy Virgin again, and in true Nyxian fashion. For it is not the sublimely beautiful pale-faced Marys of a thousand nativity scenes and holy cards that haunt my imagination, but rather the dark countenance of Guadalupe and her sister black and brown Madonnas worldwide. And so this evening I will burn a special incense made of rose, cedar, and frankincense, light a white novena candle emblazoned with the image of the Dark Mother of God, and begin to write about the cult of the Black Virgin.

All right, I concede. The Black Virgin is not the typical archetype one expects to find in a book written by Pagans for Pagans. She is a Catholic icon—the Virgin Mary, a semi-divine, all-merciful being who sits somewhere in Heaven between the saints, the angels, and God on high. She is supposed to be the Mother of Christ, a benevolent symbol of purity and light.

So why include her? Well, if you are going to get picky, Black Virgins are *literally* dark in appearance. Of course, there is far more to them than that. If we look beneath the surface of things, we find that this other face of Mary is figuratively dark as well. As an archetype she is akin to darkness itself: mysterious, hidden, quiet, primal, and timeless.

In hundreds of European chapels, churches, and monasteries, as well as in museums and private collections, powerful icons of the Virgin Mary are depicted with dark-tinted skin. These *Vierges Noires*, as the French call them, are perceived as anomalies: quaint and crudely wrought relics of medieval Catholicism that are far outnumbered by traditional "white" depictions of the Madonna. They are figures of mystery—little known in the United States. Even in Europe where they have been venerated since the Dark Ages, these odd representations of Mary are relegated to secluded chapels or dark corners and crypts of cathedrals. Despite their seeming anonymity, Black Madonnas are devoutly embraced by the thousands of faithful who flock to their sites year after year in the hope of receiving miraculous healings and divine intercessions.

How could black depictions of the Virgin Mary sneak past centuries of racist thinking *and* Church tradition? Hmm, there's certainly more here than meets the eye.

So, why is she black? The Catholic Church is decidedly closed-mouthed on that score. Ean Begg, author of the preeminent source on Black Virgin sites in Europe, recounts the story of the curious man who asked a priest why the Madonna in his church was black. The truly enlightening reply to his innocent query was "She is Black Because She is Black!" Of course there are those literalists who believe that these images are based on ancient portraits of Mary who was supposedly sunburned during her sojourn in Egypt! No, I'm not making this up. On the other hand, St. Bernard of Clairvaux, the 14th-century mystic and champion of Black Madonnas everywhere, said that the Virgin's blackness connotes her inherent humbleness and piety.

Okay folks, let's take a look at the symbolism of blackness beyond stereotypes for a second. From an occult standpoint this color represents mystery and hidden wisdom. In ancient times blackness was a sign of fertility—particularly the fertile nurturing earth. The Jungians equate black with the Earth and the womb, but it also signifies the power of death and man's innate fear of darkness. From a strictly "Gimbutesque" perspective, black is the color of the Destroyer side of the Great Mother Goddess.

Black images of Mary began to make their appearance in Europe as early as the 4th century c.e., but they were most popular during the 11th-century Gothic Renaissance. The majority of these representations are statues carved from dark stone or wood, although paintings and frescoes also exist such as that of Our Lady of Czestochowa, the beloved protector of Poland.

Some of these images were not meant to be black at all, but have darkened naturally over time. Regardless, they have been embraced by their respective parishes as images of the Black Virgin, so much so that when they have been cleaned by overzealous conservators, Church elders hastened to re-blacken them lest their parishioners take offense. You see, among the faithful, it is commonly believed that those icons that have been whitened or cleaned lose their ability to work miracles.

Speaking of miraculous properties, Black Madonnas are much like Pagan idols of antiquity. According to legend and folklore, they can move and sometimes speak. In fact, the Black Virgin of Affligem (in Belgium) once told St. Bernard to get on with his theological writing! Others change color or position in response to a crisis. It is said that they enact retribution on potential thieves by becoming too hot to touch or too heavy to move. The statues appear to be quite attached to their places of origin, often demanding that churches be built on the spot. They stubbornly refuse to be moved from their original shrines and will miraculously reappear there if tampered with.

The origins of these statues are shrouded in obscurity. Catholic legend claims that many of the Black Madonnas were actual portraits of the Virgin painted or carved by St. Luke the Evangelist, patron saint of artists. Of course, if this were true, he'd have had to be the longest-living saint in Christendom. Others were believed to have been brought back by the Crusaders from the Holy Land. The latter strongly suggests that some statues were not actual depictions of the Virgin and Child, but rather those of

Near Eastern deities, such as Isis and Horus. Many are said to have just "appeared" in natural spots such as caves or the clefts of trees. It is not surprising that many of these sites of origin were sacred to Pagans long before the idols were found there. Her shrines are usually located on or near the sites of ancient temples, sacred mountains, groves, and bodies of water. Often it was the locals (you know, them country folk who live close to the heath) who "found" and presented these mysterious idols to Church elders. If the clergy were wise practitioners of assimilation, they accepted them as icons of the Madonna and built a shrine on the spot—no questions asked.

All this broadly hints that the Black Virgin has a hidden archetypal ancestry. Ean Begg and Fred Gustafson assert that the Black Madonna, as both icon and archetype, represents the continuance of goddess worship in Europe. She is the echo of the indigenous goddesses of the Celts such as Rosmerta and Belisama who were never truly forgotten by the common folk. Her black coloring links her to goddesses of classical antiquity, whose worship was imported into Gaul and the other provinces. Isis, Artemis of Ephesus, Kybele, and Demeter Melania/Ceres were venerated at sites where Black Virgins would later appear. Idols of these powerful Earth goddesses were often black or dark-skinned and although it's doubtful that many of them survived into the Middle Ages, the memory of how a goddess is *supposed* to be depicted surely did.

The Virgin Mary is a lot like Kwan Yin and other Eastern bodhisattvas of compassion. Through her example or by direct intervention, she enables the believer to reach Heaven, or at least purge some of his or her sins. Like her white counterpart, the Black Virgin answers prayers, grants grace, heals the sick, and works miracles when all hope is lost. Both aspects of the Virgin are appealed to when concerning fertility, pregnancy, and childbirth. There is a long history of those wishing to conceive going to shrines of the Black Madonna in hopes of an especially potent fertility blessing.

As the darker reflection of Mother Mary, though, the Black Virgin embraces aspects of sex and procreation not normally accepted or acknowledged by Christian orthodoxy. These include out-of-wedlock or adulterous pregnancies, abortions, and stillborn or SIDS infants. This arena links her directly to her Pagan antecedents who held dominion over sex, birth, and death. One can reason that a Mary, perceived as the dark, earthy mother rather than as a heavenly symbol of purity, understands all facets of female sexuality and, therefore, is compassionate rather than judgmental in relation to a woman's right to choose.

A great many icons of the Virgin Mary, black or white, have the power to heal. As far as miraculous healing goes, different Black Virgins at different sites have their own areas of specialty, but most are believed to cure respiratory and neurological problems, and blindness. Resuscitating those who have drowned (especially children) is also attributed to the Black Madonna. Up until the 18th century, certain of her idols were believed to have the power to temporarily resuscitate babies who had died unshriven so that they could be baptized and go straight to Heaven instead of Limbo.

So who is the Black Virgin really? She is the archetype of the dark, and yet the compassionate Mother who will not be denied, regardless of assimilation and enculturation. She is evidence of a deep need, even in patriarchal Catholicism, for the dark side of the feminine. Funny how in those places where reverence for Nature and the Goddess have been disowned or neglected, it's not the pale reflection of the Mother that is most yearned for, but rather her earthy darkness. It may not be an obvious desire. Still, in our heart of hearts, our deepest levels of consciousness, human beings understand that we need to experience both sides of the Mother in order to feel whole. If this weren't the case, Church elders would have been able to expunge her memory long ago and there would be one less archetype in this book.

Pagans are often leery of anything that even remotely smacks of Christianity, and who can blame us? A great many of us left Judeo/Christian traditions that we felt abused our spirits, marginalized and condemned us, made us feel bad about ourselves

,or simply failed to fulfill our spiritual longings. This aversion to all things Christian sometimes does us a great disservice, particularly if we come from a tradition rich in Marian veneration such as Catholicism. I am an iconophile. I like big gaudy Roman Catholic churches, particularly those filled with statues and row after row of votive candles. Although the faith practiced therein is not something I embrace today, I have fond memories of kneeling quietly before the statue of the Virgin Mary, telling her my innocent problems and concerns. None of the male images impressed me as much as hers did. She was approachable and loving, not some cold and distant Father God. Although I could not articulate it then, I knew she stood for something holy and important, something that related to me directly as female. She was my first glimpse of the Great Mother Goddess of Pagan antiquity whom I would happily rediscover years later via the WomanSpirit and Pagan communities.

And so in her own mysterious, quiet way, the Black Virgin allows many Pagans the opportunity to honor and worship Mary, Mother of God. We recognize in her a syncretism where Christian and Pagan lines blur, and hate and distrust transform into healing, faith, and love.

Coatlicue: Mommy Dearest

By Lori Nyx

In the Museo Nacional de Antropología in Mexico City there stands a massive 15th-century sculpture of an Aztec goddess. This representation is so visceral and horrific in its conception that viewers having no previous knowledge of Aztec religion or myth instinctually realize that they are in the presence of some awesome and terrifying power. The block-like body of the goddess stands firmly on taloned feet. Her sweeping skirt—a woven mass of rattlesnakes—identifies her as Coatlicue, "She of the Serpent Skirt." Her taloned hands, balled into fists, are really the fanged heads of lethal coral snakes. So monstrous is her form that one would be hard-pressed to identify her as female at all, but for her her pendulous breasts half-covered by a gruesome necklace. Reminiscent of Kali-Ma's skull jewelry, Coatlicue wears only the choicest sacrificial offerings: a string of human hearts and hands with a leering skull as a pendant. The broad neck of her "collar" is in fact an offering bowl reserved for freshly cut-out hearts. Most terrifying is her head, or rather lack of one, as the goddess is shown decapitated. Still, two great rampant snakes emerge from her neck, their mirror images creating the face of nightmare, the grim visage of the primordial Aztec goddess of the Earth, the cosmos, fertility, creation, destruction, and sacrifice.

This infamous statue was found in 1824 conveniently located beneath the plaza alongside the Cathedral of Mexico. It had originally stood in the courtyard of the Great Temple of the Aztec capital, Tenochtitlan. Church elders had allowed the indigenous people to celebrate the Autumn harvest by leaving fruit and flower offerings over the spot for years, assuming that this quaint custom was a symbol of the converted's piety. And it was, but not to the religion of their Catholic overlords. The descendents of the Aztecs never forgot that there was someone very holy and powerful buried deep beneath the ground—the ancient and formidable Earth Mother herself, *Serpent Skirt*.

The Aztecs venerated a plethora of Earth/fertility/death/goddesses under a variety of names, most notably Tonantzin ("Our Holy Mother"). Many were adopted and assimilated into the pantheon from earlier neighboring civilizations. The roots of Serpent Skirt stretch back to distant time before the Aztecs rose to power, coming out of the semi-civilized peoples of the northern steppes of Mexico. She is an ancient aspect of the Earth, as both creator and destroyer who was too important to ignore, and so was absorbed into a complex and often contradictory mythos.

Coatlicue is one face of this pre-eminent Earth goddess, a force so primal that it is both nonspecific and all-inclusive. To the Aztecs, motherhood and death were the primary characteristics of most goddesses. And like Kali, Medusa, and many of the powerful and fearsome goddesses in this book, Coatlicue is a New World example of the archetypal devouring Mother who encompasses the seemingly contradictory concepts of womb and tomb.

As her statue and name attests, Coatlicue is associated with venomous snakes. It was believed that her body, the Earth itself, sheltered serpents, which habitually nest in holes and crevices. Holes in the ground, of course, also suggest burial—the symbolic return to the dark womb of the mother after death. At the same time, snakes are also a ubiquitous symbol of fertility and regenerative power, and Coatlicue as Earth Mother is eternally fertile.

In the origin myths, she is the primordial mountain from whose cavernous womb celestial beings are born. She is described as both the Earth beneath our feet and the Great Lady under the ground who makes the maize grow. As a truly chthonic force she is often portrayed in stories as a dark, dirty, disheveled, and hideously ugly crone. All of the above scariness runs contrary to her most notable myth, however, a myth about motherhood, sacrifice, and creation.

Being the fecund womb from which all things are born, Coatlicue had many, many children. Coyolxauhqui (the Moon) and the Centzon Huitznahus (the four hundred stars of the Southern Sky) were her original Titan-like offspring, sired by Mixcoatl ("Cloud Serpent"), god of the chase and the Milky Way.

Most notable to the Aztecs, however, was her youngest child, their patron and savior god, Huitzilopochtli. He was a fierce warrior, leader of the people, and symbol of the sun. It is the curious legend of his birth that makes up the crux of Coatlicue's myth—a myth not of a violent, malevolent goddess, but rather of one who is victimized by her unruly offspring. You see, it all started when Coatlicue was sweeping up one day at the temple of the Eden-like island mountain, Coatepec ("Snake Mountain"). Suddenly, a ball of white feathers fell from the sky and landed at her feet. Intrigued, yet intent on her work, she picked it up, stuffed it in her skirt, and continued sweeping. Later, when she searched for the magic fluff-ball, it had disappeared, having settled inside her ever-fertile womb. And you guessed it, folks; yet another solar god was about to be born of a divine and immaculate conception.

Unfortunately, this didn't sit well with Coatlicue's haughty daughter, Coyolxauhqui, who soon convinced her siblings that their mother had brought great dishonor to the family. Soon this bad seed was plotting her mother's death as a sacrifice to the whole clan's collective honor. Coatlicue is portrayed in this myth as rather powerless, perhaps in favor of her soon-to-be-born son, Huitzilopochtli, the Aztec hero-god par excellence. In any case, she is no match for the combined might of her offspring and is frightened for her life. Her blessed and still in-utero son comforts her, vowing to defend her in her time of need. Consoled, she grimly awaits the unavoidable battle.

As predicted, the bad kids storm the mountain. In fact, they storm the body of their mother as Snake Mountain is often described as the goddess incarnate. Now this is the point where the story splits depending upon which version of the myth one reads. Either Coyolxauhqui and cohorts overcome Coatlicue and chop off her head (hence our statue's gruesome imagery) and Huitzilopochtli pops out of the womb fully armed and ready to avenge her death, *or* the goddess is not decapitated at all. In the latter telling, just as Coatlicue is attacked her son is born and in her defense he proceeds to deliver an ass whooping of cosmic proportions.

Those of us who like to stay up late at night pondering cross-cultural congruencies in myth can't help but note the seeming similarities between this story and that of the decapitated Medusa who gave birth to her fully armed offspring, Chrysaor, or even Athena who popped out of the head of Zeus—not to mention legends of immaculate conceptions of a savior god the world over. No, I'm not suggesting a direct connection between pre-Columbian culture and Old World myth—my pre-Columbian ancestors wouldn't allow it. But from an archetypal, collective unconscious level, a damned good story is a damned good story.

The newly born Sun God then proceeds to avenge his mother's death by cutting off the head of his sister and tossing her body down from the heights of Snake Mountain where it breaks into bits and pieces. This reduces the Moon (remember Coyolxauhqui is the personification of the moon) to only a dismembered head floating in the night sky. As for the Starry Four Hundred, he chases them down as well, either destroying or dispersing them to the south. The few who manage to escape his wrath are left to illuminate their sister's nightly path across the heavens.

As for Coatlicue, don't worry—decapitated or not, being a goddess she can't really die. She appears in a later myth, dating back to the time of Moctezuma. This great monarch wished to send envoys to the place of origin, described in this context as the Seven Caves. It was there that the legendary mother of the great god, Huitzilopochtli, was believed to still be alive. Well, the envoys traveled to this mythical place and found themselves in another Eden-like land that time forgot where Coatlicue waited impatiently for the return of her son. The goddess appears as an ugly, disheveled, and filthy woman of extreme old age who informs the frightened envoys that she has been in mourning since the day her son left and will only rejoice when he returns to her once again. Although she appears frightening at first, the envoys find her to be pious, wise, and generous.

At this point you may well wonder what happened to the frightening, bloodthirsty, and supremely powerful Coatlicue depicted by her statue. I mean, is this going to be another chapter telling you that dark goddesses aren't really dark after all, or what? Not to worry, kiddies. Although the bloodthirsty side of her nature is not outlined in her main myth it certainly existed. I mean, we are talking the Aztecs here! To the Aztecs, the universe was a finite place that must continuously be renewed in order to flourish. If the gods provided life and sustenance, then it was *required* that the people return precious life to the deities. It appears harsh and violent to our way of thinking, but it was a basic and seemingly necessary part of existence to early Mesoamerican cultures.

As for the goddess, human sacrifice was certainly offered to honor both her and her son. Hearts and hands were considered some of the choicest offerings, and so are displayed in the necklace she wears. Coatlicue herself represents sacrifice. In her story she is "killed" so the celestials could be put in their proper places and the patron god of the Aztec people could be born and lead them to the Promised Land. Sacrifice ensured that the land would remain fertile and that the sun would be born anew each day. From her death comes the birth of the sun, source of continuing life.

In her even darker form as Chiuacoatl ("Snake Woman") her thirst for blood was unquenchable. Different from the Coatlicue of origin myth, as Snake Woman she served a more specialized role. She is the personification of bloodlust and the mother of Huitzilopochtli as war god. In this guise she is the inciter of battle known as "The Devourer," ever hungry for the blood of victims captured in battle. Chiuacoatl and her son were intimately tied to the Aztec Empire's desire for conquest. The hungry goddess demanded to be fed constantly and, subsequently, more victims were offered to her in this form than any other Aztec goddess.

In true dark archetypal fashion, Coatlicue teaches us about duality and extremes. She represents the strong connection that indigenous peoples had and still have with the Earth as source: the womb from which we are born and shall return to at death. She teaches us as modern Pagans about the mystery and miracle of life, death, and renewal and takes us back to the time and place of our own origins as children of the great and terrible Mother.

Hekate: Curse Not the Darkness

By Lori Nyx

Along a rocky path you walk, terrified. It is blackest night. Even the moon is not visible. You hear the howls of dogs in the distance. Your pace quickens and you pray that you are headed in the right direction. Ahead of you in the darkness you sense movement. Preternatural eyes glisten. You hear the rough panting, the yips and whines of dogs. Disoriented, you are no longer sure of your way.

Are you moving ahead or back the way you came?
Something brushes past you, knocking you off
balance. Catching yourself, you look up and start in
fear. In this shadowy world, a darker shape is forming,
it grows larger as it approaches...

Hekate is an elder goddess—belonging to the time before
Zeus and his Olympians wrested power away from the Titanic
Old Ones. According to Greek myth, she was a Titaness herself,
the brightly coifed child of other immortals, either Perses and
Asteria or those gloomy abstractions, Nyx and Tartarus. The myths
vary but the result is the same. She comes from venerable and
exalted stock.

Regardless of her origins, from the start she is described as
powerful. Unlike many of her fellow Titans, who were unceremoniously booted out of Heaven by those upstart Olympians, Zeus
allowed her to stay. Why, you may ask? It may have had something to do with her and her immediate siblings having backed
him in the great cosmic struggle for supremacy. Thus, according to
Hesiod, a grateful Zeus honored Hekate above all others and "allowed" her to retain her titanic powers, which means she got to
maintain dominion over a portion of the starry sky, the Earth, and
the Underworld. In addition, Hekate also retained her express
power to grant or withhold anything she damn well pleased from
mankind. With all this at her command you can see how she has
come down to us as the mistress of magick and the Witches' Goddess, par excellence. A Dark Faerie Godmother, indeed!

It may surprise all you Pagans out there that Hekate didn't
start her career as a particularly dark goddess. She is described in
the lyric poetry of early Greece as "the golden one," "tender-
hearted," "bright-haired," and even "the maiden with the ruddy
feet." In ancient art, she was rarely, if ever, portrayed as elderly.
Rather, she appeared as a stately and beautiful maiden holding
aloft two torches.

Robert Von Rudloff has outlined her earliest roles in Greek
religion. One of her titles is *Propylaia*, "the one before the gate."

This refers to Hekate as a guardian and protector. Her triple symbol was placed at the threshold of even the humblest domus and her shrines, known as *Hekateria*, stood guard at every crossroad.. Hekate shrines or statues were even set up before large temple complexes to keep evil at bay. Von Rudloff also identifies her as *Propolos*, "the attendant who leads." This describes her important role in myth as a helpful and caring attendant to other deities such as Demeter and Persephone whom (if you remember the story) she leads to and from the Underworld. He believes that the goddess (or a priestess impersonating her) played a similar role at Eleusis, guiding initiates through the "darkness" of the mysteries. Hekate was also often depicted as a kind of helpmeet/lady-in-waiting to Artemis, Kybele, and Aphrodite.

One of her most common titles was *Phosphoros,* or "light-bringer," which surely reflects those two flaming brands that she carries around. It's not certain whether the torches are meant to evoke the moon or the stars in the night sky or if they refer to her role as guide in the darkness, but I tend to think the latter.

Hekate transformed from the beautiful maiden with the starry brow into the patron goddess of sorceresses and Witchcraft in the Hellenistic and Roman periods. Hekate, as goddess of Witches, draws mainly from her legendary abilities (described in late Greco-Roman literature) combined with her connections to Orphic and Eleusian mystery traditions. These emphasize her power to give and take away and her knowledge of herbcraft, which was often employed to transform, kill, or bring forth life.

Over time, Hekate became intimately connected to the Underworld. Legend dictates that she keeps Queen Persephone company there while she waits to return to her mother in the Spring. In this, her infernal aspect, she has the power to both send and banish ghosts. The ancients invoked her to do both. In Greco-Roman literature she is often described as the scary goddess who presided over necromancy. Still, she is perhaps less of a psychopomp (that is the role of her sometimes associate and consort, Hermes) than a chatelaine: the Chatelaine of Hades who opens the way for shades to pass through.

It is generally believed that she is a goddess of threes. Certainly, her most well-known representations depict her with three heads on a single column-like body or as three conjoined women, each facing a different direction. In this last guise we know her as Hekate Triformis, the goddess of the gates and the crossways. Of course, if you take it back to the Bronze Age (and I always do), Hekate was another name for Brimo or Bendis, a tri-form Earth goddess especially revered in Thrace—legendary homeland of many a dark and spooky Greek archetype. She was also known as Enodia in Thessaly, the place where all of those wicked sorceresses in Greek and Roman plays like to hang out.

Although she was described in ancient verse as a goddess of the starry sky, the Greeks and Romans also knew her as an Earth and lunar deity. In the tradition of most mother goddesses of Old Europe, Hekate was most probably an Earth goddess first. Her altars always stood low to the ground, a clear sign of her chthonic connection. She was said to have lived in a cave underground, perhaps the womb of the world. Nevertheless, by Hellenistic times she was firmly identified with the moon.

The Greeks and Romans had more than their fair share of goddesses who represented La Bella Luna. Artemis, the Virgin Huntress (whom Hekate is most often associated, merged, and conflated with), was the primary moon goddess. Yet, she was most often associated with the waxing moon. The brightly shining, fully rounded moon was identified with Selene. Hekate, by default, came to represent the hidden mysterious moon in its dark and waning aspect.

I suspect this is where the whole modern concept of Hekate as a crone got started. You see, contrary to popular belief, a triune goddess representing Maiden, Mother, and Crone is *not* well-attested in ancient Greece. Nevertheless, most modern day Pagans perceive Hekate as the third aspect of a triple goddess form that mirrors both the stages of the lunar cycle *and* the three stages of womanhood.

Before you throw that flaming cauldron at my head, I am not saying that Hekate does not manifest as Crone energy. If it isn't already apparent, Hekate as an archetype is hardly one-dimensional. She has transformed over time into what her worshippers most needed and desired her to be. Certainly, she manifests today as the Crone, though not always in the form of the wizened hag. Sometimes she is the wise grandmother, the established matron, the compassionate nurse, and even that sexy sorceress of "a certain age." Perhaps if we push past that image, we can even see her as that sprightly Greek maiden with the starry brow.

Hekate was also called *Kourotrophos* or "nurse" by the Greeks. Myth and art rarely present her as a nursemaid per se. Nevertheless, she was the patron goddess of midwifery and nursing. How very crone-ish of her! This aspect connects her to the frog-headed Egyptian deity of fertility and parturition, Heket, as does the obvious similarities in their names. It is interesting to note that Heka in ancient Egyptian means "magick speech." Not to imply that Hekate means the same. No, her name has been translated as "the Distant One." Nevertheless, Hekate is also the goddess of sorcery who, like Egyptian deities, can cure or curse via powerful incantations.

Dogs are sacred to Hekate. In fact, they were her preferred sacrificial offering in ancient times. Like Artemis they accompany her in her travels. But these are no ordinary hunting dogs. They are hell-hounds (perhaps the shades of all those canines sacrificed in her honor) or Cerberus himself, who stands by her at Hell's Gate. On the earthly plane, it is said that the howling of dogs—a sound she is believed to delight in—heralds her arrival.

She rules the dark hours, the hidden paths, the hinges of decision, and the transitional moments of birth and death. Her symbols are the torch that illuminates and guides us through the darkness, the key that opens gates to other worlds, the scourge that stings and purifies, the dagger that cuts the umbilicus, the libation bowl filled with a dark red liquid, the crown of stars that designates her dominion over the heavens, the Earth, and the nether regions. She is the snake hibernating in its hole, the wild-eyed mare, and the hound baying at the moon. Her sacred places are crossroads and thresholds, where she waits to bless, guide, and protect the traveler or to send back evil spirits.

Ah, dear reader, I know all of the above faces of the dark goddess are confounding. It is difficult to define a goddess who seems to stand on the outskirts of myth, yet means so many things to so many Pagans past and present. Of course, all of her aspects throughout the ages mesh well with a goddess of transitions. To me, Hekate stands at the threshold of change. She is a goddess of midwifery and a goddess who tends the dead. In myth and cult she is present at the most important markers in life: at our birth, as we give birth, and at points of pivotal decision and sudden change. Ultimately, she lays us to rest and will care for us in the afterlife. She is both the light-footed torchbearer who guides us through life's changes and the stern but loving nana who disciplines with the words: "I brought you into this world, Child...and I can take you out!"

The dark figure looms before you...a flash of phosphorus dazzles your eyes. You clutch your throat, cry out and then gasp. Before you stands a maiden dressed in a white chiton and a dark mantle, her hair crowned with a circlet of golden stars. She holds forth two flaming brands. She smiles reassuringly and turns to run lightly ahead of you down the now visible path. Relieved and comforted you follow, knowing that you are never truly alone in the darkness.

Hel: Feelin' Hella Good

By Denise Dumars

"And Hell at one dark window,"
—*The Highwayman*, by Alfred Noyes

How strange it is that we so often confuse the name of a deity for the name of the place he or she rules. It happened with Hades, who is the ruler of...well, Hades, a word we use as a synonym for Hell. And what is Hell? A place ruled by a goddess named Hel, of course!

Now, your authors tend to think the Norse Eddas sounds a lot like Klingon opera, so it's hard for us to take this stuff seriously. Literally all of the Norse deities have a dark side; hey, it's dark for six months in Scandinavia. But there is much to sympathize with in the myth of Hel. Her father is Loki, another trickster like Set, and she was thrown out of Asgard, the Norse Heaven, by Odin, who demoted her from goddess to cemetery caretaker. Banished to the outer darkness and the eternal mists of the icy Hell of the Vikings, *Niflheim* (sometimes called *Helheim*), Hel languishes there like a character in a Samuel Beckett play, her body below the waist either mired in some nasty green slime or else made of decayed, greenish-black flesh. Ick! Or maybe I should say, Ich! From the waist up she is sometimes described as a beautiful woman, but sometimes her face is seen as hideous. She never smiles and one source says that one look at her face can provoke projectile vomiting, so we see some similarities here with Medusa. She has two brothers: Fenris, the grotesque wolf who is eternally chained lest he break free and destroy the world, and Jormungand, a sea monster who is eternally chained lest he...oh, you get it. She vows to rejoin her brothers at Ragnarok, a sort of worldwide Lollapalooza that ends in the destruction of Earth and its inhabitants. Well, at least she's not chained up like her brothers.

In fact, she has a rather cushy job and lots of company, for in the Norse myths nearly everyone goes to Niflheim, with the exception of men who died in battle or women who died in childbirth. Sheesh. Dying of disease or old age was grounds for going to Hel according to the Northmen, it appears.

There is never enough to eat in her realm—and worst of all, she has to share whatever she gets with everyone else. She calls her china pattern "Hunger" and her silverware design "Famine." And in Niflheim time goes by so slow that no one can tell if anyone else is moving. Wow, are you depressed yet? Hel became a place name when the early Christians decided that the description of her realm was perfect for the place where sinners go when they die. Hel has another similarity to her buddy in the undertaker's union, Hades: She has a big scary watchdog named

Garm who patrols ceaselessly, lest anyone actually try to escape from Hel. Unlike Hades' Cerberus, however, Garm only has one head.

Hel is also called Hella; her myth in Scandinavia came from an earlier German goddess called Holda, who is also known as Frau or Dame Holle. Holland, a.k.a. the Netherlands, is named after her. Holda/Holle is a more benign deity who merely blankets the northern climes with snow, rather than consigning everyone in them to eternal Hell! Our word "hail" also comes from her name, so she is originally a goddess of bad weather rather than queen of the frozen Underworld. Where Hel hangs out is sometimes thought of as a kind of shamanic Underworld, as Dutch author Freyja Aswynn points out. Like the descent of Inanna, one can go to Hel and back and survive by utilizing mind-altering practices.

To really deal with this myth we have to go way back—back to the Vanir, the original Norse gods, who were overtaken by the Aesir, or "Asian" gods (think Indo-European) or, if we see this as a Vedic reference, the "Asuras," or demons. Hmm. The Norse pantheon is more clearly linked to its origins in India than any other European myth cycle. In any case, Hel is related to Gullweig, the first Witch, a sort of Baba Yaga figure among the Vanir. She was burned at the stake three times by the Aesir and still didn't die. Loki ate her heart, probably in an attempt to absorb her magickal powers. Gullweig is thought of, through this absorption, as something of an aunt to Hel. With the burning of Gullweig, which didn't quite take, for in Norse mythology no man—not even a god—can kill a goddess, the events that led to the war between the Vanir and the Aesir took place.

If you aren't creeped out enough just yet, remember that the rune called Hagalaz comes from her name and not only is it the origin of the word "hag"—again, probably a reference to Hekate or Baba Yaga-like Gullweig—but it is actually what is being invoked by the word "heil," which of course means "to hail."

Hel's festival is, not surprisingly, held around Halloween, when all the other creepy dead gods get to come out and play.

This time of the year was called The Month of Blood by the Nordic types, as this is when animals were sacrificed, and as in other European mythologies, it is also the time of year when the veil between the worlds of the living and the dead was believed to be at its thinnest. Want to go visit Grandpa? Go to Hel. Use of the rune Hagalaz in ritual at this time can give one access to the Underworld. Charms made with the Hagalaz rune, dedicated to Hel, could repel curses. Hel is not only the deity through whom you can access your ancestors; she is also the great spell-breaker, the goddess of uncrossing.

Lest we confuse Hel with Holda a bit too much—which leads us, in many popular goddess books, to wrongly equate Hel/Holda/Frau or Dame Holle with Habondia/Dame Abonde—let's return to the original myth. There is much of the rivalry between the Vanir and the Aesir in the story of Hel. Because she is related, in a way, to Gullweig, the beloved Witch of the Vanir who was seen as an evil sorceress by the Aesir, the Aesir hate Hel, but can't really do much about her because of the power of her father Loki—a.k.a. the Father of Lies. To the devil a daughter, as they say. All the more reason, when the Christians come to town, to name what was properly called "Gehenna" in the Bible—the Jerusalem town dump, I believe it was, and Gehenna probably had a mean junkyard dog too—after Hel.

There's also a curious sort of sexism in Hel's story. How come her brothers are monsters, but she's a woman? And why, if she is dead and decaying, is she only doing so from the waist down? Talk about your biological clock running down! A reference to venereal disease, perhaps? This stuff seems to point to a woman-hating society; the historical record, however, shows that Viking women had more civil rights than nearly any other European women at the time.

The myths go on to say that if you want to visit your ancestors in Niflheim, you can put on a magick "hel-met"—yes, we get this word from her, too—and walk unseen and unmolested into the Netherworld. Vikings tried to wear their magick helmets to make them impervious to injury in battle—needless to say, it didn't work.

But we can meet Hel if we want to, and she can protect us from much bad juju. Her amulet can protect you against curses, the evil eye, and possibly even road rage, and visiting her can be a powerful shamanic journey to rebirth.

Speaking of rebirth, it is time to reclaim the Vanir and the Aesir from the taint that Hitler's evil SS put upon them. The Norse pantheon is just as valid as any other and has nothing to do with the darkest chapter in the 20th century's history. And even though Hel conspires with her brothers to bring about the end of the world, it's hard not to feel some sympathy for her. After all, she reclines in the dark, cold mists of eternal time, with never enough to eat, and only her ire to keep her warm. When she and her legions remain after her father and brothers are killed at Ragnarok, the Earth will renew itself and a new Golden Age will appear. Now ain't that just like something a goddess would do—sacrifice herself for a better world to come?

Kali: Fire, Walk With Me

By Lori Nyx

She stands before us, frozen in a whirlwind dance of destruction. Framed against the billowing blackness of her hair, her multitudinous arms brandish terrible things: bloodied swords and cleavers, freshly decapitated heads, and arcane weapons. All evidence of shocking violence, death, and destruction.

Here in the West, we are confounded by Kali, the darkest of all Hindu deities. Instinctively, we recognize the force inherent in her iconography. How can we not? There is power in raw violence, power in blood, power in shocking images of death and dismemberment. Once we see her, it is impossible to forget her blue-black nakedness adorned with skulls and body parts, her lolling tongue and breasts besmeared with blood.

Kali reminds us that the universe, or that which we imagine the universe to be, is far from neat and tidy, safe or sane. The world is a dangerous and inexplicable place. Shit happens, shit way beyond our understanding and control: violence, death, disaster, abuse, cruelty, blind ignorance, and injustice. We can try to deny, suppress, and disown these things, but they are an unavoidable and necessary part of the human condition. As much as we may rationalize, pray, or "chant and be happy," it seems that we cannot escape the shadow side of existence. The Dark Mother confronts and shocks us. She strips away our flimsy constructs of propriety, civilization, and order. Her glittering eyes pierce us with the knowledge of our own mortality and beyond that—the very dissolution of the cosmos.

The name Kali translates as both "dark" and "time." Hers is the darkness of the womb, of death, of the void, and of vast and fathomless space. Kali is Time; her three red eyes symbolize the past, the present, and the future, but she is also that which is beyond the concept of time. She is the primordial feminine force that existed before the universe came into being. She gave birth to it, nurtures it, and will eventually cause its destruction. But don't worry. When this world is no more, Kali will give birth to the next in a never-ending cycle of creation, preservation, and destruction.

But look closer at the Black Mother. She shows us more than the harsh realities of life, much more. As an archetype she symbolizes the quintessential union of seemingly contradictory concepts such as sex and death, horror and bliss, violence and calm, and beauty and ugliness. Severed heads adorn her, yes, but they smile mysteriously as if the secrets of the universe have been revealed to them. Beneath her dancing feet lies the corpse-like body of her husband, Shiva. He too smiles dreamily. In fact, at second glance he appears hardly dead at all. His pale body is soft, pliant, and decidedly aroused as if he is being gently awakened by a lover's kiss. The touch of a goddess (regardless how rough) must surely bring bliss. Not all of Kali's arms brandish weapons of destruction. Her rouged palms also make the *mudras* (sacred gestures) that "confer boons" and tell us to "fear not." Thus, while she pushes horror and gore in our faces, she also blesses and soothes us as any mother would a frightened child.

What is this paradoxical image of deity trying to tell us? According to Tantric belief, what Kali teaches us is the ultimate truth that all of these supposed oppositions are *illusory*. She shows us that within all things—no matter how debased, awful, or dark—there exists God(dess) force. Once we accept the dark side of life and of ourselves, we can move beyond it and beyond fear. With this knowledge, the mystics say, comes true liberation.

Now you know why Hindu saints like Sri Ramakrishna sang Kali-Ma's praises and wrote her love poetry. To her devotees, she is a stern but loving and adored mother whose message leads them to salvation and bliss. What to the Western mind may appear maddening, horrifying, uncontrollable, threatening, loathsome, and debased is to believers a vehicle by which to transcend the illusions of pain, suffering, and death and to become one with She who pervades all aspects of creation.

Hmm, perhaps I've gotten a little too esoteric here. By now you are probably wondering about all those amazing myths where Kali is one nasty, butt-kicking, She-demon. These too teach us important lessons about accepting the darker side of life and just why this darkness is so damned necessary. There are many stories of Kali's manifestations. In her most ancient form she was supposed to have been one of the black tongues of the fierce fire god, Agni. Of course as a force beyond time she is never really born, but rather she tends to manifest when the universe needs her the most.

According to one origin myth, Lord Shiva teasingly makes mention of his wife Parvati's dusky complexion, calling her Kali, the Black One. Insulted by his words, Parvati leaves Shiva and embarks upon a series of spiritual austerities to rid herself of her "black skin." Upon achieving her goal, she returns to Shiva as Gauri, the beautiful "golden one," and all's well that ends well up on Mount Kailasha. Yet, in Eastern thought, nothing is truly destroyed—just transformed. And so the goddess' dark side survives, just as the indigenous dark-skinned peoples of India survived despite the yoke of Aryan oppression. Parvati's dark sheath turns into a terrifying, devouring goddess of the battlefield and cremation grounds: Kali. In myth, Kali represents the negative, violent, take-no-prisoners side of the divine feminine.

This doesn't mean that Kali is bad or evil. Come now—haven't I shown you that she is beyond such classifications? Rather, she is pure Shakti, the unbridled energy of both creation and destruction. This energy is what stirs the male aspect of god into action and makes the universe manifest itself. It is the thread that holds the universe together. According to Hindu belief, without the instigation of Shakti, male deities would remain complacent or impotent in the face of grave danger. A case in point is the following myth.

The Asuras are demons of pride and vice whose greatest wish is to take over control of the universe. Through treachery, trickery, and the practice of spiritual austerities, they sometimes gain the upper hand or at least give the gods a darn good thrashing. It's at times like these that Kali's power is most needed.

You see, it's all the fault of the demon Daruka and his evil minions. He is about to wrest control away from the gods (male deities like Brahma, Vishnu, and Shiva) who are powerless to stop him. Oh, they try, but they are curiously impotent in this case. Daruka can't be defeated because he has been given the boon that only a female can best him, which is a nice way of saying that sometimes it takes a woman to do a man's job. Upon finding this out, Shiva asks Parvati if she would destroy the demon and keep life, the universe, and everything from spinning wildly out of control. With the help of the terrible poison stored in Shiva's throat, the normally benign goddess transforms into the awesome and terrifying Kali, who with her hoard of flesh-eating ghosts attacks and defeats every demon in sight.

By the way, one of the most fascinating things about Kali is that she doesn't have an animal as her divine vehicle. As a rule Hindu deities have a special sacred animal as a mount. In Kali's case, she rides on a ghost! How appropriate for a goddess of death, destruction, and the cremation grounds. Ah, but back to Kali as demon slayer.

The goddess Durga is another demon-slaying aspect of Shakti who is closely associated and often interchangeable with Kali. One day Durga found herself in the midst of a frustrating battle with the demon, Raktabija, who, as you suspected, had the unmitigated pride and audacity to try to overthrow the gods. This demon had the magickal ability to reproduce himself whenever a drop of his blood touched the ground. The warrior goddess wounded him again and again, dealing blows so vicious that they should have destroyed him. Yet, the situation only became worse as a multitude of Raktabijas sprang up with every cut. Durga became so infuriated that her outrage took physical form and manifested into Kali. The Dark Mother of entropy and the void proceeded to neatly suck the blood of the demon (and his countless clones) dry and toss their bodies into her gaping mouth.

Although the moral of these stories is that Kali is born out of righteous anger in response to ignorance, arrogance, and an overweening ego (definitely not the path to enlightenment), to me this last myth illustrates a more important lesson. And no, it's not a lesson of turning the other cheek in the face of evil or injustice. Rather, Kali-Ma teaches us that sometimes when all fails, when you are faced with insurmountable odds, it takes a bigger bad-ass—the *mother* of all bad-asses, in fact—to defeat evil and set the universe to rights. There is hope and yes, bliss in the knowledge that even the vilest of forces can be subsumed back into the source and rendered harmless. This is why I sing her praises: *Jai Jai Ma!*

Lilith: They Call Me "Demon Lil"

By Lori Nyx

"This is a man's, a man's, a man's world..." When I began to research Lilith, the lyrics to that old James Brown song kept revolving around my little brain. What must it feel like to be diminished, disowned, demonized, and deleted by both God and "His" story? As women, perhaps we already know the answer to that question.

I did my time in Catholic school, all the way from kiddy-garden through high school. I was baptized and confirmed. I spent a lot of time at Mass. I am more than acquainted with things biblical. Yet it wasn't until I read some feminist literature in the 1980s that I found out that Adam had a wife *before* Eve, and her name was Lilith. Huh? What? Talk about your cover-ups! Maybe it would have been different if I were Jewish or descended from another Middle Eastern tribal culture. Her memory, tainted as it is, still survives in the more esoteric texts, old husband's tales, and admonitions of Semitic peoples, but in mainstream Christianity she is the original *persona non grata*.

Who was this mysterious first wife of the first man, and why was she replaced by Eve? Even more aggravating, why was her existence kept from me—this woman eternally scorned by man and God? Even a demonized wife for Adam would have been preferable to simpering little Eve, the scapegoat for the world's troubles. Well, even Eve had her good points. She realized that the serpent was a far better companion than her husband. Oh, all right, I'll *try* to keep the Adam bashing to a minimum.

As I learned more about her via books on goddesses I could not help but like her. After all, she was the original bad girl, the troublemaker of the forgotten Old Testament—a complex and much maligned child of God who began on equal footing with Adam but ended up a demon, a succubus, a killer of babies and the unborn, all because she refused to be less than who she was.

So who is Lilith? If we look back far enough we can trace her origins to the ancient deities, spirits, and demons of the Fertile Crescent. In Sumer she began as Lil, meaning "storm" or "wind spirit," a force from the time of creation. In the story of Gilgamesh (circa 2100 B.C.E.) she is Lillake, the goddess/demon who lived in the primordial tree tended by Inanna. By the time of Babylon she had transformed into the Lilitu or the Ardat Lili, phantoms of the night, the most ancient of all succubi. In Babylon and Assyria she was conflated with the goddess of the starry heavens, Belit. According to Hebrew esoteric tradition, Lilith, in her most primal state, emanates from a combination of fiery and lunar energy. In

Judeo/Christian folklore she is best known as the primordial
succubus: that creature who mounts and mates with the sinful or
weak-willed in their sleep causing nocturnal orgasms, emissions,
and those embarrassing stains. For this very reason, medieval rabbis forbade married people to sleep alone in the house, lest Lilith
have her wicked way with them.

But the bad press doesn't stop there. Lilith is also a baby-killer
and birth demon. Her sister in spirit is the fearsome Lamashtu, a
Babylonian demoness who was thought to cause the unexplained
deaths of children, babies, pregnant women, and the unborn. Similarly, Lilith holds diabolical power over babies in their first few
weeks of life. These she will try to kill, stealing away their breath or
strangling them in their cribs, unless proper binding rituals (or
circumcision, in the case of Jewish boys) are performed.

On the one hand, Lil is portrayed as seductively beautiful and
heavily ornamented. She is a true painted woman, rouged and
perfumed, bedecked in marvelous jewels and diddlibobs. She does
not cover her head decorously, but rather sports the kind of long,
sexy mane that all men love. Her glorious hair flows free, sinfully
unbound. For shame! At the same time, she is described in Semitic
folklore as horrific, repulsive, and excessively hairy. A real She-
Devil, she is often attributed with dragon wings, goat or bird legs,
and the claws of a raptor. She may also appear with the upper
torso of a beautiful woman and a lower half of pure flame, like
some *Arabian Nights* effrete.

This last manifestation ties in with her most abstract and powerful form: the ever-revolving and flaming sword of God that bars
mankind's way back into the Garden of Eden—the same flaming
sword that will denounce sinners on Judgment Day. In this ab-
stracted form, she is a symbol of divine retribution and the wrath
of God, an essential tool in Yahweh's arsenal. Birds of prey are
sacred to Lilith, particularly the owl—a bird of ill omen. In the
King James Bible she is referred to as "Screech Owl." According
to Barbara Black Koltuv, even today in Near and Middle Eastern
countries, the cry of a raptor is thought to be the evil spirit of
Lilith intent on mischief.

So where was I? Yes, Lilith, the first wife and helpmeet of Adam—a whole being in her own right, not just a spare body part made over into a female form. You see, according to Genesis 1:27, the Hebrew God created man and woman together and plopped them both down in our garden, Earth. *Male and female he created them* are the words. Don't be fooled by that other conflicting passage a little later in Genesis—that whole rib deal. The rabbis of old weren't. In fact, all discrepancies were ironed out according to a story in the *Alphabet of Ben Sira*, a 9th-century C.E. collection of post-Talmudic legend and law. With a great deal of license, I will recount the legend here.

Feminist reworkings of the Lilith story like to paint Adam as a dolt, but he couldn't have been that much of one if Lilith liked him in the beginning. Adam was just...well, different...the yang to Lil's yin, the sun to her moon. They played together in the beginning, experiencing everything for the first time, touching, tasting, and learning about the world around them and within them. I like to think that their exchanges and sharing was mute, sensory, and telepathic. The pulses in their freshly formed bodies beating out point and counterpoint, their glances and smiles revealing all.

But then came the naming. We all know the power of words. The Near Eastern father gods loved their words of power. Yahweh had created all but the void in this way, and he passed on this power to his human creations. Since they were made in His image, they too could name things. In fact, he expressly ordered Adam to go around and name the beasts and birds and swimmers and creepers in the Garden, and to make matters even sweeter, he threw in the part about dominion over all on this Earth. And so Adam, the first man, began to wield the power of words; he became the first primitive scientist, naming and classifying things in his own special cabinet of curiosities. With each naming, there was individuation and separation until the thought of dominion and control over something outside of himself came as natural as breathing.

So what about Lilith? Adam must have hit a brick wall when he came across his other half. I mean, she had probably watched over all the naming with curiosity and some amusement, not thinking that such nonsense would ever apply to her. After all, she was made in God's image, too.

In any case, she and Adam found themselves on the opposite sides of an issue—an issue that plagues us to this day both literally and figuratively: Who's going to end up on top? I don't think that Lil really cared about lording it over Adam. It was just the fact that he felt it was his place, his God-given right to give the orders and to try to define her. I mean, sex was no dirty word to Lilith, neither was love, but somehow everything went horribly wrong when Adam opened his big mouth and said: You are no longer me, we are different, and I call all the shots BECAUSE GOD SAID SO.

She must have laughed at first, thinking he was teasing or playing some new game. No, she countered: I'll be the one on top! Won't that be fun…you liked it that way last week! And when this pronouncement was met by cold, stony silence or reiteration of his newly ordained husbandly rites, she may have tried to reason with her soul mate: Why does anyone have to be on top or on the bottom? We are equals. We are one. Come now, my beautiful darling, let's play and love and be as we are.

Well, things change, times change, and people change. Adam was a new man, the first man of a society that viewed deity as male, light as good, and the darkness and warmth of the womb as old-fashioned, barbaric—demonized. And Lilith, ancient Levantine goddess that she was, suddenly found herself out of vogue. If she would not obey and transform into something more suitable to Adam's plans, then she would be ostracized, deleted, forsaken, and forgotten.

In essence, the story of the first couple is about power imbalance, dominance, and individuation. Lilith refused to submit to Adam. Adam never even thought of submitting to her. Lilith knew that to submit would be the death of who she was: a slow death of slavery and the sting of memories of what once had been in the Garden. So she refused, much to Adam's dismay and Yahweh's disapproval.

The story goes that Lil preferred to disappear into the waste-lands beyond the security of Eden than to give in. She chose a dramatic exit. All of the early warm fuzziness of their relationship was obliterated in a burst of molten kundalini. If he would wound her with words, then she would fight fire with fire. Like the Egyptian goddess, Isis, she knew the secret name of God, the ultimate word of power. I'm not even sure it was the true name of Yahweh that she called forth; perhaps it was the name of the mother of us all, the Void.

Regardless, daring to call upon the name of the untenable enabled her to escape the prison of a life separated from herself. And so Lilith fled on dark wings, her body adapting to flight and freedom, leaving behind her twin soul, who in his newly acquired self-centeredness would not miss her for long. Soon, he was dialing-up the gold-encrusted princess phone to God and ordering wife number two: "...and make sure she's a blond this time!"

Unfortunately, freedom has its price as does disobeying your creator. Lilith flew toward the farthest horizon, reaching the shore of the Red Sea where she nested in a cave. In Isaiah it is said that she escaped to a wild, wasted place where she was thought to cavort and have concourse with wild beasts and satyrs (no doubt the remnants of Dionysos' followers).

Some effort was made to bring her back. Adam initially complained to his creator, so Yahweh sent three angels (Sanvai, Sansanvai, and Semangelof) after her. These messengers demanded her return, and she summarily rebuffed them saying, "How ya gonna keep me down on the farm, boys, after I've seen the Red Sea?" As a consequence, Lilith was punished. Her inherent fertility and progressive attitude towards sex is twisted and she becomes a semi-dry goddess—unable to give birth to human offspring.

Still, you can't take all the fertility out of the crescent. Bad girl Lil continued to live it up with demons, unclean spirits, the occasional fallen angel—even Adam, who after "The Fall" ignores Eve but doesn't mind the occasional nocturnal romp with his ex.

As a result of all this canoodling, Lilith gives birth to demonic offspring called *Lilim,* born to seduce and torture wayward men and women.

Incidentally, Lil had her share of strange bedfellows. As She-Devil, she's been paired with Satan or the Hebrew version of Satan, Samael. Together they produced Ashtoreth (the demon, not the goddess). Conversely, Hebrew mystics refer to her as Yahweh's mistress until Shekinah can be restored. Huh? Lilith keeping company with the Hebrew God that kicked her out? Say it ain't so. Well sheesh, even he must get lonely sometimes. Ask your friendly neighborhood Kabbalist to explain it all to you when you have a spare week!

And so, within her cave at the edge of the world, Lilith suffers, denied her rightful place and consigned to the outer darkness simply because she refused to be tamed and shackled. Ostracized and ultimately demonized, she burns with righteous anger and is tormented by the memory of happier days. Yes, "This is a man's, a man's, a man's world..." or is it? There's more to the song of course... "But it wouldn't be nothing, nothing without a woman..."

Lilith has her revenge. What arrogance to think she could ever truly be eradicated. She is, after all, part of us. She is the fire in the belly, the primal essence of life, sex, birth, and death. She is fluid and unpredictable, like the moon. She manifests in our deepest, most constant, most searing feelings: love, lust, hate, desire, anger, and pain.

We cannot escape her, nor should we try. She comes to us unbidden in dreams, nightmares, and fantasies. Our subconscious is her medium. There she unleashes our hidden desires, our wanton lusts, and our unfulfilled longings. Across our inner eye we flirt with images of writhing bodies glistening, conjoined, pulsating, until at last the dream becomes the reality of the orgasm that shakes us and wakes us confused, dislocated from our surface selves, gasping and grasping for our veneer of rationality and civilization. In the aftermath of Lilith, we lay spent and shivering, exposed in the pale moon's light.

Medusa: You Want Your Face to Freeze Like That?

By Lori Nyx

We remember them from the popular legend of Perseus, one of the many sons of Zeus. Those three hideous gorgon sisters living on a lonely shore, guarding the liminal space between the known world and the Netherworld—horrific creatures with scaled flesh, brazen claws, dragon wings, snaky hair, and glaring eyes. According to the most popular myth, there are actually three gorgons: Medusa, the mortal one, and her two immortal sisters, Euryale ("Wide Roaming") and Stheno ("Far Leaping"). Additional gorgons are sometimes referred to in the ancient literature, and they are exclusively female. On top of their loathsome appearance, they have the innate ability to petrify their victims with a glance. Even the 5th century B.C.E. poet, Pindar, described them as creatures of nightmare—Fear personified:

> ...Perseus himself, the son of Danae, was...like one who hurries and shudders with horror. And after him rushed the Gorgons, unapproachable and unspeakable, longing to seize him...two serpents hung down at their girdles with heads curved forward: their tongues...flickering, ...their teeth gnashing with fury, and their eyes glaring fiercely. And upon the awful heads of the Gorgons great Fear was quaking.

As mythical characters, they exist merely to test a hero's mettle. Their only crime is their monstrous form and heritage, for these sisters are children of the old Titans of the ocean, granddaughters to the primal forces of Night and Chaos. The old gods are always demonized by their replacements, and so the pre-Olympian deities were set up as target practice for the children of Zeus. Such is the nature of religion and assimilation.

Perseus, Prince of Argos—yet another by-blow of Zeus (did that guy *ever* take a night off?), was cheated out of his birthright. He and his mother came under the power of an unscrupulous king, who sent the hapless lad on a death mission to bring back the head of Medusa as tribute. In truth, foolish Perseus boasted that he could do such a thing in the first place. Luckily for him, however, the gods were on his side, and with the help of both Hermes and Athena and an arsenal of magickal weapons, he was able to sneak up on the trio of sleeping gorgons, behead Medusa, and, well, the rest is myth. What a terribly brave and intelligent hero…ahem.

But there is another part to the story, a tale that hints at earlier times when the gorgon, Medusa, was not a monster but a goddess, the consort of Poseidon, the beautiful dark-haired lord of the sea. According to the myth of her monstrous origin, Medusa was so desirable that a besotted Poseidon bedded her in a field of wildflowers. Unfortunately, said field was smack in the middle of the sacred precinct of the goddess Athena. To make matters worse, Athena, the Parthenos herself, caught the lovers in the act and in her rage transformed Medusa from a devastating beauty into a devastating ugly. Athena was often at odds with her uncle, but in distant times their names were linked in a less avuncular way. Perhaps the Greek Athena needed to destroy the memory of her former self: her shadow side, the death dealer, what we Pagans refer to as the crone aspect, who just happened to be the once and ancient consort of the King of the Sea.

Gorgon, Gorgo, Gargoyle…the word is thought to reference sound—a strangled scream or fierce cry echoed in the discordant scales first played on the reed flute by Athena. It is said the Maiden goddess was displeased with her musical creation and cast it aside with disgust as it reminded her of the angry screeching made by the gorgon sisters when they discovered their mortal sister, Medusa, had been murdered by Perseus. Then again, this mysterious gargling sound might refer to the last gasps of the gory head of Medusa herself. Gorgons are known to us via the Greek myths, but they are probably much older than that. They are remnants of the Mother Goddess at her most ferocious and implacable—the dark side, the crone aspect, the hidden face of the ancient Mother.

Medusa is more of a title than a name: It translates as "Queen." An odd name for a monster, don't you think? Taking her cue from the folklorist, Robert Graves, Barbara Walker holds this fact as evidence that Medusa may have been a real-life Amazon Queen of Libya, who, in the misty days of pre-Hellenic Greece, tangled with the "real" Perseus, a Mycenaean chieftain. Graves also suggested that Medusa was but another name for Metis ("Wise Council"), the first wife of Zeus and mother to Athena. And you thought that mighty Zeus was solely responsible for the birth of the goddess of wisdom and war? Tsk, tsk. Even more tantalizing is the fact that "Queen" is an epigram for the dark mother aspect of the *Potnia Theron* ("Lady of the Beasts"), the original Great Mother Goddess of the Bronze Age Aegean. All of these conflicting and convergent bits of lore suggest that, at the very least, the most infamous of all gorgons should command respect and reverence, rather than fear and disgust.

The 19th-century Romantics thought of her as a tragic figure, a beautiful demi-goddess who is seduced by one god, made ugly by another, murdered in her sleep by a brash hero, and ignominiously used as a weapon by her murderer. They set her up as their tragic muse, seeing her as suffering and the way in which she was misunderstood as echoes of their own sense of feeling "different" and put-upon by the establishment. Feminists and goddess worshippers embrace the gorgon as a symbol of that which was suppressed and hidden for millennia: strong, unbridled woman's power, the castrated woman as opposed to the castrating woman a la Freud. (Regardless, somebody gets a head lopped off!) To this day in story and film she is perceived as the evil bogey, the ugly hag: unfeminine, dangerous, threatening, or even worse—a comic figure. If you don't believe me, rent the film, *The Seven Faces of Dr. Lao*, and I defy you not to blow beer out of your nose when you see Tony Randall vamping it up in gorgon drag.

The gorgon is much more than a fairy tale monster of Greek myth. She is the archetypal, lethal female, a death-dealing demoness straight out of Hades, the poisonous serpent woman with death in her eyes. Hers is the face of Death, perhaps literally! In his book *Medusa: Solving the Mystery of the Gorgon*, Stephen R. Wilk suggests that the gorgon's distinctive features are meant to mimic those of a bloated and rotting corpse. And the power of that Death's Head is to petrify us, cause our blood to run cold and our hearts to stop, until we are as still and lifeless as the stone from which her own ancient images are carved.

There is something tremendously compelling about the gorgon image, particularly Medusa's. She haunts our imagination—Beauty transformed into the grotesqueness of death, unnatural, super-natural—the sensuous, sexual qualities of a woman contrasted with our deepest aversion to the cold, glittering eye, tightening coils, sudden strike, and burning sting of a reptile. Though be-headed, she doesn't die. Her head lives on to freeze, to destroy, as she glares her outrage at those who dare to look upon the face of Death—to pry into the secrets of the sacred, of the unknowable.

But there are other sides of this creature of myth—a beautiful side, a haunting side, a practical side. All are part of her peculiar darkness and mystery. As I pored through musty old art and classics tomes in my personal search for "Medusas," I discovered that the first image of the gorgon was just a head (referred to as the *gorgoneion*), a disembodied head straight out of Hell. Even the brave Odysseus could not face such a menace, fleeing from the Underworld when threatened with its appearance. This head combines the worst features of nightmares: large glaring eyes in a screaming ogres' face, tongue jutting out of a snarling rictus grin.

What was its purpose? The Greeks and Romans have shown us, if not in their legends, then in their art. The gorgoneion was a ubiquitous symbol, decorating everything from shields and cups to kilns and temple pediments. Its purpose was clear—to keep evil at bay. It is apotropaic, as are the gargoyles that decorate a church or even the plastic owls that you perch on your rooftop to deter pigeons. Like other monstrous deities, the gorgon was the bigger baddie, meant to out-evil whatever looked upon it. Ultimately, it was used as a protective device. Gorgons are guardians of the liminal space, ritual space, and sacred space. According to legend, the gorgon inhabited the transitional space at the edge of the Earth, far to the East/West—a twilight place where the ocean meets the sky, the land the sea. They are guardians whose presence demarcates the supernatural, the threshold to the secret and the sacred. These ferocious protectors of hidden wisdom and religious mysteries represent impenetrable barriers to the uninitiated.

We can call upon this aspect of the mysterious gorgon in our own dark workings. She will protect our sacred spaces and our secrets as she did those of the ancients. She can stop and silence those who are disrespectful of the mysteries. Sphinx-like, she can serve as an indicator and marker of sacred space.

Some may wonder at my choice of guardian. After all, the gorgons in the Perseus story were easily outwitted by the young hero. But if I have not made it clear before, the mythical gorgons are just a pale shadow of their original versions. Perseus' tale is a story told by a patriarchal culture, a culture that deified heroes. At the same time it was a traditional culture that used the image of the gorgon to protect its soldiers in battle—the noble Achilles' very own shield was emblazoned with the gorgoneion—and to signify sacred space and to demarcate the threshold to ancient mysteries. On some level the Greeks realized the power of the ancient dark face of the Mother Goddess and had no problem using it magickally. Shouldn't we feel free to do the same?

Oya: A Mighty Wind

By Denise Dumars

"Oya likes a good hard lover."
    —from a praise song to Oya recounted in
        Judith Gleason's _Oya: In Praise of An African Goddess_

Oya is the irresistible force. She is the wind that wears away mountains, the brewer of storms, the brandisher of lightning, and the guardian of the cemetery. She is a lusty, hard-drinkin', hard-lovin' woman who fights like a man. She is the whirlwind in the thorn tree. Oya's myths are plentiful, but there are three main aspects to her story.

First and foremost, Oya is a warrior. She is an Amazon. She is counted among the warrior orishas of Santeria along with her husbands, Ogun and Chango. Yes, she also practices polyandry! Chango, the most macho of the Yoruba gods, often takes Oya along with him into battle. Oya carries a horsehair flail or whisk, and she always has a weapon, usually a sword, hunting knife, or machete. Sometimes she wears armor. She is portrayed as a beautiful woman, usually bare-breasted in true Amazon fashion. Sometimes she wears layers of multicolored skirts, and it is said that a cyclone starts when she swishes them. Those who become possessed by her during Santería rituals mimic this trait.

Oya is capable of outwitting any male orisha. She outwitted Osain by getting him drunk while he was working herbal magick and learned the secrets of herbs. She sort of stole Chango's thunder—well, his lightning, anyway—by spying on him when he was making lightning and thunder, and now she knows how to do so too! Oya is married to Ogun, the god of iron, and these days, of technology. She is also married to Chango, another of the warrior gods, and one of the most important orishas. Oya is friends with the hunters' orisha, Ochosi, and goes hunting with him often, even though this sport is forbidden to West African women. In other words, Oya breaks all the rules.

Her essential myth from West Africa, however, finds her being outwitted by another female orisha. Yemaya, who in some chronologies is listed as Oya's mother, was the original ruler of the cemetery. Oya ruled the ocean and the river Niger. Yemaya was tired of the cemetery, so she invited Oya to view her properties—at a distance. Oya saw the lush green lawns and vast acreage and was very impressed. Yemaya suggested that they change places. Once the change was underway, Oya realized that the properties Yemaya had shown her were, in fact, cemeteries. But then it was too late—Yemaya became the sea goddess, and as though Oya retains her role as goddess of the river Niger in Nigeria, she is now the custodian of the dead and the ruler of the graveyard.

Perhaps this dramatic change in her own circumstances is how Oya became considered to be the goddess of violent change. She is known to afford her worshippers a change of venue—even if it means blowing their ship thousands of miles off course or knocking down their town with a tornado. She is known as the goddess of professional women since she rules the marketplace, which is run by women in West Africa. Oya is anything but a traditional African woman. She is, much like the Roman Diana, a huntress, a warrior, and an independent woman who does not cater to men's whims. However, unlike the chaste Diana and other Amazons who live without men in their lives, Oya has not one but two husbands, and many lovers! Now, who wears the pants in that pantheon?

Oya is associated with dark and destructive forces and is the only orisha who can control the dead. She is called on to dispel haunts and for necromantic purposes. Cemeteries are known as *ile yansan*, the House of Yansa, which is another of her names. Natural destructive phenomena such as tornadoes, and earthquakes, are associated with her powers. But she is not all negativity and scariness. Sometimes she uses her warlike tendencies for the greater good, for as a warrior she will fight for her followers. She is sometimes called Buffalo Woman, and some images of her are crowned with the impressive horns of the Cape Buffalo—the African animal that big-game hunters call "the most dangerous game."

One humorous story of Oya tells of Chango getting tired in battle and asking Oya to save him so that he can get some rest. Oya does so by dressing him up as herself: She cuts off her hair and pins it to his, puts him in a dress, and sends him back out to the battlefield. He walks right by the troops without attracting their attention. Later, after his nap, he gets up on a horse and goes back into battle, forgetting that he is still in Oya drag. When the fight begins, his confused enemies believed that Oya had turned into Chango! At the sound of their cries, Oya herself came out of the house with swords flashing, and the two of them (the two Oyas, it would appear) defeated the enemy. Thereafter,

Chango takes Oya into battle with him. This cross-dressing story is very interesting, as it appears to put Oya in the superior position, which is not unusual in her associated myths. It is easy to imagine Oya as Annie Oakley, singing, "Anything you can do I can do better."

Why does a strongly patriarchal society like the Yoruba and their related tribes in West Africa need a goddess like Oya? Here in the New World, it makes sense that Oya has been elevated to great status by the mostly female writers on Santeria who feel that she should have been included in the Seven African Powers, the primary orishas of Santeria. But considering Oya in the Old World and in the New calls for some variance in interpretation. In the Old World, she must have stood for something frightening: a woman who can out-smart and out-fight a man, who goes against traditional male/female roles, and who rules the destructive aspects of nature and the house of the dead. Perhaps in a moralistic sense, only a "bad" woman could rule over forces seen as negative by society. In the New World, she becomes a feminist icon and an initiator of drastic change. Oya—her name is spelled "Olla" by Spanish-speakers and she is called Yansa in Brazil—must feel proud to be considered all of the above, for she embraces her frightening characteristics while relishing helping others. She is sometimes invoked, for example, to have mercy on dying children, and at least one orphan clinic and hospice in Kenya is called Oya's House.

In the New World we ask her to help with careers. Both men and women can be devotees of Oya, as with all orishas, as the orishas themselves are not sexist. Men seeking her favor would do well to flirt with her a bit (remember, Oya likes a good hard man!) and above all respect her power. Women can use her strength to get ahead in the world.

But Oya is not for wimps. Do not work with Oya if you are afraid of change, because that's what she's all about. She is also a sort of trickster, much like the Vodou loa Baron Samedi, who, after all, always gets the last laugh—because we will all eventually die! One of Oya's favorite tricks nowadays is to cause runs in the stockings of women who are on their way to important business meetings or job interviews. If you work with Oya, always carry a spare pair of pantyhose!

Because Oya is a rule-breaker, she does not always stand on ceremony the way other orishas do. For example, the wearing of the sacred necklaces—called _elekes_—is usually only afforded to those who are undergoing initiation into Santeria. However, if one wants to wear Oya's necklace, go ahead—buy one and wear it! You can buy her beads at a botanica, or take any beads that are black and white, maroon, brown, or alternate these colors and consecrate the strand of beads to her. Garnets, amber, jet, obsidian, smoky quartz or smoky topaz (and a few pearls just to add a touch of girlishness) are her jewels. She wears nine copper bracelets, as nine is her sacred number, so a copper bracelet in place of beads would work as well.

As Oya is part of a living tradition, unlike some of the gods and goddesses we are reclaiming in this book, there are some very current guidelines for accessing her power. Initiates of Santería, Vodou (in which Oya is called Maman Brigitte or sometimes the royal consort of Damballah, Aida-Wedo) and Yoruban traditions make animal sacrifices to Oya. Most say she prefers only hens. Others say she will eat the flesh of any female animal. Our tradition, the Fellowship of Isis, forbids sacrifice of any kind, and most Pagans do not believe in sacrificing animals during religious or magickal workings. The orishas know and understand this. One can make what is called "a dry feeding," meaning that there is no blood involved, by offering Oya her favorite fruits and vegetables. Collect rainwater to offer her, and she likes her alcohol, so offer her red wine or a fiery liquor such as cachaca or aguardiente. Cooked chicken or Cornish hen can be offered if you are not vegetarian; Oya would love a nice eggplant parmigiana, some roast chicken, a side of black-eyed peas, a glass of good Merlot, and some tart plums and sweet red grapes for dessert. She also loves starfruit, which, when sliced, forms the shape of a pentagram.

She enjoys marigolds on her altar and chrysanthemums, prob-. ably because in Latin America they are the flowers offered to the dead. You can burn mugwort, camphor, cypress, rosewood, and mimosa incense for her. You can buy Oya candles in botanicas, or offer one of Our Lady of Candelaria or Saint Therese the Little Flower, both of whom are the Catholic saints associated with her. Oya's sacred day is February 2, Candlemas; the candle flames of this holiday are right in keeping with her fiery spirit. If you are troubled by "hants" you can ask Oya to take care of that problem. You can also ask her to speak to the dead for you, and she some- times allows visitations from the dead in dreams.

The aspect of Oya that scares me is change, but in fact it is Oya who helped me overcome this fear. Change, although unsettling, is a necessary part of life, but because it is so threatening to people so even fear positive change. By working with Oya you can con- front your fears and overcome them. Be aware that change is a process and sometimes in the process there are battles to be fought. And if even Chango takes Oya into battle with him, then maybe you should too. I'll be willing to bet that most of us find the boss's office to be a scary place, though with Oya along you will never feel that you walk alone while approaching that imposing edifice. Just remember that a "pink slip" is just not Oya's color or style and hold your head high.

Part Three

Bad Boys, Bad Boys, Whatcha Gonna Do? The Dark Gods

Anubis: The Soul Conductor

By Lori Dyx

Nearly every day I get to take Anubis, or "Anpu" as the ancient Egyptians called him, for a walk. Well, okay, it's not really Anubis; it's a beautiful, protective, mischievous, loving, imposing-looking Newfoundland dog. He is a great teacher, teaching me about myself, about animal intelligence, about trusting in the senses and instinctively knowing the right way to go, and how to handle life's pitfalls, merely by example. I also understand what it is to feel secure and a little humbled in the presence of a powerful, potentially dangerous, yet ultimately benevolent being. Sometimes when I look into his dark liquid eyes I fancy I see the ancient Egyptian jackal god gazing back.

Anubis, patron of embalmers and protector of the dead, is hands down one of the coolest-looking Egyptian gods. I'm sure you've seen him depicted in tomb paintings, stooping over the embalming couch or weighing hearts in the Hall of Two-Truths— that tall, tan, fit fellow in the kilt with the preternatural head of a black jackal. Impressive! That's his humanoid form, but he also commonly appears in full canine form. It's not entirely certain what kind of canine, however. Some say jackal; others identify him as a hound. I tend to favor the latter since to me he best resembles ancient Near Eastern breeds like the Ibezan. Still, the jackal is traditionally associated with him because of its habitual proximity to his preferred stomping ground—the necropolis—as well as its efficient "processing" of carrion thereabouts. Of course, as is the way of the ancients, the Anubis animal is probably a composite, combining traits of both wild and domesticated dogs in order to best represent an otherworldly being.

His coloring does not reflect that of any indigenous Egyptian wild or domestic dog. Rather, it is symbolic. As we have seen throughout this book, black often reflects the Underworld and the death aspect of a pantheon, which makes perfect sense in the case of a funerary deity. Egyptologist George Hart purports that Anubis's black coat symbolizes the color of a mummified corpse.

Well, I suppose if you dried me out in salt and lathered me in pitch I'd be black, too, but the symbolism seems a bit too pat to me. After all, black was not merely the color of a mummy to the ancient Egyptians. On the contrary, it represented fertility and the cyclic return of life as exemplified by the silt-enriched black soil of the Nile Valley. So Anubis' darkness ultimately suggests the renewal and continuance of life after physical death. His black coat and doggie form also hint at a connection to the "evil" god, Set—but more about that later in the curious story of his supposed parentage.

Anubis is a very ancient god dating back to Egypt's distant pre-dynastic times. He was the original god of the dead and was called "Lord of the Sacred Land," meaning the necropolis. In fact, he preceded Osiris as judge in the Afterlife and ruler of the Netherworld. On the walls of Old Kingdom tombs, called *mastabas*, there are inscribed petitions asking Anpu to help the deceased cross over safely and live again on "the Other Side." He, and similar funerary jackal gods, were widely worshipped throughout ancient Egypt with the center of his cult situated in Middle Egypt at Cynopolis—Greek for "City of the Dogs." Obviously the Greeks also viewed him as a hound! However, with the rise of the cult of Osiris (circa 2000–1550 B.C.E.) Anubis relinquished many of his former duties and instead became a kind of executive assistant to the new Lord of the Dead. Regardless, he always was (and is) a most important and powerful funerary deity.

Anubis is also called "Chief of the Divine Pavilion," as the embalming tent was known, because he invented and performed the very first embalming and funerary rites on the remains of Osiris. This set the mythical model for the well-known practice of mummification. To the ancient Egyptian the deceased's body (or a reasonable facsimile), had to be preserved. With no body or representation in the tomb, there was simply no chance for life eternal. Funerary priests costumed as Anubis and acting as the god himself were responsible for the important "Opening of the Mouth" ceremony, which revived the senses of the deceased or animated his effigy so that his soul could live on in the hereafter.

At the same time, renderings of Anubis acted as guardians for both the mummy and his *ka* (the part of the soul that remained connected to the tomb).

Anubis also retained his most important funerary role, that of psychopomp. He is the soul conductor who guides and protects the deceased along the perilous journey into and through the Netherworld. The trip from this life to the next was apparently a really scary one full of traps and pitfalls for the ill prepared. Any mummy worth his natron would not be caught dead entering the tomb without the appropriate Anubis amulets and spells of passage. In his capacity as guide, Anubis is often referred to as the "Opener of the Way," meaning he opens the gates between this world and the next.

Once the deceased makes it through to the Underworld kingdom of Osiris, Anubis acts as his advocate, describing all his good deeds and qualities to the Lord of the Dead and his testy tribunal of forty-two judges. His most important function in the Afterlife, however, is the famous weighing of the heart (the seat of the conscience) against the feather of Ma'at (the personification of Truth) in the infamous "Hall of Two-Truths." Anubis' role here is crucial. He makes sure that the balance of the scale is even so that the heart of the deceased can be fairly judged. All of this goes down before the throne of Osiris with the Ibis-headed god, Thoth, standing nearby to record the results of the weighing. When the heart passes the test, the deceased is a shoo-in to enter the Kingdom of the Dead and live forever. If for some reason the heart is not feather-light, it is Anubis' grim task to toss it like a Scooby snack to the menacing, ever-hungry she-monster, Ammit. This is a fate literally worse than death for the soul, which is then irretrievably lost.

The etymology of Anpu's name is curious. It may come from a root word meaning "to putrefy," which certainly links him to the processes of death and decay. It is curious to note, however, that his very purpose as patron of embalmers was to *prevent* putrefaction of the body. It has also been translated as "Royal Child" or "Prince," which suggests the noble heritage described in the myth of his conception and birth.

In the really "olden days" of Egypt, Anubis was believed to be the son of the sun god Re, and either the cow goddess Hesat, the cat goddess Bastet, or Nephthys, Isis' dark twin. However, once he was "adopted" into the Osirian mythos, his origins changed. According to the story he is the offspring of Nephthys and one of her brothers. The big question of course is: Which one? Either it's her uncouth and cranky consort, Set, or it's the very studly and oh-so-forbidden brother-in-law, Osiris, for whom she bore a *tendre passion* (and possibly a puppy-faced boy). Now, if you just go by looks alone, Set could well be her baby's daddy. Yet Old Sutek wasn't called the "dry god" for nothing, and the scandal is so much juicier if we think of Baby Anpu as the result of an illicit tryst. In defense of Nephthys, though, some ancient texts say that both she and Isis were rightful wives of Osiris. Remember, incestuous polygamy was the norm for both ancient Egyptian royals and their gods.

If Anubis was a love child, then Nephthys' actions after he was born make more dramatic sense. After his birth, the goddess abandons him in the papyrus swamps. Yes, I know it sounds heartless and cruel, and her motivations are never entirely explained. Some say that it was fear of what an angry Set (not to mention an angry Isis) would do to her and the baby when he found out about her infidelity. Before you go throwing stones at Nephthys, however, there may be another explanation. The scholars Dimitri Meeks and Christine Favard-Meeks describe the papyrus thicket as a kind of safety zone where Set, the desert god, couldn't penetrate. Isis would later use it to conceal and keep safe her royal baby, Horus. Perhaps Nephthys was being protective rather than punitive. Ultimately, she changes her mind and rushes to Isis to confess the whole sordid tale. This is when Isis springs into action and quickly retrieves the baby. She decides to adopt Anubis as her own and to foster him in his "real" father's household. Isis' motivations aren't entirely clear either. Perhaps she saves Anubis out of pure compassion or because he is the offspring of her beloved, or perhaps she just wants to take him in as her own in order to rub things in her little sister's face. You be the judge.

Regardless, from then on Anubis' loyalty is mainly to Isis and Osiris. He becomes the dutiful nephew/son and boon companion who accompanies the living Osiris on his very pharaoh-like conquest of the known world. Later he will assist Isis in her search for her missing (and dissected) consort. Gee, this faithful and noble companion sure sounds like a deity's best friend. Little is said about his relationship with his real mother. Still, all three— Isis, Nephthys, and Anubis—worked in tandem to put Humpty Dumpty (so to speak) back together again. I figure that things couldn't have been all that strained between them. As far as myth is concerned there was little love lost between Anubis and Set, though from a magickal standpoint I have seen both deities work together without incident. Aw, Heka, it's all in the family! Although a specific consort of Anubis is rarely mentioned, according to the Pyramid texts he has a daughter named Kebehwet. The name of this goddess of purification means "Cooling Water," and she is described as a celestial serpent or ostrich that carries the water to refresh and purify the body of the deceased prior to mummification.

It would be remiss of me in a discussion of Anpu to not mention a deity often confused with him—Wepwawet, another important jackal god that looks a whole lot like him and shares in some of his duties. Wepwawet is a fierce and protective deity who often works in tandem with Anubis. He is the jackal-headed god who guides the solar boat of Re through the night sky and is a patron of warriors. Sometimes he is depicted as having a gray wolf's head rather than a black jackal's. However, most depictions present him as Anubis' twin. Wepwawet's name actually means "Opener of the Way," a function he shares with Anubis. When both gods are mentioned in this capacity, Anubis is described as opener of the roads or gates of the North and Wepwawet as opener in the South in the Netherworld. On the flipside, Anubis is the personification of the Summer Solstice and his 'brother' is the personification of the Winter Solstice.

Anubis is an austere and enigmatic god, spooky at times, which is why modern Goths and old-fashioned occultists like him so. At the same time, there is a touch of the trickster about him like his

Greek counterpart, Hermes Psychopompos. Those who work closely with this deity often say he has a sardonic sense of humor, sort of like the undertaker who apologizes for his cold handshake. Personally, I have always found him to be like that Newfie I walk— a little scary and imposing on the outside but playful, loyal, and protective to those who are close to him. I hate to be accused of cutie-fying a funerary god, but my experience of him has at worst been mischievous and at best protective and companionable. Sorry folks, I can't help it if he repeatedly appears to my inner eye in his hound form with tail a-wagging.

Still, don't be fooled. Anubis is a very serious deity, as serious as Death itself. My coauthor had a frightening encounter with him in a lucid dream. The large merciless canine face of the god loomed over her and frightened her into wakefulness. In this case, it was not the canine aspect of the god but the implacable mask of the embalming priest that she encountered. YIKES! Much later she came to realize that this archetype was not preparing to whisk her away to the other world before her time, but rather desired to get her attention in order to convey an important warning, much like the "faithful watchdog" trying to wake its owner when there's danger outside. With Anpu as your soul's "best friend," Death truly has no dominion.

Dionysos: I'm in a Frenzy!

By Lori Nyx

I've always wanted to be a Maenad. I mean, think about it: You're a woman living in a repressive society. First, you are under the thumb of your father; once married you are under the thumb of your husband. As a good Greek woman you stay up on the second floor of your *domus* (house) and card or spin wool or some such necessity. If you ever so much as look or talk to a non-familial man while you're drawing water at the well, your rep is ruined. Believe me, Xena, Warrior Princess is even more hooey than you thought.

Luckily there are outlets in every society. Public festivals of the gods were ways for the common folk to blow off steam and drop the yoke of Apollonic logic. Drama, games, blood sacrifice, sharing of food, and mysterious rituals certainly helped to balance out the lives of the logic-loving ancient Greeks. When it came down to it, the good mothers and daughters of Greece were kept under a tight reign—except, of course, when they chose to follow the Lord of Wild Abandon, Ecstasy, Violence, and Divine Madness: Dionysos, the most exquisite of the dying yet triumphant gods, bringer of terror, frenzy, chaos, and the sweetest bliss.

There is nothing logical or restrained about Dionysos. He is the antithesis of the golden god, Apollo. He is sensual and androgynous: dark wild hair, long curling beard, fair girlish complexion, large dark eyes glazed with excess, dressed in panther skins and flowing Phrygian robes. It was thought that his orgiastic cult practices came out of the decadent East—the mysterious foreign places that the xenophobic Greeks both envied and disdained.

Archaeological evidence, however, suggests that he is as much a homegrown as an imported deity. His name, meaning "Zeus of Nysos," was written on tablets in Linear B attesting that he originated with the Proto-Greek cultures of Crete and Mycenae. Mount Nysos is where, according to later myths, he would spend his formative years. His name suggests that Dionysos was once a form of Zeus. By the time the Greeks got around to telling the approved version of his story, Dionysos had become the son of Zeus and the mortal, Semele, daughter of King Cadmus of Thebes. Okay, kiddies gather round. It's time for Auntie Nyx to open up her _Big Golden Book of the Golden Age of Greek Myth_ and relate the tale of Dionysos, The Twice Born.

Zeus became enamored with the lovely Semele. Always wary of the sharp eyes and tongue of his wife, the randy old rascal disguised himself as a mortal and carried out a semi-discreet love affair. Soon Semele conceived Dionysos and all was well until Hera found out. The mother of the gods disguised herself as Semele's childhood nurse and convinced the girl to ask her mysterious lover to reveal his true self. Well, via a bit of wheedling and a hasty vow, Zeus ended up reluctantly granting his girlfriend's request. Of course, no mere mortal can withstand the experience of the Full Monty view of a god, and so poor Semele perished as if struck by a bolt of lightning.

Not wanting to lose his son too, Zeus retrieved the fetus from her womb right before she turned to ash and had it sewn with golden thread into his beefy thigh. The storm god then carried the child to full term and at the appropriate time Dionysos was born—literally twice. To keep the child out of harm's way, Zeus sent the young demi-god far from Olympus, entrusting him to the care of the elder gods and spirits of the forest primeval: the nymphs of Mount Nysa and the ancient half man/half goat, Silenus. From that point on the Dionysos of myth would go through a series of adventures and harrowing escapes, spreading his mystery cult and bringing his peculiar brand of joy, chaos, mayhem, and enlightenment to the Greeks, Romans, and their neighbors. Along the way he invented viticulture and passed the precious gift of wine to an unsuspecting and eternally grateful world.

But back to my modern day Maenad fantasy. Women of his cult called to the god in special ceremonies and festivals in wild sacred places like mountaintops, forests, and caves. The god was believed to appear among them mysteriously and join in the revels. At his coming, his followers would become divinely possessed. According to myth and drama, the frenzied bacchanals of Dionysos were frighteningly unrestrained. Dressed in animal skins and carrying the phallic symbol of the god—the thyrsos staff—Maenads intoxicated by their lord were known to hunt down animals and rend them limb from limb, dining on their raw flesh. It was thought that followers of the god consorted and sported with all manner of satyrs, pans, and fauns—the horny elder gods. Nothing was prohibited. Lust, joy, epiphany, and the ever-present threat of violence and death surrounded the mysterious rites of Dionysos and his merry followers.

As a female living in a society where excess and abandon are kept in check (for although our society is far more permissive than many, we are the inheritors of the Greeks, make no mistake), the above sounds good to me. Okay, not the violent part...but a good old-fashioned session of wild abandon deep in the sacred woods with a mysterious, sexy, and woman-loving god to guide me. Hmm, where do I sign up?

Yes, woman-loving and beloved of women. He was nursed by the mountain nymphs of Nysa who kept him safe from the wrath of a jealous Hera. Oh yeah, Hera that long-suffering consort of Papa Zeus, who would kill baby Dio if she could. He was...ahem... succored by several goddesses, including his ageless granny, Kybele, who taught him her mystic, orgiastic rites. Then there was the sea nymph, Thetis, who welcomed a frightened young god with open arms after he had been unceremoniously chased into the sea. The Orphics won't let me forget their Underworld Queen, Persephone, who, in their esoteric tradition, was his mother instead of Semele. Then there was that tryst with the Cypriot bombshell, Aphrodite, with whom he is said to have fathered the John Holmes of ancient deities, Priapus.

Of course we can't forget the groupies, the nameless bevy of willing nymphs and mortals (male and female, old and young) who gleefully danced attendance on their lusty god—that is, when they weren't being persecuted for their beliefs or tearing forest creatures to bits. However, as Greek gods go, he certainly wasn't as love 'em and leave 'em as his dad, and he seemed to genuinely like and appreciate the feminine side of existence.

Can we not forget the episode of Ariadne, she of the famous Minotaur story who was spurned by the boorish hero, Theseus, after her usefulness was exploited? Her grief caught the sympathy of our wild-eyed god who made her his bride. There is a famous painting by Titian of this mythic event: a desolate shore, the tear-stained face of Ariadne caught in an expression of amazement as the clamoring Bacchic throng appears before her— Maenads and satyrs and fauns—*oh my*! Amidst the chaos, her divine, soon-to-be bridegroom half flings himself, half falls out of his golden chariot to embrace her. Intoxicated and intoxicating, he will sweep up his beloved and carry her away to his realm of wondrous possibility and devastating loss. Now, that's an offer no princess with a well-cultivated streak of melancholy could refuse.

But there is a downside to all this free love and romping around in the woods. With Dionysos, as with Life itself, the heights of joys are married to the depths of despair. Dionysos has a dark side; he is a god of bitter sacrifice and violent death, as well as a god of the sweetness of life and the fruits of creation. Like his Near Eastern counterparts, Osiris, and especially Jesus, he is a semi-divine being who is persecuted, who dies a sacrificial death and will rise again. In the myths, Dionysos enacts retribution on those hapless enough to cross him. His inherent feralness often called for the blood of the innocent and not so innocent.

This is why he is the dying lord: What he perpetrates comes back to him. According to the Orphic tradition, just at the point when young Dionysos starts to reach manhood, Hera ordered the Titans to hunt him down and destroy him. This they eventually manage to do. Being only semi-divine, the son of Zeus is felled in his burgeoning prime in the form of a bullock. Primal forces tear *him* limb from limb and consume him. The circle is complete. Yet as the seasons turn, he will rise again, called forth from the dark womb of the Underworld.

This is the mystery of Dionysos. He is both darkness and light, both death and life, both bliss and terror, but ultimately Truth. He appears when least expected and at the height of his triumph he is cut down. Yet those who know his mysteries realize that he is beyond death. He is "the resurrection and the life," via the alchemical miracle of decay and fermentation—he is born anew as potent and inspiring wine. He is also called the Roarer, the Bellower, and the Thunderer. No delicate plucking of Apollonian lyres here. The rambunctious rock and roll of panpipes, hand drums, cymbals, and timbrels causes all to flee in terror or bliss or to be struck dumb in some bizarre mix of fear, shock, and desire. Hmmm, reminds me of my first rock concert.

So what does Dio do? Why is he dark and dangerous? His behavior is notably erratic. He gave man the blessing of the grape—a dual edge that makes our hearts light and strengthens our passions, yet at the same time awakens our hidden animal nature. When we embrace Dionysian energies we come face to face with our shadow side—that part of ourselves that we must embrace in order to become a whole human being, connected and at one with the universal flow.

A word of caution when invoking this archetype: Dionysos works in mysterious and often unexpected ways. Although this archetype appears chaotic (and can certainly bring a boatload of chaos into your well-ordered, in-the-box life), Dionysian energy is all about balancing what is out-of-whack or against Nature. If you are too rigid and out of touch, he loosens you up and teaches you to appreciate your most basic urges and desires. If you are addicted to excess, he will slam you against the wall and force you to treat his gifts of wine, women/men, and song with respect and reverence.

In my own workings with him I have discovered many surprising things about myself and about hitherto unrealized sides of my personality. Some of these lessons have been pleasantly surprising and delightfully ecstatic, while others were excruciating, painful, and as shocking as being hit with one of Zeus' thunderbolts. But all have been enlightening and ultimately healing. So you see, my Maenad aspirations have been realized, after all.

The Grim Reaper: He Kindly Stopped for Me

By Lori Nyx

Why is death so elusive? Well, at least the popular icon of the Grim Reaper is. Let's face it; I've had a crush on this guy for years. He's just my type: exceedingly tall, thin (well, you can't get thinner than bones), doesn't say much, always grinning, a palpable presence whenever he walks into the room, and he has a great big...scythe. Did I forget to mention snappy dresser? Shrouded and hooded, sometimes sporting dark angel wings...that spells cutie to old Nyx.

Seriously, folks...when I began to research "the Grim One" I was amazed to find so little written about him. Here's an archetype as well known as Santa Claus but with no definitive sources. But wait, we all know our modern conception of the Reaper has ancient roots. Surely we've seen those scythe-wielding skeletons wreaking havoc across medieval landscapes. So, as often is the case I turned to art and found a plethora of Death images from the Middle Ages. Many come out of France and Germany, though the Italian and Dutch have their share of skeletal types, most of which adorn churches, tombs and the stern pages of religious tracts. Hans Holbein's woodcut series on the Danse Macabre pretty much defined the European conception of Death among us sinners. And how can we forget the Black Plague personified as the "Gimmest of the Gim" flying over Europe, scythe in hand, decimating entire populations?

Nevertheless, I knew the Reaper had a longer pedigree than woodcuts and church frescoes. Spanning backward I could see his relationship to Cronus, Greek god of time, and even some of the biblical/Islamic dark angels. And what about his peasant origins among the Celts, where he haunts the lonely lanes at dusk on his way to the next person in the village fated to die? Like the duties of his office, my search for Reaper info seems never-ending, but I will gladly share what I have unearthed so far.

The person or personage of Death is tied up with European allegory and folklore. The medieval Reapers and skeletons caution us to repent and be good, for there is no escaping our own mortality. So accept the inevitability of death and prepare for the next life by being a good little Christian...you get the picture. As Robert Alton Harris, "The Laughing Killer," said: *You can be a king or a street sweeper, but everybody dances with the Grim Reaper.* Death is quite a dancer. When I look at medieval woodcuts and murals illustrating the Dance of Death, I invariably think that "he" (if the skeletal figure of the Grim Reaper can be defined as having a sex) would feel quite at home cutting his swathe through a rave.

There he is. Grinning jaw hinge to jaw hinge prancing the steps of a pretty farandole amidst a cross section of humanity. He is equally at home with peasant and king, soldier and clergy, and the doddering and the newly born. Sometimes the dead dance with him. They seem so festive and animated with their viscera spilling from between gaping rib cages that one can almost hear the bone xylophones rippling some quirky melody accompanied by the hollow thump of femur bones hitting skull drums. This is the Danse Macabre, where Death is a combination Lord of the Dance and Pied Piper, leading us all inextricably toward oblivion. The allegory continues with Momento Mori. Here the Reaper or his skeletal counterparts inform us in no uncertain terms the simple facts of Death. Often decorating tombs or shrines in churches, he may recline atop a sepulcher and say "Rich Man, Poor Man, Beggar Man, Thief...You will one day be here, where I am."

You wouldn't think it by looking at him but apparently Death digs the chicks. The somewhat kinky proliferations of Death and the Maiden imagery attests to this. Again, a skeletal Death is supposed to be showing us that Life is as fleeting as the sweet bloom of youth and beauty. Death and his girlfriend are sometimes found locked in an embrace, a chaste kiss or something far more compromising. The apparent eroticism of nubile flesh being groped by a skeletal hand both repels and titillates. When Death and his hoochie are portrayed together in this way they also define life's other great mystery, the bridge between birth and death: sex, and perhaps a reference to *le petit mort*.

Is Death an angel? Certainly the Bible tells us so—you remember, firstborn sons and lamb's blood and Passover seder. But did he look like our Reaper? I would disagree. Nevertheless, this is the image we encounter most prominently amongst the Goth and Dark Romantic set. There, he goes by the name Azrael.

Azrael as Grim Reaper has been conflated with the ancient Judeo/Islamic fallen angel of the same name. I have always viewed him as more the serpent type of Old Testament nasty than the Reaper. But Leilah Wendell makes a good case for Azrael as the archetypal Angel of Death, and I say whatever blows the hem of your tattered black gown up is fine with me. For those who are intrigued by this extremely dark romantic view of Old Boney, read one of her books...if you dare.

Pamela Coleman Smith portrays "the Pale Rider" in her illustration of the tarot's Death card as a knight trampling all beneath his mount's hooves. This image of the Reaper was popular in Italy during the Middle Ages and the Renaissance, probably due to all those warring city-states: the rider on the pale horse, the skeletal figure on his skeletal horse-hacking, slaying, and trampling our bones to dust. This Death's origins are biblical, where he appears in the Apocrypha, laying waste with his brother riders until the Second Coming makes him obsolete.

The Reaper is well-known in European folklore, and the French in particular have a penchant for Mr. Grim. Although he served an allegorical purpose in church frescoes and in cemetery monuments, his Gallic roots go deeper...back to the days of the Celts...who yes, were not merely confined to the British Isles. In Old Breton the country folk told tales (and may still) of L'Ankou, the silent reaper who comes to harvest the souls of the dead. Sometimes called the Workman of Death or even Father Time, this personification of Death has many guises. He may appear as an unusually tall, painfully thin old man with long white hair. He is dressed in peasant/laborer's garb, his face stylishly obscured by a wide-brimmed black hat—kind of your early undertaker/gravedigger gear. Yet L'Ankou is often described as the archetypical Grim Reaper: a terrifying animated skeleton cloaked in a shroud. To make matters worse, the skeletal version has the neat ability to spin his skull completely around *a la* Linda Blair so that he would be able to survey his domain in a single glance! Death must be ever vigilant lest someone try to cheat him.

Either version—Tall Man or Bone Man—carries the infamous scythe, an ancient tool/weapon employed wherever Indo-Europeans settled into farming communities and linking L' Ankou and the more contemporary Reapers back to the Greek Titan and personification of Time, Cronus, and his Roman cousin, Saturn, and even earlier harvest gods who reap human souls. Oddly enough, L' Ankou doesn't seem to actually use his scythe in the stories. He is most commonly talked about as a collector of the recently deceased. "Bring out your Dead." He sits astride a rickety cart not unlike the death carts of the medieval gravediggers.

This idea would evolve into the Romanticized "death coach" known to haunt empty country lanes on moonlit nights in gothic novels.

Death's creaking rig makes an awful clatter due to the pebbles and stones that he keeps in the back of it. One can hear his approaching cart in the death rattle of the dying person. Part of the ritual of collecting the newly deceased is an exchange. L'Ankou knows that it is only polite to give as well as to take, so each time he collects the newly departed he drops a stone from his cart. Surely this has the added benefit of making room for...one more.

There is something rather intimate about this country version of Death that appeals to my peasant roots. I suppose the Celts wondered how Death, being so prevalent, could be in so many places at once. According to folklore, L'Ankou is not an omnipresent personification in charge of the entire planet, but rather the local parish Reaper. Villages were thought to have their own particular Ankou, who only did his duties for one year. The person unlucky enough to die last (or first) during the year was thought to become the Ankou, to be replaced the following year by another unhappy soul.

Lastly, is Death Father Time? Isn't it funny how gods of Time are often gods of Death? Look at the Hindu Kala (Shiva) or Kali. These destroyer gods hold dominion over or are Time personified—the Great Entropy in action. As previously mentioned, Reaper iconography is borrowed from the Greeks. His symbols are the hourglass and the scythe given to him by Gaia to wreak a little emasculating havoc on his father, Uranus. Of course, Cronus, who appears as a dour old man, is technically not the Greek god of death. That would be Thanatos, who appears winged and in full armor. Still, old age and death go together.

The Reaper no longer serves the same allegorical function that he did in olden days. Most don't believe in the Christian afterlife or the punishments of Hell. To most of us the Grim Reaper is a fairy story, a logo for beer or a heavy metal band, a mocking icon on an over-the-hill 40th birthday card, or the little wind-up toy that sits on my desk. I suppose this is because we really don't like to acknowledge death here in the West. It is a subject rarely spoken of and rarely witnessed by the majority of people. We hide death, sanitize it, and keep it shrouded and buried. Ours is a culture of life, young life, and green growing youth. Death never comes to us as friend. His entry into our safe little constructed world is always shocking. We are rarely prepared for this "grave" visitor.

But Death can teach us so much. He serves as a reminder that life is short and to make the best of every day (eat dessert first and dance now), to cut away the dead wood and move on and ahead. Every gardener knows that in order to get lovely blossoms next year, you must prune today. Hey, as Blue Oyster Cult said: "Seasons don't fear the Reaper." Nor should we.

The Reaper also reminds us to care for our dearly departed. Go to the cemetery and lovingly tend a grave; go to the funeral service and speak the words of praise and prayer; remember those you miss, however painful. Each year at Hallows, The Day of the Dead, All Souls Day, remember to honor those beloved dead.

It is mid-December as I sit and type. Saturnalia is fast approaching; the end of the year creaks and groans towards a new one. The Holly King will end his reign, and his brother will take his place. Even at this merry time we see the Reaper (for Winter is his season) in the gray skies, barren trees, and bleak fields. It is no mistake that the ghost of Christmas future is portrayed as Death.

Loki: And for My Next Trick

By Denise Dumars

Loki's myth reminds me of the kind of news story you hear now and again. You know, the one about a much-decorated firefighter who has saved lots of kids and puppies from burning houses...only to be arrested later when it is learned that he was the instigator of the fires! Loki represents to me this very same mindset. He sees that important implements of the Aesir get "lost" and then retrieves them, ingratiating himself with the Norse gods. He's like an annoying teenager who always needs attention.

Loki is a highly combustible mixture of Fire and Air. Indeed, he may be a primal fire deity, at least as old as the Vanir or perhaps older. In fact, according to Peter Andreas, the ice of Niflheim, Loki's daughter Hel's realm, was there at the beginning of creation, placing Loki in a much older place indeed. His magick is deadly, and when in trouble he flies away. He is a destructive god of chaos and uses trickery to get much of his dirty work done, so he is the prototypical trickster god. Many of his battles are verbal in nature. In the myths we know, Loki becomes one of the Aesir by becoming a blood brother to Odin. He is also, inexplicably, Thor's friend.

Loki is of the race of giants, primal beings in the myths. The giants—frost, mountain, and fire—represent the raw forces of Nature in Norse mythology. Loki, therefore, may be very old indeed as a force of Nature, with modern connotations put upon him in the myths. The Vanir, the elder gods, are the gods of Water and Earth; the Aesir are the gods of Fire and Air. So Loki isn't really Aesir, the ruling gods of the Norse and Germanic peoples; he may represent the forces of Fire and Air as they relate to the older gods, the Vanir. Barbara Walker theorizes that he may have been a "genius loci," a spirit of a place. His name may come from Logi, "Flame," or may be Lodr, a foreign word. He is also called Loptr, which means "Sky Traveler," hence his relationship with the Element of Air. Loki may be a foreign, demonized god, like Set.

He is related to the Vanir in a strange way. It is Loki who eats the Vanir Witch Gullweig's heart, thereby taking in her powers and in so doing passes on some of her magick to his daughter, Hel. Some of the myths see the beginning of the end with the death of Gullweig, far earlier in the saga than the beginnings of Ragnarok.

Loki has three monstrous children with his giantess (sometimes called an ogress) mistress Angrboda ("Distress Bringer"): Hel, Jormungand, and Fenris. Indeed, through Gullweig's magick, we presume, Loki is sometimes blamed for fathering every female monster on Earth! He also has, by the way, an Aesir wife, Sigyn, who is faithful to her womanizing husband to the end and with whom he has a "normal" son (though he seems to prefer his monster progeny). No wonder Loki is also called "the burden of

Sigyn's arms." Poor Sigyn! In this way, she reminds us of the long-suffering (though not always faithful!) Nephthys, wife of Set.

Researchers feel that there was no cult of Loki. Is that so? Well, that's not true of his daughter Hel. Her followers, even according to Norse myth, are legion. It is Hel and her minions who will ultimately bring about the end of the world at Ragnarok, but not before Loki sets things in motion.

Loki is always jealous of someone or angry about something. Though often described as "fair of face," Loki becomes murderously jealous of the beloved sun god, Baldur, son of Heimdal. Baldur can do no wrong. He's blond, he's gorgeous, he has the gift of gab, he brings sunny days and tra la la. Hell, I'm starting to hate him! Anyway, Loki planned to kill Baldur, but before he could get around to it Frigga made every possibly fatal object swear not to harm Baldur. The gods had fun trying to do so, but spears wouldn't pierce him, clubs wouldn't harm him, and even Thor's hammer bounced off of him. Loki, in fine sex-changing form, turns himself into a woman and with his gift of gab befriends Frigga. He gets her to admit that she had forgotten to have mistletoe swear the oath—hey, what's so dangerous about a little mistletoe, anyway, right? Well, wrong. Loki had an elfin smith fashion some mistletoe into an arrow. He fires the arrow (in some versions of the story he has the blind god Hod do it), and of course it kills Baldur. Loki is found out as the perp. As punishment he is chained to a rock for eternity, or at least until Ragnarok. Frigga places a snake above his rock on a tree limb, and the snake drips venom down on Loki. Sigyn is powerless to do much except stand by her husband with a bowl to catch the drops of poison. Whenever she leaves to empty the bowl, the poison falls on Loki, giving him convulsions that are felt by us humans as earthquakes.

Loki hangs around with dark elves and other creepy beings, and they assist him in his magick. He also has a way of talking his good pal Thor and sometimes other gods into inadvertently aiding his evil plans. He's nothing if not devious and persuasive.

His anger erupts in another famous story, this one surrounding a banquet given for the Aesir at the home of the sea god Aegir.

Loki gets mad and bitches out each of the gods in turn; Munch quotes his insults to Freyja: "I know you only too well. There is scarcely anyone in this company, whether of Aesir or of Elves, whom you have not had for a lover; you are a Troll [trull, trollop], wicked through and through; once the gods surprised you with your own brother!" After he is through ranting, Odin shouts at him and accuses him, among other things, of being a pederast.

Come Ragnarok, Loki will escape, as will his three monstrous children. He will instigate the war that brings about the end of the world, but he and Heimdal will kill each other before Ragnarok is over. Fenris and Jormungand, after doing much damage, are also killed, and then it is left to Hel and her legions to finish the job. Come the end of the world and the end of the gods, one prophecy is that a new Earth will arise, ruled by the One, a male/female shining god not unlike certain depictions of Shiva/Shakti.

Even if there was no sect of Loki in ancient times, modern Odinists do call on him. I've been in attendance more than once at one prominent Pagan author's home when he called on Loki. Something always caught fire, immediately! Freya Aswynn warns against invoking Loki, but admits that she's been warned against invoking Odin also, and does so anyway. Why would someone want to call on Loki? To start an "insurance fire?" It's a good question. Perhaps the best answer is that it's naughty to do so, so it's fun. That's a pretty good description of Loki's motivation for doing things, so perhaps that's his followers' *raison d'etre*.

But Loki has important functions in the sagas. He's a convenient "human" sacrifice to have around when you need one, as he always comes back to life. One story says that, being the class clown as tricksters often are, he made the gods laugh by tying his testicles to a goat. (Don't look at me like that! I don't make these stories up! This is what happens when you drink too much mead and write the Eddas.) The goddess Skadi had vowed never to laugh again, but then the goat runs off, and Loki's naughty bits are torn off and fall into Skadi's lap. Skadi, whose more fanatical followers left their severed penises as offerings to her, laughed, causing Spring to return. Needless to say, Loki then gets sacrificed to scary Skadi each year to bring Spring around. It is appropriate, after all, as the reason Skadi had vowed never to smile or laugh again was that her father had been murdered. Guess who was his murderer? Loki, of course. Skadi/Scotia/Scatha is the goddess for whom Scotland was named—and yes, the Highland Scots followed the Norse, not the Celtic pantheon.

Another creepy tale of Loki tells of his mummified head and lips being sewn together with thong, as a scary oracle. This may be a mistake in interpretation that relates to a very interesting representation of Loki as part of a triple godform. Odin/Hoener/Loki is one such godform. Hoener has a messenger called Mimir, and in some stories Mimir's mummified head is used as an oracle. Turville-Petre believes that as a triple god it should be Odin, not Loki, who is considered the origin of all evil in the Norse myths, considering Loki is one of his three faces, just as Bhairava the demon is one of the three faces of Shiva in Hindu legend.

Researchers have traced Loki's legends, and various versions of his name including Lodr and Loptr, back to the Caucasus. One of Loki's homes is named Kvasir, a word that has origins in the Ukraine, where *kvass* is a popular alcoholic drink. These examples and others, plus some of Loki's legends that bear strong likenesses to Set's, lend credence to the "foreign god" theory, for like Set, Loki is a rapist, a womanizer, a homosexual, and a sex-changer! In fact, he's the mother—yes, mother, as he turned himself into a mare and became pregnant—of Odin's horse Sleipnir, the gray, eight-legged horse who is the fastest in the world but who is also a death spirit. The eight legs may be an arachnid allusion; some theorize that the word for "spider" in Swedish, "lokke," comes from the god's name. Hel also has a supernatural horse, this one with only three legs, who—like Sleipner—is also a psychopomp.

The more I write about Loki the more I think of him as Lodr, or Lodur, as it's usually spelled. Turville-Petre believes that "Loki" may be a pet name for the proper name Lodur. "Lodur," which means "fire-bringer," may also be related to the old English word "logiper," which means "magician."

The mistletoe aspect of the legend of Baldur's death is an interesting one as well. Mistletoe, sacred to the Druids, is not a "nice" plant. It's a parasite to the trees it grows upon and is poisonous. Its white berries symbolize sperm, and together with the red berries of holly, symbolizing menstrual blood, the alchemical cycle of fertilization is represented. But mistletoe, because of its unusual characteristics, is an occult symbol of chaos and disorder. Enter Loki, and so much for the romantic illusions about The Golden Bough. But wait, there's more. Some versions of the myth say that the mistletoe was "too young" to be asked to swear an oath. This is very interesting. What does it mean? Perhaps it's a way to absolve Frigga of failing to make it take an oath; it's better to say it was too young than to state that she forgot and missed it.

The myth is something every medieval Cabalist and every 21st-century quantum physicist would understand. Baldur was perfection; in Nature, there is no such thing. Randomness is built into the equation, as quantum mechanics has revealed. Chaos is part of life. But for a people who do not see things this way, a people for whom, like most people, believe that everything has to have a reason for its existence, then Chaos must have a capital C, which rhymes with deity, and which is where we get Loki.

Today, in the post-heathen world, we view mistletoe in a positive light, and this may fit in with one very interesting aspect of the Baldur story. Mistletoe has no sinister associations to moderns; quite the contrary. It is hung up at Christmas, and if you catch someone under it, you are allowed to kiss the person. It is associated with lovers and those wishing to find one.

Which brings us back to Baldur! One version of his myth has him sent straight to Hel after his death, the implication being that he is to then be her consort. Now, let's review the story: Loki fires a magickal arrow made of mistletoe through Baldur's heart and kills him...and he ends up—the most perfect of the gods—with Loki's daughter. Are we seeing a very twisted version of Cupid's arrow in this story? Or is Loki just doing his best to provide a good husband for his daughter in his own sick way? Still another version of the story calls Baldur Odin's son, and when Odin visits Helheim (another name for Niflheim) he is surprised to see the usually gloomy place all decked out for a party. He learns that the festivities are for a "Welcome to Hel" party for Baldur!

Yet another story of Baldur's death places Hod squarely as the assassin, and Loki is not even mentioned in this version of the tale. Turville-Petre states that it is not known which version of Baldur's death is the earlier one, but with the doubt this casts, there is the suggestion of Loki as scapegoat.

Loki is one of few gods around the world who are associated with volcanoes. Indeed, he is linked to both volcanoes and earthquakes. No wonder the Icelanders kept him around long after the Scandinavian countries had become Christian. Loki's myths have also been traced back to the cradle of the Caucasian race, the Caucasus, whereas most of the Aesir are essentially Vedic gods with bleached hair ("Aesir" may come from the Sanskrit "Asura," according to Jakob Grimm).

There are many curious similarities between the Slavic and the Nordic Pagan religious practices. The Arabic anthropologist Ibn Fadlan—which is what he was, though there was no word for it at the time—recorded, for example, Viking and Russian funerals that followed essentially the same ritual. Obviously, there are many crossovers in their beliefs. It is natural, as we have seen with Set, to see "foreigners" as scapegoats when things go wrong. But whereas the "foreign" god Set becomes the eternal boatman, living a relatively tranquil retirement, Loki's role at the end is far more active. Curiously, Loki's dad, the giant Farbauti, has his name translated as either "cruel striker" or "the boatman"!

Though Loki brings to a close the saga of the Aesir, and indeed the end of all of us, in the process he ushers in a brave new world—one in which, as is described in some of the myths, returns Baldur to life in a new Golden Age. Once again, sometimes it is darkness that leads us into light.

Lucifer:
Just Call Me Angel of the Morning

By Lori Nyx

It may come as a surprise, Gentle Reader, but Lucifer didn't start out as the biblical Satan. In fact, it wasn't until the Middle Ages that church elders like St. Jerome declared the name Lucifer a synonym for that of Satan, the fallen angel—based on an erroneous translation of an Old Testament passage. Even the legend of Lucifer that has come down to us via Judeo-Christian folklore and apocryphal text has less to do with canonical scripture than with out and out plagiarism.

You see it all started in Canaan. The ancient Canaanites (later known as the Phoenicians) were Semitic peoples who occupied areas of present day Palestine, Syria, Israel, and Lebanon. In the hazy days of Hebrew history when the holy books and their commentary were being put to scroll, there was a great deal of borrowing from local legend. In fact, the ancient Hebrews prior to the whole "there is only one God" thing were polytheistic and worshipped similar if not many of the same deities as their cousins. Hence, the myths of the gods and goddesses of the Canaanites and other Near Eastern cultures pop up in the Old Testament with the names changed to protect the "hack writer."

The father and mother gods of the Canaanite pantheon were the sky god, El, and his consort, the wise Asherah of the Sea. Their firstborns were the twin deities, Shaher the Dawn, and Shalim the Dusk—considered to be the gracious deities who ushered in the rising sun and put it to bed at night. Barbara Walker identifies Shaher and his brother as the Morning and Evening Stars, a.k.a. the planet Venus. However, most scholars refer to the Morning Star who heralds the rising sun as Helel—either the son *or* the father of Shaher, depending on who's translating what. In any case, it is the Hebrew noun, *Helel,* which will later transmute into the Latinized name, Lucifer—meaning "Light-bringer." Follow me so far?

Okay. Let's get back to Canaan. According to the myth, Shaher (or Helel) stopped being so gracious and began to covet the throne of the chief god, presumably El in his aspect as the Sun. One day he tried to usurp the high god's position in the heavens. Unfortunately, the solar deity made short shrift of him and cast him down like a bolt from the blue. The following lament for the Morning Star's fall is taken from 7th century B.C.E. Canaanite scripture:

> How hast thou fallen from heaven, Helel's son Shaher! Thou didst say in thy heart, I will ascend to heaven, above the circumpolar stars I will raise my throne, and I will dwell on the Mount of Council in the back of the north; I will mount on the back of a cloud, I will be like unto Elyon. (Albright, 232)

Fast forward several hundred years to the prophet Isaiah (or his ghostwriter) comparing King Nebuchadnezzar of Babylon to the personification of the Morning Star:

> How art thou fallen from heaven, O Lucifer, son of the morning! How art thou cut down to the ground, which didst weaken the nations! For though hast said in thine heart, I will ascend to heaven, I will exalt my throne above the star of God: I will sit also upon the mount of the congregation, in the side of the north; I will ascend above the heights of the clouds; I will be like the most High. (Isaiah 14:12-14, *King James Bible*)

To paraphrase Dana Carvey's Church Lady character: Whomever could Isaiah be referring to? Could it be *Shaher*? Regardless, this is the first mention of the name Lucifer in the Bible. Curiously, the name appears in only a few other places in that Holy Book and not as a pejorative, but rather as a metaphorical description of greatness and LIGHT! According to NewAdvent.org, even Jesus Christ is given this epithet in II Peter 1:19 and Apocalypse 22:16!

Nevertheless, this did not stop St. Jerome from mandating that Lucifer be the sanctioned name of the principle angel in the legend of the fall from Heaven. He and other Church fathers mistakenly and stubbornly interpreted the Isaiah passage and the name Lucifer as a reference to the rebel angel. St. Anselm, Archbishop of Canterbury in the 11th century, further elaborated on the legend in a treatise, and from then on Lucifer was a synonym for Satan.

By now it should be obvious that the whole Judeo-Christian concept of the rebel angel who is cast down into the pit was lifted from poor old Shaher/Helel's myth. Those familiar with Islamic lore will also recognize the link between the morning star god, Lucifer, and the legend of Iblis, demonic king of the Djinn, who is cast out of Heaven by Mohammed. Yes indeedy, a good story travels well. So, let's take a look at this view of Lucifer as Satan. Since, like it or not, the Brightest Star in the Heavens transformed first into the brightest and the best of Yahweh's heavenly host and subsequently into the Prince of Darkness.

Now, if you go back far enough you'll see that even Satan didn't start out as a bad guy—not that he didn't become one. Yes, his name means "adversary" or "opponent," but this initially reflected his role as one of the _bene ha-elohim_ ("Sons of the Lord"). The _bene ha-elohim_ were the mysterious pantheon of the Israelites prior to their commitment to monotheism. They would later be described as angels—not deities, and according to Hebrew Apocryphal texts they made up a council of Yahweh's advisors, enforcers, and personal assistants. Chief among them in looks, style, and grace was Satan who often acted as prosecuting attorney attached to the Almighty's Seat of Judgment. Hmmm, I always knew the Devil was a lawyer.

You may well wonder what this early version of Satan/Lucifer looked like. Literature may paint the Devil as the red guy with the horns and the cape but there is a very different description of him in the book of Ezekiel. There he is described as the sum of all wisdom and beauty. He is the winged cherub anointed by God and covered with precious gems and shimmering gold. In short, the guy is sheer perfection. Unfortunately for him, he knows it. This is part of the reason that, like the Canaanite god before him, Lucifer gets a little too cocky and as they say, Pride goeth before one hell of a fall.

So, here we have Lucifer, the superlative Angel of Light, a god himself if you go back far enough, committing the sin of hubris—with perhaps a little envy and ambition thrown in. What exactly the conditions of said sin were is a little sketchy depending on which Rabbinical or Christian non-canonical text you read. Some sources say he refused to bow down before the Great White Throne of the Lord. Others say he actually dared to place his golden posterior on the Celestial Seat itself, no doubt whilst Yahweh was on a coffee break.

I prefer the Talmud's telling of the tale. Here, it is not Yahweh or his throne that Lucifer refuses to bow down to, but his latest creation, Adam. When Yahweh presents man to the angels they are required to worship him—since man was created in God's image. This does not sit well with Lucifer who knows his rightful place in life, the universe, and everything—and that sure ain't low man on the totem pole in relation to a human. The Archangel Michael tries to force the issue but Lucifer refuses to submit, vowing to set himself above the stars and become like the Highest—a god himself. As you can imagine when this gets back to the Boss-Man, poor Lucifer and any of the angels who dared to side with him get 86'd out of the celestial sphere. It is said that they plummeted like fallen stars.

In this light, the rebel angel reminds us a little of Lilith, the first woman and Adam's mate before Eve. Both she and Lucifer are somewhat like the older children of Yahweh's "first marriage." Initially, they are close to him and well-loved, but when things don't work out they are replaced and made to feel inferior in lieu of younger, cuter siblings with less baggage.

So, this is the Lucifer handed down to us: the flawed and fallen Angel of Light who suffers and rages because he is forever banished from the celestial realm. And although he rules in the infernal regions and has supposedly retained certain angelic powers, secular writers will come to portray him as eternally tormented by his lot. As Mephistopheles puts it in the novel *Dr. Faustus* (by Christopher Marlowe):

Think'st thou that I, that saw the face of God,
And tasted eternal joys of Heaven,
Am not tormented with ten thousand hells,
In being depriv'd of everlasting bliss?

As a result of all this eternal rage, pain, and angst, Lucifer is believed to inflict his revenge on God by tempting mankind to sin, and the rest you can read about in Sunday school.

Lucifer in popular imagination appears as a sort of tragic anti-hero. Much of this comes out of Milton's magnificent depiction of him in *Paradise Lost* where he appears as a flawed Superman scheming and brooding in his Fortress of Solitude instead of as "The Fiend." The Romantic poets embellished this depiction by embracing him as an ultra-cool radical set to tear down the status quo. No doubt they picked this idea up from medieval mystery traditions, such as the *Luciferians* who worshiped Lucifer as the brother of god.

Such traditions were heavily influenced by Gnostic Christianity. According to Gnostic doctrine, Lucifer was not the enemy but rather a sort of noble Promethean figure. In their eyes Jehovah was the bad guy and Lucifer the savior of mankind, because he gave us a remarkable gift—knowledge—which a jealous Yahweh would have denied us if he could. And as we all know knowledge is power.

I would call down the curses of my Italian ancestors if I didn't at least mention Lucifer, or Dianus-Lucifer as he is viewed in the Stregheria tradition. A tradition, which I may add, I am no expert. So, all you *Strega Nonnas* out there, please keep your evil eye to yourself and accept my *mea culpas*. As I understand the tradition, Lucifer is considered to be the brother, lover, and son of the great goddess Diana, with whom he fathered Aradia, Queen of the Witches. He is known as the lord of light and magick, the spirit of the crossroads, ruler of the powers of the air, the true creator of the world and, of course, the morning star. He is a fascinating mix of the Roman god Apollo and the fallen angel forged in the crucible of Etruscan and Roman Paganism, late classical and medieval mystery cults, and Italian familial traditions. If you wish to know more, read Leland's *Aradia: Gospel of the Witches* or modern sources on Italian Witchcraft. Better yet, ask your Strega Nonna.

But what of our morning star, the herald of the sun? Ancient cultures seemed to have a love/hate affair with the planet Venus. The Canaanites not only equated Venus with Helel but also with their goddess of love and war, Astarte, who the Greeks and Romans equated with Aphrodite/Venus. As a goddess the star is considered beautiful and mainly benevolent. Even the Virgin Mary has been described as the morning star. Underlying this are the myths of Shaher and Lucifer. It seems that wherever we find the predominant god as solar or celestial, there is often this backlash and demonization of his "herald." Related to Astarte in name is the Persian deity, Athtar, called "The Terrible." He was the evil personification of the Morning Star. We even see it in New World cultures in Tezcatlipoca, the Aztec "devil" whose form as the dastardly Evening Star battles the savior god, Quetzalcoatl, across the Milky Way.

Ultimately it appears that Lucifer is not as dark as most would paint him. He is literally the antithesis of Darkness, a true Lord of Light. Yes, he "sinned" if you believe in that word. Yes, he tried to overthrow the status quo and ended up taking the fall. But was he really a bad guy? Is it a sin to be glorious? Is it a sin to know one's self-worth? Is it wrong to want to shine? Gee folks, I'm sorry; I just don't think so. Hey, I'm not advocating conceit and arrogance, but what the devil is wrong with reaching for the stars?

Set: The Original Green-Eyed Monster

By Denise Dumars

Something really spooky happened when I sat down to write about the guy who was, until I did my homework, probably my least favorite dark deity. See, I was trying to type "Egyptian." Well, I type really, really fast. The word that appeared as I attempted to type "Egyptian" was "Typhon." Yes, Typhon is the Greco-Roman name for Set, and it's where we get our word typhoon (which is really weird as the word "typhoon" supposedly has Chinese origins; back to the drawing board, etymologists!) Okay, so who's the role model for Cain, Satan, and Judas? The Egyptian god Set. I mean, the seven deadly sins could serve as his personality profile. We will present only one really safe ritual to do involving him; if you wish to go deeper into his mythos, see the References for Don Webb's books.

Set is the brother of Isis, Nephthys, Osiris, and Horus the Elder. They were all together in the womb. That is where Isis and Osiris fell in love (these are god-archetypes, people, so don't freak out about this). Isis and Osiris are married, as are Nephthys (Isis' identical twin) and Set (who don't look like any of the other kids...we'll get to this in a minute).

Osiris and Isis ruled over the Earth and Set was jealous. Even worse, his own wife had a major crush on Osiris, and even schemed to put the horns—or at least those funny-looking little giraffe ears—on Set. Set is often called "the dry god," and apparently for good reason. The story goes that Nephthys, unhappily married to Set and plagued with a major jones for Osiris, tricked Osiris into thinking she was Isis (well, they are identical twins) so that he would sleep with her. From this union came Anubis.

Anyway, back to our soap opera. Set, who has auburn locks and green eyes, unlike his dark-haired, dark-eyed siblings, schemes to kill his brother, and he and his henchmen trap Osiris in a sarcophagus. But Set isn't content to just kill Osiris; no, he has to dismember him and throw his penis into the Nile where it is immediately eaten by a fish. Okay, let's back up a little into our vegetation god archetypes.

Osiris is a vegetation god; he is the god of the fertility of the black land—the rich silt that is deposited on the banks of the river when the Nile floods. Without this annual phenomenon, life in Egypt would not have existed. Osiris is sometimes shown with green skin, in typical Nature God fashion, or with black skin, as representative of the black, fertile earth of Al-Khem, the black land of lower Egypt that he rules. Osiris has to die, like all vegetation gods, so that the cycle of life can continue. If you wish to look at him as a sacrificial god, then it was necessary for Set to kill him so that he could die and save his people. Sound at all familiar? Judas Iscariot is often depicted with auburn hair, just like Set's.

Set, on the other hand, is the god of the cruel desert of upper Egypt; he is the drier, redder god. His color is red, like his hair, like the hair of the okapi whose coloring and face look a lot like Set's. In ancient Egypt, this was the color of evil; what is called "black magick" they would call "red magick." Red was a bad-luck color; ancient Egyptian women did not even wear red lip rouge; they wore magenta or vermilion, but not pure red, as it was dangerous. So Set is a death god, the god of the killing sun of the desert.

And what mysterious animal is that head of his supposed to represent, anyway? The Setians think he's a donkey. Others call him a composite animal, a kind of griffin, or an unknown animal. What is that face supposed to be? What? What? I still like the okapi theory (it even works with the funny ears, as okapis are related to giraffes and Set has somewhat giraffe-like ears), but then he also looks to me like an aardvark, and some scholars have suggested a long-nosed desert mouse, sort of like a kangaroo rat. In the glyph that stands for his name he is portrayed as having a dog-like body, so perhaps jackal-headed Anubis is his natural son after all. And in this form he also has a forked tail that stands straight up.

Anyway, Set the different one—the one who came out with those bright red cornrows—is a lord of chaos. Set's killing of Osiris panics the gods of Egypt. Isis flees from Set who is intent on raping and killing her. In the process, while undercover as a nurse, she finds various parts of Osiris in the bulrushes (starting to sound familiar again?) and puts him back together. She never finds his phallus, but this is of little concern to the Lady of Magick. She just makes one herself and then has sex with her reanimated (or, if you're really into the necrophilia thing, still dead) husband and conceives Horus through the artificial penis she created. Talk about parthenogenesis! No wonder we all worship Isis.

Isis continues to hide out, as a beggar and whatnot, and her son Horus grows to manhood and vows to avenge his dad. He fights with Set—and man, do they fight dirty. Set pokes out one of Horus's eyes; Horus castrates Set. At one point in the fight Horus sodomizes Set, though in some versions of the story it's the other way around. Horus finally defeats Set.

Horus goes and gets Mom and says, hey, let's execute Uncle Set for murder, high treason, attempted murder, attempted rape, and just plain bad manners. Isis says no; to kill Set would be to be as bad as he is. Horus gets pissed and chops off Mom's head; Uncle Thoth sticks a cow's head on her body and I suppose this makes some kind of sense if Isis is identified with Hathor, a much older Egyptian goddess who is also a cow deity (and in one version of the Horus story, Hathor nurses him back to health, heals his eye, then marries him.) Then Set lives out the rest of his life on a fishing boat on the Nile, content to be a simple fisherman, or perhaps a character in a zen parable or a story by Albert Camus. Who can tell?

Neither do the contradictions in Set's myth make sense. On the one hand he's sterile and probably impotent. On the other hand, in the popular mythology he's a womanizer who comes on to married as well as single women. On one hand he's a god of chaos. On the other, he's a god of reason and has some things in common with Thoth, his uncle, the god of academics, writers, and gamblers, who is also one of the few gods who can rein Set in when he's on a tear. One particularly weird version of the myth is that Thoth is the son produced from the homosexual union of Horus and Set! Set is also a mean drunk, like his cousin Sekhmet, who, it is theorized, was originally paired with him in marriage. (Red, the feared color of the Egyptians, is Sekhmet's color as well, as it represents the blood she loves to drink). And he is equated with Typhon, a sea monster who causes storms and rough waters in Greek mythology, in stark contrast to Set as lord of the parched desert. To make things even more confusing, there are some representations of a two-headed god that has both Horus' and Set's heads atop one body—looking in different directions, of course.

So. According to TeVelde in *Seth, God of Confusion*, Set is really a foreign god. All the negativity heaped upon him in the myths is just a bit of ol' Egyptian xenophobia. My favorite epithet for Set is the one which TeVelde translates as "blockhead." And there's plenty of evidence that Set did indeed get the short end of the stick in the myths because he's a foreigner (which explains why he doesn't resemble his "siblings"). For one thing, he is equated often with Baal, one of the Middle Eastern gods. His mistresses include two foreign goddesses, Anat and Astarte. Complicating the matter is the fact that Anat likes to dress like Marlene Dietrich and be sexually ambiguous, but hey, that just turns Set on. And I'm not even going to tell you what he poked out Horus' eye with…

If we want to really rush headlong into foreign lands with Set, then this next reference will not surprise you: He's likened in literature to one of the Guedes, the Vodou gods of death. You know, Baron Samedi and the gang. Both Set and Guede are considered, as are many chaos deities, as divine tricksters who have perpetrated the ultimate practical joke on mankind: the fact that we all have to die. It's a sick joke, but then Set probably tells dead baby jokes too, as he is the god of abortion. Women with unwanted pregnancies would pray to him for spontaneous abortions, and women wanting children would wear amulets against his influence so that their babies would come to term safely. Set also is symbolically dangerous to childbearing women as he was not born "naturally"; he tore through his mother's side rather than waiting to take his turn in the birth canal. Some other shocking myths of Set include his sexually abusing Horus when he was a child, and there is one document—talk about a shock—in which Isis is instructing Horus on how to be Set's catamite! Yikes!

Akhenaten started the whole monotheism trip in Amarna that set up Aten, a sun god, as the Supreme God, and Set as the inevitable Devil. Déjà vu all over again! Ramses II was a devotee of Set, dyed his hair red with henna, and ran his country with an iron fist. Many pharaohs held Set in high esteem. He is spoken of favorably in the literature in many ways: "Set the great," "Set is kind," and my favorite, "Set rules." Many people in ancient Egypt had names that translated to mean "Servant of Set," "Daughter of Set," or "He who is Set's." At least one of the pharaohs named Seti was so named because he was a natural redhead. So Set was not always a negative figure in Egyptian religion. What we have here is a demonized god.

So, in the final analysis, what are we left with? A god of chaos and death…a god of forbidden practices, a god who is at once sterile and impotent yet is also deeply involved in sexual matters, some of them very much forbidden in Egyptian culture. So how shall we work with Set? How shall we let him back into the Egyptian pantheon, where he reminds us that none of us will escape death?

Even Setians acknowledge that you'll run into danger when working with Set. Just having that red light on in your ritual room might give people the wrong idea, for one thing…isn't it interesting that the red light is symbolic of prostitutes, considering its Setian connotations?

Maybe we really don't want to know what goes on behind closed doors with Set, but as a trickster who boots our butts out of the material world and into the Afterlife, perhaps we can safely meet him there. After all, perhaps the most compelling myth of Set is one in which we find the story of someone arriving in the Afterlife and encountering a veiled, seated Set. If you approach Set and remove his veil (Set wears a veil? *Glen or Glenda, or I Changed My Sex?*) then, like Clive Barker's Pinhead, he has such things to show you…but if you prefer to be in the dark and not see any secrets, then do not lift the veil. It's your choice. I say, who could resist just taking one peek beneath it? But beware: there be dragons here, or at the very least, sea monsters.

As I researched the mythology of Set I came to feel more and more sympathy for him. Look at all that mythology has heaped on Set; it reads like a catalog of issues that even 21st-century society has yet to truly come to grips with: infidelity, homosexuality, abortion, alcoholism…sounds like a lot to put on that funny-eared head of his. Maybe he's not a donkey after all; maybe he's a scapegoat.

Shiva: The Sensuous Yogi

By Denise Dumars

Isn't Shiva just the coolest Goth guy you've ever seen? I mean, no one should be surprised when Sati's father didn't approve of her marrying a guy who is smeared with crematory ash and hangs out in a cemetery with ghosts, vampires, and other unsavory types. But that's just the beginning of the Shiva story, and just the beginning of the love/death saga that he represents. I'm going to ask you to stop walking like an Egyptian for a moment, and think like a Hindu because we're visiting Aghora...no, not the city in the San Fernando Valley...Aghora, another name for Shiva, and the name of Hinduism's Left Hand Path. First, here is your attitude adjustment: Western mysticism ascribes godhood to beings both bad and good. Gods like Set and Loki are bad, but they're still gods. And hell, Satan's even an angel! In Eastern mysticism and religion, however, it's more like gods and monsters; if you're a god you're not bad. The bad guys, for want of a better word, are called demons. This viewpoint is widespread throughout Asia.

Aghora means "not terrible." Well, Shiva is plenty terrible, but of course it's bad luck to say that, so don't. In the usual Hindu creator trinity, Brahma is the creator, Vishnu the preserver, and Shiva the destroyer. His role, therefore, is already leaning toward what most of us would call negative. Shaivites, as Shiva's followers are called, often consider him all three: creator, preserver, and destroyer, as followers of Vishnu would count their own patron deity too. Brahma is more of a Re type; he created the universe, then evidently retired to South Florida.

Ah, to be a medieval Shaivite mendicant! To smear yourself with ashes, and walk the Earth with a skull for your begging bowl! Those were the days...

But back to our narrative. When Sati married Shiva, Dad pretty much disowned her. He refused to invite her to her sister's wedding, but she showed up anyway. Dad was angry enough to kill, and she offered herself as a willing sacrifice. This sets the tragedy in motion. Shiva goes mad with grief; he carries her body for eons mourning, he becomes a necrophile, and he retreats to Mount Kailasha in the Himalayas to meditate in the icy wastes.

But Shiva, always the babe magnet, is never at a loss for female companionship. Soon he is beset by the attentions of Parvati, who fasts and prays and has to out-yogi Shiva in order to impress him. But one day, she sneaks up behind him and playfully puts her hands over his eyes, you know, the old "guess who?" flirtation. Well, this is *Shiva*, remember? Covering his eyes makes a third eye erupt in the middle of his forehead (hmm, that pineal gland...) and a thermonuclear beam of light erupts from it, nearly destroying the Earth. Oh yeah, forgot to mention that nowadays Shiva is also thought of as the god of nuclear power. Yikes. Guess we really are living in the Kali Yuga, or as the Chinese curse might say, "interesting times." In visual depictions, Shiva's third eye usually resembles a yoni.

Parvati becomes his main squeeze, and after meditating for so many eons Shiva is now ready to copulate for many eons, for one of his names is "the sensuous yogi." One of my favorite Shiva tales relates his visit to a shrine where sages studied his practices. Shiva arrives, naked, and the wives of the sages are so incredibly aroused by his presence that they throw themselves at him, and he has sex with each one of them. For this, too, is a way to study Shiva. Well, when the sages eventually get their noses out of their books and see this guy shtupping their wives, in a rage they fall upon him and cut off his penis. As soon as it is severed, Shiva's phallus became an immense lingam, and the sages finally figured out who they were dealing with.

But Parvati and every other gal in town aren't enough for Shiva. He has Ganga in his dreadlocks, spitting out the water that becomes the Ganges River. The water is made fertile by sluicing through Shiva's hair. Shiva is also part female. His Trimurti form shows his usual handsome (though often gray or white as a corpse) face; the boar-tusked fearsome demonic face of Bhairava; and the face of Uma, a sex goddess, as the third part of this triple god/dess. Sometimes he is half of the eternal couple Shiva/Shakti, which

can never be separated. So he has plenty of female companionship, but never denies a woman who would desire him, and many
do.

Women in India pray to Shiva to find them a husband—
hopefully one who is as sexy as he is. In our practice as Pagan
followers of Hindu deities, Dr. Joni Abbatecola, psychologist and
guru, recommends that a female devotee of Shiva ask him be her
husband while helping her to find an earthly one. As the magickal
initiator of sex, Shiva accepts female desire as few gods do. There
is nothing judgmental or negative in Shiva's reaction to the woman
who worships him and lusts after him. How refreshing to find a
god who does not judge women as "bad" for wanting sex, or for
wanting him. It is liberating indeed.

Shiva has many myths, for though the god called "Shiva" is
relatively new, gods with his characteristics go back to the most
ancient forms of religion in India. Take Pashupati, for example.
He is shown as a horned god, seated in a lotus position, holding a
trident. He is called The Lord of Beasts, and manifests in later
years not only as Shiva, but also as nearly every "horny" Indo-
European god you've ever seen, from Pan to Cernunnos to Herne,
as the residents of the Indus Valley move west. Pashupati pre-
dates the Aryan invasion of India, going way back to the Harappan
culture in what is now Pakistan. He is very, very old. Like Isis, he
is connected to Sothis—the Dog Star, Sirius.

Another old-timey version of Shiva is Rudra, "the red one,"
who embodies Shiva's scarier aspects as destroyer. In this case,
red does not just refer to blood but also to Rudra's red hair. Shiva's
dreadlocks are sometimes red as well, linking him with other red-
headed gods in some ways, and there are many of them, from Set
to Quetzalcoatl.

Shiva is most often paired with Kali in modern myths. He is
the only one who can quell Kali's murderous rage, and he does so
by letting her dance on his corpse and distracting her with his
erect phallus. Yet another cool necrophilia story! Indeed, he is
sometimes referred to as "the erotic corpse." For Shiva is gray/
white for a reason. He *is* a corpse, in many ways, and to hang out

in the cemetery is something his followers do, and which you can do too as a way to venerate Shiva. Shiva is also sometimes blue, as are many of the Hindu gods, but he has a specific reason for being so tinted. Shiva captured the most dangerous poison in the world in his throat to keep the rest of us safe from it, and in so doing turned his throat—and eventually the rest of him—blue.

One of Shiva's names is Nataraja, Lord of the Dance. When Shiva does his dance, the universe will end. But Shiva can also dance the dance of life, because where there's sex, there's life. He is the cycle: life, death, rebirth.

Shiva is portrayed as more virile and macho than most of the Indian gods, at least to our Western perspective. He is lean and muscular and wears a tiger skin. The trident is his most important prop, and it should be no surprise that this "pitchfork" he carries ends up in the hands of the western Satan, for many scary deities, not just Shiva, carry this weapon (think Neptune and Poseidon.) He is often shown seated in the cold Himalayan wastes upon an elephant skin. Shiva is worshipped by displaying his most symbolic prop—the lingam—an abstract ovular form that represents the phallus. Sometimes it is paired with a vessel representing the yoni as well, and together the two resemble a mortar and pestle (see Baba Yaga for more on this). During a Shiva *puja* (worship) the lingam is bathed with water or milk. Offer Shiva flowers, scented candles (I feel that he responds well to mango-scented ones), sandalwood incense, and pistachios or other nuts. The mantra to chant in praise of Shiva is *Om namah Shivaya*.

Shiva is the paradox, and one which Westerners have a hard time wrapping their imaginations around. He is both asceticism and license. He is both intellect and emotion. He is both life and death. Shiva's followers are not ascetic yogis and yoginis; they are men and women who incorporate the body into the very worship of Shiva, blessing each of their limbs and their genitals in Shiva's holy name. They equate each of the chakras to a particular Element and sense, and glorify each body part as sacred. That the body itself can be holy and not something merely created to rise above is an idea that perhaps most Western religions and many

Eastern ones find hard to understand. In other words, perhaps ironically, Shiva represents the opposite of the famous Tibetan saying "You are not that body." In Shiva's world, and to the glory of him and to the pleasures and trials of the flesh, "You *are* that body."

Tezcatlipoca: Smoke and Mirrors

By Denise Dumars

Leave it to the Aztecs to peel back the veneer (sometimes literally) and reveal the truth within. Tezcatlipoca, at one time nearly the head honcho of the Toltec nation and who, after becoming victim to the "foreign god syndrome" as we've seen with Set and Loki (to whom he is often compared), finds himself in interesting roles as both a dark god and a revealer of truth.

Demonized by the Aztecs who conquered the already-fallen Maya and then vanquished the Toltecs, Tezcatlipoca, along with many other gods of the Toltecs, Mayas, and other Mexican tribes, was integrated into the pantheon of what would become the Aztec Empire. Quetzalcoatl—another of those anomalous red-headed fellows who crop up often in the mythology of dark-haired peoples—falls victim to one of his brother's nastiest tricks in Tezcatlipoca's most famous myth, which portrays ol' Tez at his most malicious. The dark brother of Quetzalcoatl is about to put one over on his brother and teach him a lesson.

Quetzalcoatl is ill, and Tezcatlipoca, whose name means "Smoking Mirror," appears to him in the form of an old man who says he is a healer and has medicine that will make him better. He gets his brother to take the draught, which is not medicine but rather *pulque*, a very strong liquor made from the maguey cactus. This renders Quetzalcoatl drunk and at the mercy of his brother. Tezcatlipoca eggs him on until he commits the heinous act of raping his own sister. Somewhere along the way Tezcatlipoca has lost a foot (sometimes in the tale the whole lower leg) and has had it replaced with a sort of peg leg that ends in an obsidian mirror—hence the "smoking" or dark mirror.

Quetzalcoatl has no idea what has happened when he wakes up the next day with the universe's worst hangover. But Smoking Mirror puts his new prosthetic to good use—he holds it up, and makes Quetzalcoatl gaze upon himself in the reflective obsidian surface. Quetzalcoatl sees his evil deed and blackened soul in the mirror and flees the abode of the gods in shame, leaving the Aztecs to await his second coming...we'll get to that story later.

There are many illustrations of Tezcatlipoca. Some show him wearing the mirror on his chest as a kind of pendant, sometimes on his back, but always as a prosthetic foot. He can have up to four mirrors on him at any one time, perhaps to reflect (no pun intended) his former glory as a quadruple-form god. The four Tezcatlipocas created the universe. Unlike his relative (and sometimes a version of himself) Xipe Totec, he does not have to flay your skin from your body to reveal what is inside you—all he has to do is hold up his mirror, and bid you look inside. Mirror, mirror on the wall—who's the ugliest of them all?

Because of the Catholic excision of much of the literature of the Mayas and other peoples of Mesoamerica, the exact origins of Tezcatlipoca and crew are vague. He is one of the oldest of the indigenous gods of Mexico; he goes back to the beginnings of the Nahuatl peoples before they split into various tribes, such as the Olmecs, Mixtecs, Huastecs, Toltecs, and finally the Aztecs, who came from the north (Aztlan, which is rumored to actually be Atlantis) and would one day rule them all.

Artistic renderings of the Aztec cities in their heyday would put any science fiction artist to shame. Great pyramids and broad avenues flanked with sacred ball courts (where the winner was beheaded), fences topped with skulls, and city centers where the temple and its sacrificial altar took center stage are almost beyond modern imagining. No wonder that other tribes banded together with Cortes to overthrow their Aztec oppressors. Little did they know that overthrowing one tyrant usually brings another to power.

At one time nearly a supreme deity, in the later myths from the Aztec empire Tezcatlipoca comes off as a bitter, angry god, a god demoted, someone very much like Milton's Satan. Sometimes in later depictions he wears a cloak and floppy hat and hides in the bushes at night, and like a divine highwayman he attacks those who travel alone along lonely stretches of road. He is also, as are many gods of his type, a lord of the crossroads.

But Tezcatlipoca's origins are grander indeed. The four Tezcatlipocas, in the earliest myths, symbolized the four Elements and the creation of all that is in our age, the age of the Fifth Sun. In later stages, the Toltecs took Tezcatlipoca and made him one of two creator gods—Tez and his brother Quetzalcoatl. Joseph Campbell relates the story of the two creators in a way that reveals the inherent violence in the peoples' beliefs: Tez and his brother essentially turn themselves into monster snakes, and ambush and tear apart the goddess Tlalteutli, using her body parts to create the heavens, the Earth, and even the other gods.

Now suddenly Tez is down to two forms: the "red" Tezcatlipoca, who will later be identified separately as the flayed god Xipe Totec, and the "black" Tezcatlipoca, who is the one with which we're concerned.

The "black" Tezcatlipoca has several myths, two of which attempt to explain why he has an obsidian mirror for a foot. In the first story, Tez and Quetzalcoatl, the "plumed serpent," are fighting a river monster that bites off Tez's foot. In the more modern myth, Tezcatlipoca breaks his foot after he falls from Heaven and has it replaced with the truth-telling dark mirror. Tez's sin? It is called lubricion—he seduces the beautiful flower goddess Xochiquetzal, who is already another god's wife.

As a tempter who is cast out of the abode of the gods, ol' Tez seems very similar to that certain fallen angel mentioned earlier. After falling from Heaven he bunks in the dark Land of the Dead, which is already ruled by a Lord and Lady of Death, so he is only a boarder, not a ruler.

Tez is a god of war and warriors; like the Berserkers of Scandinavia and the Norse god Loki, he is able to shape-shift, and in battle can turn himself into a jaguar—the most fearsome predator in Mesoamerica. The jaguar is also an important symbol for Tez because its spotted coat recalls the starry night sky, which is one of his aspects of Nature. Followers of his would sometimes paint white spots on their bodies to symbolize the stars, and cells of his cultists in the military called themselves the Jaguar Knights or the Ocelot Knights after the indigenous spotted cats. The bear is another fierce animal associated with him, and so Tez's constellation is the Great Bear, Ursa Major. In his myth he is seen as the evening star, chasing his brother Quetzalcoatl across the heavens in eternal conflict.

Tez has many names. The longest is "He Who Causes Things to be Seen in the Mirror." One of the most revealing is "The Enemy of Both Sides." His most sinister name is "Left-Handed Jaguar." But there are other versions that are not so dark: His name "Four Times Lord" reveals his former glory as a creator. In the valley of Toluca, he was seen as a god who dies and is reborn each year. This god was portrayed in ritual as a beautiful young man (as is Xipe Totec, or the "red" Tezcatlipoca) and was called "The Virginal Youth." Clearly there are stories and versions of Tezcatlipoca that are strikingly different from the more prominent ones.

Bits and pieces of Tez's former glory complicate his darker myths. For example, not only is he the god of the night sky, he is also seen as a sun god, as one of the original four Tezcatlipocas was the god of the sun. He is the creator of our current age, the Fifth Sun, which—not surprisingly—has many similarities with the turbulent Kali Yuga, as our age is called by the Hindus. And we all know the Mayan calendar ends in 2012 C.E.!

Though he is a warrior, a sorcerer, a tempter, and a trickster, Tez is also seen as the benevolent protector of slaves, indentured servants, and prisoners. Masters who abused their slaves could be afflicted with diseases such as leprosy as punishment from Tez. It was said that the smoke from his mirror quelled the physical and emotional pain of slaves and others in bondage, and when one of them was chosen for sacrifice, the intended victim would pray to Tez to ease the pain of having his heart cut out from his still-living body.

One wonders whether this particular function of the "smoking mirror" had to do in some way with smoke used literally as an analgesic. In working with Tez, Aztec sorcerers inhaled hallucinogenic herbs, including a heady mixture of tobacco, marijuana, poisonous mushrooms, and the dried and ground bodies of scorpions and poisonous snakes. It would seem reasonable to assume that a narcotic mixture similar to this one could be given as an anesthesia to a sacrificial victim.

The Head of Tezcatlipoca is considered to be the finest piece of Aztec sculpture ever found. Tez's sacrificial ritual was similarly beautiful in contrast to other sacrifices in which a slave would be dragged kicking and screaming to the sacrificial altar, have his heart excised, and then have his body unceremoniously tossed down the stairs of the temple. In stark contrast, Tezcatlipoca's sacrifice would be the handsomest young warrior available. For a year, eight priests would work with this young man, teaching him in princely ways and treating him as a prince. He would learn to play sacred songs on the flute. He was given four beautiful young women as consorts. When the year was up, the young man would be dressed up, and the eight priests would lead him to the temple. Incense would be burned and people would throw flowers and wear their best costumes. On the steps up the side of the temple to the place of sacrifice, the young man carried several flutes and would play each and then break it. When his heart was cut out, his body was then reverently carried down the steps, and the people mourned. His head would go onto the rack of skulls beside the temple.

The coming of Cortes was seen by many in the Aztec Empire as the second coming of Quetzalcoatl. Some say the followers of Tezcatlipoca aided Cortes in his conquest of the Aztecs as payback for the elevation of Quetzalcoatl to supreme deity status and the demotion of Tezcatlipoca to Chief Bad Guy. Demonized though Tezcatlipoca was for hundreds of years, in Guatemala adventure tour outfitter, Stephen Beck, found a cult of Tezcatlipoca very much alive today, especially in the region of Tikal. There ol' Tez has recouped some of his former glory. It is very unusual for a demonized god to find himself redeemed and his cult status reclaimed. Perhaps we really are living under the Fifth Sun. Perhaps every dog—or jaguar—does have its day. Maybe in 2012, we'll know for sure.

Volos:
Even the Man Who Is Pure of Heart

By Denise Dumars

Who is Volos and is that even his name—a word that comes from the same root as the Russian word for death? Who were the Volkhvi—whose name comes from the same linguistic root as `folk`—and why should we care? Because when we talk about Volos—Lord of Beasts, and, not unlike Osiris, god of agriculture and the Underworld—we're talking about werewolves. And everyone loves a good werewolf story, right?

But who is Volos, really, and why is it that—somewhere in our collective memories—the legends of werewolves come from Eastern Europe? Well, my Akashic record player needs a new needle, but I'll bet it's because we somehow remember Volos, the werewolf god, the patron of the Volkhvi, sorcerers who, unlike the kolduns and koldunyas (the Russian version of Wiccans or "white" Witches), practiced a magick of a darker kind, as well as shape-shifting.

Many cultures have shape-shifting myths. The most famous aside from werewolves are probably the Berserkers (werebears) of Scandinavia and the Leopard Men of West Africa. These shape-shifters, like the werewolf, are considered frightening, dangerous—and very powerful. It is likely that the Volkhvi had shamanic practices, and perhaps did don wolf skins and in a trance "became" wolves. For shape-shifting has a lot to do with the indigenous shamanic rituals of many of the world's peoples.

Who is Volos/Veles/Volkh or whatever you want to call him, and why is he so important that when the Greek Orthodox Christians and their business partners, the Viking Rus, converted the Eastern Slavs to their religion they did not do away with him as they did with many other Slavic gods and goddesses? Instead, they turned him into St. Vlas (St. Blaise in English), the patron saint of domestic animals and animal husbandry. Just as the Catholics in Ireland could not get rid of the goddess Brigid and so replaced her with St. Bridget, so too was Volos remembered...but tamed.

Volos, like so many of the old gods who represent the active male principle, needed to be domesticated in order to fit in with, well, the New World Order. Perun, the Russian Thor, had his gold and silver statue flogged and then dumped into the Dneiper by the new "converts," many of whom, according to *The Russian Primary Chronicle*, were "converted" at sword-point. Volos, on the other hand, was considered to be either the son of the river goddess that the Volga is named for, or the son of Mokosh, "Mother Moist Earth," Mother Russia herself, and was not so easily dispatched. According to Sergei Zaroff, when a treaty was signed with the Byzantine Empire, the soldiers took an oath on the name of Perun, and the commoners—farmers and the like—swore on Volos. However, he states that it is much more likely that the civilians swore on Mokosh, for whom Volos was the guardian, and, in some myths, Her son.

Apparently the cults of Perun and Volos were competitors. Some say the two gods hated each other; others say it was not they, but rather their worshipers, who hated each other and created the conflict between the two. Perun has many characteristics in common with sky-father gods such as Thor, Odin, Zeus, and the like. Volos is closer in theme to Cernunnos, Pan, Pashupati, and other earth gods and half-human godlets such as satyrs and centaurs. So maybe the real conflict here is a truly ancient one: sky gods vs. Earth gods.

The Baltic states also had their version of Volos, called Veles or Velnius. Sound familiar? In the 13th century Russia went back to being Pagan for a time when it was conquered by the Lithuanians; the Baltic republics did not become Christianized until the 16th century! It is almost certain that the Greek port Volos is named for the eponymous god, as is the Bulgarian city of Veles. Velnius of the Balts was a god of the dead, sometimes seen as a demon who could grant the worshiper clairvoyance and other supernatural powers. In an even spookier correspondence—

and the UFO people will love this—in Serbia one of the names of the six sister-stars called the Pleiades means "children of Veles." Marija Gimbutas, among others, believes that Vilnius, the capital city of Lithuania, was named for Velnius.

So what are we to make of a god so widespread that his name reaches from the Baltic to the Aegean? Well, he is definitely an earth god, both of the Underworld and of the beasts of the earth and the farmers' crops. His rituals, like those of most of the Slavic gods, were performed in the forest. Like many dark gods, such as the Yoruban Babalu-Aye or the Mesoamerican Tezcatlipoca, he is sometimes accused of causing disease or epidemics, especially among animals, and an amulet picturing him was thought to protect against such illnesses; breaking an oath to Volos could bring them on.

Kenneth Johnson states that the Pagan priests were called Volkh, and perhaps in later years these were demonized into the Volkhvi, or sorcerers. Russian Witches no longer call themselves by this name. But it all makes sense if you look at Volos this way: Let's say you're a peasant living on the Ukrainian steppes, the breadbasket of old Europe. You have crops to grow, animals to tend, horrific weather to deal with, and every now and then some guys from the north with bad braids and hammers come down and smite you. And when they're not raping and pillaging here come the guys from the east knocking you upside the head with their shields whenever they're not cooking barbecue on them. Who can you count on to protect your land? Your crops? Your animals? Perun, the sky father, who's sitting around the samovar having tea with Odin and Zeus and the other CEOs of the gods? No, you need the meanest guard dog you can find, and that would be Volos.

If you're a peasant you probably don't mess with Volos' magickal workings. You leave that to the shaman/sorcerers who study the black arts under Volos' tutelage. Either way, Volos is a god of covert power, whereas Perun is a god of overt power, which is probably why the Christians found him more threatening. The monks turned the werewolf into a nice old sheepdog. Right.

Clearly, the monks who equated Volos with the peaceful saint of barnyard animals—a shepherd, and quite a Christ-like image, if you will—were missing quite a bit of the myth. They totally left out the stuff about his role in magick, divination, and clairvoyance, as well as his "manimal" status. In his Osirian context he is both god of agriculture (offerings of bread were left for him in the fields) and death, and this too is left out of the Christianized version. Volos truly has two sides: the peaceful St. Vlas, barnyard guardian and healer of the sick; and Volos the werewolf, he of unbridled power, Lord of the Underworld, sacrificial god of vegetation. If all these attributes are given to one god, then it is not surprising that at least one source calls him the most powerful Russian god after Perun.

But enough of myths and syncretization; let's talk about the werewolf. For Volos was depicted as one—a creature both man and beast. A charming 19th-century woodcut depicts Volos as a shepherd watching his flocks—a man dressed in traditional medieval Russian costume but with the head of a wolf. The Eastern Slavs of Pagan times, like their cousins the Celts, did not put pen to paper. The same Greek Orthodox monks who converted them to Christianity also made them an alphabet. But Kievan epics tell of a poet/folk hero named Volkh Vseslavovich—a son of Volos—and these epic poems and stories were handed down in the oral tradition until someone eventually wrote them down.

It is very likely that there were two sides to the Volkhvi. On the one hand, they were seen as priests, seers, magicians, and oracles. On the other hand, they were a secret society that often practiced "black" magick. Prince Oleg of Kiev, one of the most powerful early Russian rulers, was rumored to be a Volkh. But then again, anyone who has seen portraits of George Washington or Teddy Roosevelt in their Masonic regalia knows that world leaders often belong to secret societies.

Joanna Hubbs, in *Mother Russia*, tells a horrifying story of the Volkhvi's misuse of power: Summoned to figure out if supernatural forces were behind crop failures in the year 1070 (this is post-Christianization, mind you) in the town of Rostov-Suzdal, the

Volkhvi blamed some of the most socially prominent women of the city for the disaster, and killed many of them, appropriating their property. Hmm, sound familiar? The desire to grab property was a common motivation for accusing women of witchcraft during the Burning Times. Hubbs believes that the women had their own secret society, which may be the same as that of the "Vilas" spoken of in Miriam Robbins Dexter's *Whence the Goddess: A Source Book*, and that jealousy and a need to wipe out a powerful women's group was behind this appalling example of human sacrifice. The Russians like to brag that while the rest of Europe was in the throes of the Witch hunts they never burned their Witches; I'm not so sure. One would like to think that misappropriating the dark power of Volos eventually brought the Volkhvi down.

Werewolf stories spread with the Indo-Europeans across Europe. Germany had quite a problem with werewolves at one time; the mental illness, appropriately called lycanthropy, came from the notion held by some homicidal maniacs which was that, upon donning a wolfskin belt or performing a magick ritual, they actually became wolves. In medieval times through the Renaissance there were many famous cases in which these men were executed for their crimes (they had a tendency to kill and eat children, you see). By the 18th century they were being placed in asylums and by the 19th century a later-debunked theory of human evolution called "atavism" was blamed for lycanthropy. The great American writer Frank Norris wrote *Vandover and the Brute*, a novel based on such a theory, in which the main character devolves from graduating from Harvard to drinking, debauching, and finally barking at the moon. Legends of French werewolves, called the *loup-garou*, evidently came to the Americas with their people, which explains the legends of the loogaroo, the werewolf of Haiti, in a country where there are no indigenous wolves!

Polish-born writer Ioanna-Veronika Warwick speaks of the loss of werewolf and other Pagan lore in Polish mythology. "Unlike the Orthodox Church in Russia," she begins, "the Catholic Church in Poland effectively wiped out our Pagan traditions. We have to go to Lithuania to learn about our Pagan heritage." But Warwick remembers some talk about the werewolf in her childhood. Sometimes he was spoken of like the American bogeyman. Sometimes he was a big eater: "I remember someone being called a 'werewolf' if he were very hungry or ate a lot at a meal," she says. Sort of like our "hungry as a wolf," or "wolfing down one's food." But there's more: "The most important thing I can remember about werewolf lore is that if the werewolf sees himself in the mirror, he will remember his true self and turn back into a human being." Aha!

Each of us has an inner werewolf. Each of us is both the domesticated St. Vlas and the wild Volos. In an over-civilized era in which anger is often stifled until it erupts like Set from his mother's side, we need to learn positive ways to access our inner werewolf. We need to become comfortable with him, and if in doing so are seen as monsters, then we need to deal with that as well.

We need to applaud being "different."

We can start with the man or woman in the mirror.

Part Four

Rituals, Spells, Talismans, and Correspondences

To Protect and Serve: An Anubis Talisman

By Lori Dyx

Anubis in his role as guardian can be called upon to protect and guide you anytime you are out of normal waking consciousness. Just as he protected the Egyptian mummy and led the soul on its perilous journey to the other side, he can watch over your consciousness, astral or ethereal bodies, and even guard your physical body when you are away from it. According to Alan Richardson, the ancient Egyptians kept a statue or talisman of Anubis near their bedsides to protect them in the mysterious and possibly dangerous other-world of sleep and dreaming. Having studied and taught techniques of dream interpretation and lucid dreaming for several years, I keep a consecrated and charged statuette of the god on my night table for a similar purpose.

However, Anubis as guardian and guide is not strictly limited to dreamwork. Look to him as guide dog, teacher, and protector whenever you are in a meditative or trance state or if your astral double goes a-traveling. As a healer and reanimator of the body he can be called upon to guide and protect your consciousness during medical procedures. For instance, anytime you must undergo anesthesia, call upon him to ensure that you return to your body (and waking consciousness) safe and sound.

In this working you will purify and consecrate a statue or image of Anubis to act as your own personal guardian and guide. Statuettes of Anubis, particularly reproductions of him as he appeared in Tut's Tomb in his "recumbent hound" pose, are readily available in museum or Pagan stores and catalogs. Of course, if you are crafty you may wish to sculpt your own out of polymer clay.

Part of the consecration is my own version of the "Opening of the Mouth" ceremony in which you will ask the god to infuse some of his divine essence into the talisman. For this part of the working you will use a small ankh to symbolically imbue life into the image. You can find ankh charms at all the aforementioned sources or make one yourself.

I have chosen to call on Anubis in his canine form; you may of course visualize him in either form. Some Pagans believe it is dangerous to work with Anubis in his canine form, particularly if you are calling down the god into yourself. I strongly disagree with this line of thinking; you should work with a deity in whatever form he or she wishes to appear to you. Anubis as canine is not a dog or beast; he is always first and foremost a supernatural and divine being.

Before you begin the consecration of the statue, you should determine its primary purpose. Do you wish this talisman to serve as a protector and guide in dreams and other altered states such as meditation, inner plane journeys, or astral travel? Perhaps you would rather focus on healing, guidance, and protection when you are undergoing a medical procedure or if you have health problems that can cause unconsciousness or spontaneous out-of-body states. Although technically one charged statue can handle all of the above, if you prefer to specifically focus on the healing aspect of the jackal god (and trust me, any deity that can reanimate the dead is a healing deity) feel free to fine-tune your intention to suit your needs.

Supplies: a statue (or image) of Anubis in canine form, a small ankh, clean sand, charcoal tab, incense censer/holder and myrrh resin, a tablespoon of "natron" (a 1-to-1 mixture of baking soda and coarse or Epsom salt), a bowl of moonlight-charged water (see following), and 2 beeswax taper candles in holders. Optional: white linen altar cloth or tray, white feather or fan for smudging, and an aspergillum for sprinkling water.

The ritual should be performed on the night of the full moon and should take approximately two hours including prep time.

Prior to performing this ritual you will need to charge some spring water out under the moon. Although Anubis is generally considered to be a solar deity, I prefer to use the cool properties of lunar energy when working with him in this way. If you are in no hurry you can choose to do so on the night of a full moon and wait until the following month's full moon to consecrate your talisman. Otherwise, it is perfectly acceptable to charge the water using waxing moon energy on the night before the ritual. This can easily be done by placing the container outside or on the sill of an open window once the moon has risen; make sure to bring it indoors before the sunrise.

Prepare your ritual working space several hours before dark. First, choose a place close to your bed like a nightstand or shelf. Choose carefully because this space will be the eventual "home" of your statue-talisman. Clear and clean that space and set up a mini altar in the following manner: Wipe the surface down with a little of the moon-charged water. Next, sprinkle a thin layer of sand on the tabletop—you may wish to lay down an altar cloth or use a shallow tray to cover the surface first. A layer of clean sand was often used in ancient Egyptian rites to instantly purify and designate sacred space. Mound a little more sand on the spot where your statue will rest.

Place your statue or image on top of the sand flanked by the candles. Arrange the incense holder, water bowl, and other supplies. Don't forget to have matches handy.

At dusk on the evening of the full moon begin the ritual proper. It begins with self-purification. The Egyptians truly believed that cleanliness was next to godliness. A clean and pure body was essential when working with the *neteru* (gods). So bathe and dress in freshly washed clothes or ritual-wear.

When you are ready and the moon has risen, dim the lights and light the candles. Light the charcoal tab and burn some of the myrrh. Allow the pungent resin to permeate the room and your senses. Take a few slow, calming breaths and say: "May I be purified by Air and by Fire. I am pure. I am pure. I am pure."

Next, take the natron and mix it with your fingers into the bowl of charged water. Quiet your mind, anoint your forehead at the third eye with the moon water and say: "May I be purified by Water and by Earth. I am pure. I am pure. I am pure."

Now you must do the same to the statue. Cense the rendering of Anubis. Say: "May you be purified by Air and by Flame. You are pure. You are pure. You are pure."

Lightly sprinkle the statue with the water. If you are using an image or statue that will be damaged by contact with water, hold up the bowl in front of the rendering instead, and visualize the essence of the charged water permeating it in the form of soft white light. Say: "May you be purified by Water and by Earth. You are pure. You are pure. You are pure."

Now it is time to ask Anubis to preside over your magickal working. Hold out your arms in front of you. Bend your elbows up at about a 60-degree angle with palms facing forward. This is called the *Ka* position. Start to slowly chant the name Anpu *(Ahn-poo)* to raise energy. When you are ready call out to Anubis:

> *Anpu, Guardian of the Gates, Opener of the Way, Lord of the Hallowed Land, He who protects the Ba and the Ka. Come in peace and preside over this magickal rite.*

Lower your arms. Now focus intently on the rendering of the god. See it not as an image, but with the help of your inner eye see the true face and form of the jackal god surrounded by a nimbus of shimmering golden light. Open yourself to his dark but benevolent energy. When you feel that the god is present, you can begin the Opening of the Mouth part of this ceremony.

Pick up the ankh in your dominant hand and say: "In the name of Anpu and the neteru of Kemet, may this image be awakened to serve as his vessel." Touch the ankh to the eyes of the image, saying: "Your eyes are open so that you may see with the eyes of Anpu." Touch the ankh to the ears of the image, saying: "Your ears are open so that you may hear with the ears of Anpu." Touch the ankh to the mouth of the image, saying: "Your mouth is open so that you may speak with the voice of Anpu."

Finally, touch the ankh to the body of the image, saying: "May the divine presence of the Jackal god enter here to guide, protect, and instruct me." Concentrate on the statue or picture of Anubis, envisioning shimmering golden energy surrounding and infusing it with his divine essence.

Put aside the ankh, refresh the incense and waft it towards the consecrated statue as an offering to Anubis.

Next, assume the Ka position and say the following prayer to charge the talisman with your intent.

> *Anpu, Guardian of the Gates, Opener of the Way,*
> *protect my spirit and guard my body when I am traveling*
> *through the Netherworld of the unconscious. Guide me*
> *in dreams and in sleep, in meditation, on the inner and*
> *outer planes, and whenever I am out of consciousness*
> *and away from my body. Keep all evil away and lead me*
> *safely back whole and unharmed.**

Fold your arms across your chest like a mummy. Now thank and praise the god:

> *Anpu, Guardian of the Gates, Opener of the Way, Lord*
> *of the Hallowed Land, He who guides and protects the Ba*
> *and the Ka, I thank you for your divine presence and aid*
> *in this magickal rite.*

Maintaining the mummy position, bow your head in gratitude. Know in your heart that Anubis has heard your prayer and that a part of his divine essence has found a home within your talisman. Remain in this position as long as you wish. Let the incense and the candles burn out. Leave the altar set up until the following morning and then clear up and arrange the charged talisman in its appropriate spot next to your resting place.

* This prayer may be repeated each night before going to bed or whenever you feel the need for Anubis' guidance and protection.

CORRESPONDENCES

Symbol: Jackal, wild or domestic dogs, embalming bier, sarcophagus, shrine box, the hieroglyph of the speckled animal hide on a pole, the *sekhem* and *was* scepters, flagellum, embalming tools, adze.

Color: Black, gold, saffron, white.

Direction: North, West.

Element: Earth.

Day/Holiday/Season:
21st day of the month, Summer Solstice, Summer.

Incense/Oil: Kyphi, myrrh, frankincense, cedar oil, lotus oil.

Associated deities:
>Wepwawet, Imy-wt, Khenty Amentiu, Nephthys, Set, Isis, Osiris, Horus, Thoth, Horus, Re, Hesat, Bastet, Kebehwet.

Party Like It's 1599: Baba Yaga's "Hen" Party

By Denise Dumars

Listen up, gals! It's time to take Baba Yaga's Crone energy and make it your own. She won't mind; she'll just eat a few more nice young people and have her strength back in no time.

A few years ago my former boss and her gal pals went out for lunch. When the waiter came around he surveyed the group and said, "A hen party, huh?" Needless to say, she was very offended. Well, I'm here today to propose a radically different kind of Hen Party! Cronies (the male version of "crone" is "crony," or so we figure) may now leave the building and go out in the woods looking for Robert Bly and beating their drums. This working is for girls only.

And by that I mean crones, hags, feminists, womanists, riot grrls, wimmen, dames, chicks, broads, and any other females who dare to feel the power of wise blood! We'll use Baba Yaga's house on chicken feet on our party invitations, and who cares if the boys snicker. Little do they know...but then they never did, did they?

You may feel that this type of "covert power" is obsolete. I mean, for one thing, when was the last time you attended a women-only event? It's sort of politically incorrect nowadays, isn't it? And now that women are out in the world and have overt power they no longer need the covert stuff, right?

Sorry to burst your bubble, baby, but you haven't come all that far. Last time I looked, women still make 79 cents for every dollar men make. That's up a whopping 10 cents on the dollar since the 1960s. The only way we've become equal to men is in having stress-related heart attacks and, oh yes, cigarette-smoking related lung cancer. A long way, indeed. So, as Peggy Lee would say, if that's all there is, then let's break out the booze and have a ball.

Baba Yaga's crone party may be set up for crones only, if you prefer. A crone is defined in the Craft as a woman who has completed menopause—specifically, a woman who has not had a menstrual period for a year and a day. Oftentimes women have a "croning party" to mark this passage in a woman's life. You could certainly utilize the Baba Yaga party for this occasion.

But we will present a more general event, and you can adapt it as need be. Baba Yaga's Hen Party calls for the celebration of women in all three stages of life. In Russian mythology, Rusalka is the Maiden, Mokosh is the Mother, and Baba Yaga is the Crone. Each will have her say.

Ahead of time, recruit a young woman to portray Rusalka, and have her dress in white or in a diaphanous, multi-hued gown. She should wear silver jewelry. A woman in her prime should play Mokosh, dress in earth tones, and wear gold jewelry. A postmenopausal woman should play Baba Yaga, dress in black, and wear bone jewelry: It is easy to find Tibetan skull beads and other ornaments carved from bone in import stores and in catalogs.

These women will be the party's honored guests. Invite as many friends from as many different backgrounds and as many different generations as you can. Try to have regularly scheduled parties in which different participants play the three roles; begin on Midsummer Eve, the most magickal day in Russia, when women would go into the woods to search for healing herbs and magick mushrooms. Hold subsequent parties on or near St. Demetrius' Day, the Autumnal Equinox, and the Spring Equinox if possible. In olden times, Russians would honor the dead at these four times of the year, and by association, honor Baba Yaga.

Bring your business cards, flyers for upcoming events, pix of the grandkids, poems you've had published, and any other networking tools or what we writers call BSPs (short for Blatant

Self-Promotion). This is about empowerment, in the secular world as well as in the sacred. It is about bridging generations and cultures.

Suggested refreshments include Russian snacks such as pierogies and blinis (blintzes will do), which can be found in the frozen food section. Chicken and dumplings would also go well, and deviled eggs with caviar. Offer vodka on ice for the braver souls and smoky Russian Caravan tea for the rest, drunk out of glasses. If someone has a samovar from which to serve the tea, so much the better. Check the Sovietski Collection catalog for supplies.

Floral decorations should include ferns, poppies, and sunflowers. Have a mortar and pestle, of course. Candles should be gold, green, red, and black. You will also need a natural beeswax candle. Burn birch, fir, pine or Russian amber incense. Music could include recordings of traditional Russian folk songs; Eastern European classical music, especially music based on magickal themes such as *Night on Bald Mountain*, *The Rite of Spring*, or *The Firebird* is always appropriate.

The ritual is simple:

Rusalka is given a bowl of water; Mokosh a censer; Baba Yaga the mortar and pestle into which you have placed coarse salt and herbs such as valerian or patchouli—any earthy scented herbs. The three women stand in the center of the room and the others form a circle around them. The *koldunya* (priestess, usually the woman in whose home you have assembled) casts a Circle with an athame, a birch branch, or a broomstick. Rusalka approaches each woman in turn, asperging her, and states: "I am Rusalka, the rarest fern flower. I grant you beauty." Each woman she blesses then states: "Rusalka, I honor your playfulness and beauty," then bows. Mokosh follows, censing each woman, stating, "I am Mokosh, the bounteous one. I grant you prosperity." Each woman blessed says "Mokosh, I honor your industry and beauty," and then bows. Baba Yaga then follows, dipping her hand into the salt mixture and touching the center of each woman's forehead, stating: "I am Baba Yaga, lady of the two worlds. I grant you long life." The women reply: "Baba Yaga, I honor your wisdom and beauty," and then bow.

The koldunya starts the music. After each woman has been blessed by the three, the women join hands and weave a spiral dance between and around the women portraying the goddesses. The "goddesses" may lay down their burdens and clap to the beat. Continue until everyone is dizzy! Then each participant should clap her hands and press her hands to the floor to ground herself. The koldunya ends the ritual with a circle drawn widdershins. Now it's time for snacks! The women honored as goddesses are served first, of course.

Networking, bragging, or gossiping are now the approved activities. Other acts of magick may follow; I strongly suggest a discussion of herbs, aromatherapy, or natural hormones, for example. The women may agree to make a potion or two in the mortar and pestle and give some of it to each attendee to take home.

End the event with candle wax divination, a method which is as popular in Russia as tarot cards or crystal gazing is here. Light the beeswax candle and pour cold water into a bowl. Drip candle wax into the water. The koldunya or one of the "goddesses" may do this for each participant. As the wax hardens into shapes in the water, ask the person who is being read for what the shapes mean to her. In this regard, it is much like reading tea leaves. Then ask the priestess or goddess for any prophecy she sees in the wax. Alternate reading tea leaves or tarot cards at subsequent Hen Parties.

The swearing of oaths was an important part of Pagan Slavic culture. If each woman present agrees, at the end of the party have each place her dominant hand over the bowl of Baba Yaga's mortar and pestle. Have her swear in the name of Baba Yaga to help and support her sisters in the Craft. Depart after kissing the hostess/koldunya and the three goddesses on each cheek.

In the Baltic republics, Paganism remained until the 16th century. In Russia and other countries converted by the Eastern Orthodox faith, the people were allowed to keep many of their "folk" customs, which were then combined with Christian beliefs. Baba Yaga lives! Throw her a bone.

CORRESPONDENCES

Symbol: Mortar and pestle, skull, bones, hut, babushka, chicken.

Color: Black, red, bone.

Direction: North.

Element: Earth.

Day/Holiday/Season:
Vernal Equinox, Midsummer Eve (June 21), Autumnal Equinox, St. Demetrius' Day (October 26), Samhain (October 31), Autumn.

Incense/Oil: Birch, fir, cedar, Russian amber.

Associated deities:
Koschei, Mokosh, Rusalka, Volos, Perun.

The Black Virgin: A Novena

By Lori Nyx

"To thy most merciful face of night I kneel..."
—G. K. Chesterton, *The Black Virgin*

A Novena is a nine-day devotional practice performed by Catholics and those influenced by Catholic practice in order to obtain special favors or grace. You may be familiar with special Novena Masses attended as part of mourning to help the recently departed make a smooth transition into Heaven. However, the most popular type is the Novena of Prayer whereby the petitioner asks a holy intercessor for help in dire and distressing situations.

Novenas consist of the repeated performance of a pious exercise such as attending Mass, the recitation of prayers or the rosary, or meditation over a predetermined amount of time. There are often extra conditions attached to this exercise; for instance, having to repeat the entire process within a certain time constraint. The purpose of this practice is for the petitioner to receive help, healing, relief, blessings, and absolution of sin(s). On a very basic level, however, the petitioner is asking a higher power for a special favor/indulgence for themselves or another in exchange for an offering of devotion. This practice has its roots in ancient Pagan customs like the Parentalia Novendialia—a Roman nine-day mourning ritual and commemoration of ancestors. In a broader sense, a Novena is the Catholic version of the time-honored tradition of petitioning a deity for healing, fertility, prosperity, love, luck, and so forth, in exchange for a votive or sacrificial offering.

Before all the Pagans in the room reach for their athames and loudly accuse me of Popery of the foulest kind, stop for a minute and think. Doesn't the above sound familiar to you? Certainly the concept of asking a deity or interceding spirit/power for a special favor in times of need is commonplace in the Pagan community, as is the practice of repeating a magickal working over a set period of days before the hoped-for results manifest. In essence, a Novena looks and acts very much like spellcraft. And to further belay your fears of Christianity intruding on our Pagan ways, fear not—the Catholic Church has condemned Novenas from time to time as being suspiciously Paganish. Okay, now all the Catholics can burn me at the stake—but then that's to be expected.

Appropriately, the Novena of Prayer is thought to have arisen during the Middle Ages among the faithful in France, Belgium, and neighboring areas—Black Virgin territory. Since we are calling upon Mary as the Dark Mother, what would be more appropriate than a *spell* in Novena form?

The purpose of a Novena of Prayer is meant to be both personal and specific to the petitioner. With this in mind, I have not created the following spell toward a particular end. Nevertheless, there are themes specific to the nature of the Black Madonna mentioned in her chapter. Recall that in the Middle Ages she was concerned with more earthly than celestial matters. Her province is life and death, sex, procreation, healing, forgiveness, and release from suffering, grief, danger, and enslavement. She is protective as well as merciful and does not judge the past sins of the repentant. Traditionally, she has been implored to in times of desperation and despair. She brings hope to battered souls and healing to broken bodies. One area I believe she can be extremely helpful in is that concerning female reproduction, whether it's a desire to conceive, to terminate a pregnancy or coming to terms with infertility, stillbirth, miscarriage, or infant death.

When you call upon her, know that she is the Divine Mother whose memory cannot be erased from our consciousness. Remember that she is Black Isis who purifies us with her tears; Kybele, bliss-filled and raving Earth Mother; the many breasted/ever-nurturing Artemis of Ephesus. In Judeo/Christian mystery traditions she is called Sophia, Shekinah, and Mary the Magdalene. Her most distant roots stretch back to the Great Mother Goddesses of the Indo-Europeans. She is our Mother in Heaven and on Earth who cannot be denied, and conversely, she will not deny bestowing grace upon us, her beloved children.

If the need is great enough this Novena to the Black Virgin can be performed at any time, but an optimum time to start is at the New Moon. Potent times of the year to invoke her are Candlemas, the months of February, May, and December, or any feast day sacred to the Virgin Mary—preferably a Black Virgin such as Our Ladies of Guadalupe or Regula. The working is a nine-day, daily meditation that includes the burning of a candle and incense, the recitation of a special prayer/petition and an offering of flowers. The meditation and prayer at a set time each day are the integral parts of the working and should not be omitted.

Ritual supplies:

- A black, brown or dark green candle in a glass container. What is commonly called a "seven day candle" will suffice, because I do not hold with keeping a candle burning unattended for long periods of time. This candle is to be used throughout the working and will be burned consecutively for *at least* an hour on each day. With a little luck you may also find and choose to substitute the candle with votives emblazoned with an image of one of the New World Black Madonnas. These candles are usually white, yellow, or pink. In my personal devotions, I have used candles dedicated to The Virgin of San Juan de los Lagos, Our Lady of Guadalupe of Mexico, and Our Lady of Regula of the Philippines.

- Incense in a holder or censer: a mixture of frankincense or myrrh, ground cedar, and either rose or lily.

- Nine fresh flowers: rose, iris, or lily in the darkest color you can find. There are specialty strains of black iris that I feel are particularly pleasing to La Vierge Noire. Offer one at a time in a bud vase to be replaced by a fresh blossom each day.

- A half-gallon of spring water (optional) to which has been added a teaspoon of milk or a few drops of rose oil.

Decide to perform the Novena at the same time on each consecutive day. Strict adherence to this schedule is required. As in all magickal workings, a quiet place where you will be uninterrupted is essential. If you have time, take a purifying bath or shower before you begin. If not, wash your face and hands in the spring water mixture. On your altar or on a clean place in your home, set up the candle, bud vase with flower, and censer. Light the incense and let its smoke permeate your surroundings and clear it of any negative influences. If you wish to further consecrate your space you may sprinkle the room with a fresh supply of the spring water mixture.

Next, light the candle. Sit comfortably or kneel in front of your altar and begin to meditate on the Black Madonna. Think about how she has performed miracles of healing and deliverance to the faithful over the centuries and has survived under different names and in different guises but is still, beneath it all, the ever-nurturing Earth Mother. Know that she hears your petition, understands your pain and difficulties, and does not judge you for embracing your own dark, earthy side. Now concentrate on whatever you have come to ask her for, even if you have only come to open your weary heart up to her guidance and solace. Speak freely and from the heart, share your desire, suffering, grief, confusion, pain, or longing. When you feel truly ready, recite the following prayer with great intention and piety.

> *Salve Regina, Black Virgin, Most Holy Dark*
> *In your compassionate wisdom you understand my desires and my suffering*
> *I come seeking your guidance, solace and aid.*
> *Turn to me the beauty of your midnight face*
> *And look with mercy and love upon me.*
> *Grant that I may* (say your petition here). *
> *Oh Gracious Mother, both Dark and Bright, hear this my prayer, bestow your grace upon me and grant me the favor I ask.*

* For instance: enjoy health of mind, body, and spirit and be delivered from present sorrow and pain.

Sit in quiet contemplation for a while, knowing in your heart that your request has been heard and will be answered. Allow the candle to burn as long as possible before snuffing it. Ideally, it should burn all the way down by the end of the ninth day to "cement the intention." However, it has been my experience that the length of time such candles last is highly variable. If the votive has not burned all the way down by the end of the ninth day, continue to light it thereafter until it has finished. If you are able to keep your candle burning safely for extended periods and it burns down before the Novena is completed, have a spare votive on hand to get you through the ninth day.

After the ninth day, your prayers will be answered. The Dark Mother will not fail you. *Salve Regina*!

Correspondences

Symbol: Fleur-de-lis, crescent moon, five-pointed star, distaff, crown.

Color: Black, brown, green, gray, silver, gold.

Direction: South, West.

Element: Earth, Water.

Day/Holiday/Season:
Monday, Friday; Candlemas (Feb. 2), Holy Days sacred to Mary and to specific Black Virgins worldwide; Spring, Winter.

Incense/Oil: Rose, lily, frankincense, myrrh, cedar.

Associated deities and Biblical figures:
Isis, Kybele/Rhea, Artemis of Ephesis/Diana, Demeter Melania/Ceres, Lilith, Brigid, Sophia, Shekinah, Kali, Jesus, Queen of Sheba, Mary Magdalene, Sarah the Egyptian.

Coatlicue: An Aztec Fertility Charm

By Lori Nyx

Initially knowing Coatlicue only from the fierceness of her iconography, I was surprised to discover that her most popular myth revolved around motherhood and miraculous birth. I shouldn't have been; Coatlicue is, after all, the Great Mother Goddess—the fecund Earth in which seeds germinate and from which green shoots arise. Regardless of their emphasis on the destroyer aspect of many of their female deities, the Aztecs also viewed their goddesses, even the most fearsome, as nurturing life-givers.

A tuft of white feathers was worn in the hair of Aztec warriors, which is why the fluff ball in the story anticipates the warrior god to be born, Huitzilopochtli. The Aztec's believed that a woman in labor was like a warrior fighting a life and death battle. Similar to the Vikings, they praised the spirits of women who died in childbirth, viewing them as honored warriors in the Afterlife.

They understood that the miracle of birth was nothing to be sneered at. I witnessed the birth of my oldest and dearest friend's baby from the initial labor pains to his arrival the next day. The experience was awesome, both beautiful and primal. It was as real and fierce as any warrior's battle in intensity and sheer physicality. Perhaps birth is the closest thing to physical combat experienced in this day and age.

When it came time to create a magickal working for this goddess, I had thought to focus on her darker side in some über-aggressive, in-your-face fashion. Yet, as I sat down to write up something suitably awesome and spooky, my mind kept returning to the image of that little miraculous fluff ball.

Fertility magick was one of the most popular and important kinds performed by our Pagan ancestors. Just think of all those little female fertility figures found in prehistoric and ancient sites the world over. Funny how today we seem to be more concerned with *not* conceiving than with conceiving. Still the desire to procreate and bring another life into the world someday is something many of us take for granted as one of our most basic god/goddess-given rights.

The miraculous nature of Huitzilopochtli's conception made me think about fertility magick today. I recently met a young Pagan couple who is trying to conceive via artificial insemination. When I looked at these two vibrant and healthy people, it struck me that fertility is not as simple a process as we think. It certainly isn't a given. In fact, more than five million people of childbearing age in the U.S. experience infertility and the emotional upheaval that such a condition may cause.

So I thought, why not a fertility charm inspired by Coatlicue? Why not use the magick of the fertile Earth Mother to help you conceive? Of course, I am not advocating the use of a fertility charm in lieu of the many medical treatments for infertility today. If you believe that you may be infertile or are having trouble conceiving, please go to a doctor and look into the variety of medical procedures available, as well as other alternatives such as surrogacy and adoption. I would also advise checking the information and resources available at the Website of **Resolve**, The National Infertility Association (*www.resolve.org*) for more information.

However, once you and your spouse or significant other have explored your medical options, or if you are in fact fertile and in the process of trying to get pregnant, feel free to make the following charm as a little extra insurance on a successful outcome. Oh, and don't think this is another one of those "woman only" workings. After all, it takes two to tango and 40 percent of all infertility is due to the male factor. A couple can each make a charm for themselves or better yet, make one and charge it together and hang it over or near their bed.

One last word of caution: Don't make this charm for somebody else. It is meant to work for the person or couple who creates it. It is also not meant to be manipulative in any way. Make sure everyone involved wants a little fertility in his or her life before you start working this kind of magick. It is necessary that the parents-to-be are in accord about such an important and life-altering matter.

Supplies needed for the charm: about 6 inches of white marabou boa (readily available at craft stores), a 4x4-inch square of snakeskin patterned cloth, waxed cord, needle and thread, a small tumbled piece of green turquoise, scissors, and fabric glue. Optional: short straight pins, and a little bit of actual snakeskin.

Ritual supplies: the finished charm, turquoise-colored or Mexican blanket, seasonal fruit and flowers and living plants for decoration, an ear of corn (fresh or dried), an offering plate, copal or dragon's blood resin in a small incense burner, a white feather for censing, charcoal tab and matches, and a representation of Coatlicue or of a serpent.

As for the assemblage of the fertility charm, that is better done inside. It won't take long to make—even if you are craft-challenged. You can start it on the morning you plan to charge it or prepare it a few days before. I strongly advise making the charm with your partner if you have one. Before you begin, clean your workspace and assemble your supplies. Light some incense and cense yourself (and your partner) and the supplies. While you are putting the charm together, you should think about the child you wish to bring into your life. Do not stress about conception. The experience should be fun. Just think about what your child will look like, how it will be to have a little person running around the house, and what it will feel like to hold this much-anticipated baby in your arms. Talk about your hopes for the future with your partner. Keep things light, happy, and loving. Don't worry about making things look perfect; it is the intent of the charm that contains the magick.

Begin by wrapping the turquoise stone with the fabric to form a roughly circular little package. If you have a piece of real snakeskin that you wish to incorporate into the charm, wrap that around the stone first, then wrap both up in the cloth. Yes, the result will be lumpy. You may have to rewrap a couple of times or cut the fabric down to a more manageable size. Work with it until you are satisfied. Aim for something about an inch or two in diameter, but don't stress. Remember: There is no perfection in Nature! When you are satisfied with the size and shape of this little care package, wrap some of the waxed cord around it and tie it securely together. You may need to use pins to anchor things in place while you do this, but be sure to remove them once the bundle is secure. To really secure things you can take needle and thread and sew the bundle up.

Next, apply a thin layer of fabric glue to the bundle's surface, just enough to make things tacky so the feathers will stick. Then wrap the marabou strip around and around the bundle until it is completely covered with feathers. This part can be a little tricky. You may need to anchor the boa with pins while the feathers adhere to the surface. Check the instructions on the container of glue for recommended drying time. Once the glue is dried, carefully remove any pins. For additional security, you may need to tack the boa securely into the fabric using needle and thread. A few stitches here and there should be enough to hold things together.

I know that this seems like a lot of work for those who consider themselves craft-challenged, but believe me, it is not as difficult as it sounds. What you want to end up with is a circular ball of white feathers. The last touch is to attach a length of waxed cord or strong thread around the charm for hanging purposes. You can choose to tie the cord around the inner bundle (and hide it with a quick fluff of the feathers) or you can sew a suitable length of thread to the bundle itself.

The consecration of your charm is best performed outside on the day of the full moon. If you are monitoring your own or your partner's peak fertility days, you may substitute one of those as long as it falls during the moon's waxing cycle. The consecration must be done outdoors, because you really need to feel the Earth Mother beneath your feet. An ideal location would be a lush garden or grove of fruit trees. Do whatever is necessary to get in contact with fresh earth, even if you have to spread a 20-pound bag of potting soil on your concrete patio and surround yourself with potted plants! The ritual should be performed during the day. Dress appropriately for the weather but your hands and feet should be bare. It is necessary that you make physical contact with the Earth.

Set up your altar area in a central position orientated towards the south (you will be facing North). The altar will be on the ground so choose as flat a spot as you can to spread out your altar cloth. Place your rendering of Coatlicue at the center, surrounded by seasonal fruits, flowers, and living plants. Place the offering plate to the right of this and the incense to the left. Arrange the other supplies as you wish.

Light the incense tab in the holder. Take the white feather in your dominant hand and hold it out before you. Now, it is time to orient yourself within the cosmos. Address the Aztec Lords of the Five Directions and ask them to sanctify and protect your space and the working:

Begin by facing East and say:

Hail to he who is Lord of the East.

Face North, say:

Hail to he who is Lord of the North.

Face West, say:

> *Hail to he who is Lord of the West.*

Face South, say:

> *Hail to he who is Lord of the South.*

Turn back to the altar and kneel before it, saying:

> *Hail to He that stands in the Center.*

After you greet the fifth direction, pour incense on the tab and say:

> *Lords of the Five Directions, bless this space as sacred.*
> *Let no ill will or evil thing enter here.*

Now call to Coatlicue, ask her to enter the sacred space and to preside over your spell, thusly:

> *Great Serpent Skirt, Coatlicue, Mother Earth, mother of the stars, the moon and the sun that brings life, rise up from deep beneath the ground, come down from Snake Mountain, come forth from the holy places of the ancestors. Sanctify this rite with your awesome and nurturing presence.*

Then pick up and present the ear of corn and some of the flowers to her by placing them in the offering plate and say:

> *Serpent Skirt, Mountain of Creation, I offer you these symbols of burgeoning new life.*

Now the one who is to conceive should lie or sit upon the ground. Your partner may do the same or stand next to you. Feel the power of the Earth beneath you. This is the body of Coatlicue, the Earth Mother: she who gave birth to the Four Hundred, the moon, stars, and sun; she who provides sustenance and life to us all. Feel her energy building in your body (have your partner do the same).

Bring forth the charm. Hold it before you toward the altar. Concentrate and bring the Earth energy up through your body and into the palms of your hands. Have your partner do the same and put his or her hands over yours to intensify Coatlicue's potent energy.

Ask the goddess to consecrate the charm:

> *Coatlicue, you who show us that sacrifice begets new life.*
> *Bless this charm with your potent power of fertility.*

Now, toss the feather-ball lightly up in the air. If it falls to the ground, or on the altar, or on your body, that's just fine. You may choose to have your partner stand up and drop it in your lap instead. Pick it up and hold it in front of your womb or genitals and say:

> *Serpent Skirt, Bless my genitals so that they may bring forth life.*

Tuck the charm into your waistband, shirt or pants pocket. Close your eyes and visualize a successful conception, a peaceful and easy birth and a child as beautiful as the shining sun.

Thank Coatlicue for her patronage and bid her return to Snake Mountain:

> *Serpent Skirt, Mother Earth, mother of the moon, the*
> *stars and the the life-giving sun, thank you for the honor*
> *of your presence. Thank you for consecrating this charm*
> *with the potent force of the fertile earth. Thank you for*
> *your protection and nurturance. Return to the holy place*
> *of the Ancestors, you who are the holy place.*

Thank the Lords of the Five Directions for their protection in the order that you summoned them (East to the Center).

Once the charm is consecrated, hang it over your bed or put it in a prominent place in your bedroom. Make physical contact with it before you and your partner make love, undergo any fertility treatment, or proceed with an adoption or surrogacy.

CORRESPONDENCES

Symbol: Serpents, necklace of hearts, hands and skull,
                primordial mountain, white feathers, rabbit.

Color: Black, turquoise, earth tones.

Direction: South, North.

Element: Earth, Fire.

Day/Holiday/Season:
                Spring, Autumn; according to Aztec calendar, year
                1 Rabbit (when the Earth was created).

Incense/Oil: Copal, dragon's blood.

Associated deities:
                Chiuacoatl, Tonantzin, Mixcoatl, Huitzilopochtli,
                Coyolxauhqui, Centzon Huitznahus.

Dionysos: En Vino Est Veritas

By Lori Nyx

According to Plutarch, all one needs to worship Dionysos is a wine jar, a vine, a goat, a basket of figs, and a phallus. Hey, sounds like a party to me! There were many ancient festivals of Dionysos, most of which celebrated the intricate and miraculous process of winemaking, as well as important and symbolic moments in the god's mythos. Many of the more esoteric cultic practices were kept under wraps, but we do know that processions, ritual reenactment of myth, theatrical performance, singing of dithyrambs, dancing, feasting, sex (both ritual and secular), and of course imbibing in the fruit of the vine took place. These ancient mystery practices revolved around the changing of the seasons and the miracle of growth, harvest/sacrifice, and inevitable rebirth. The cultivation of the vine and the production of wine acted as metaphor for the life, death, and resurrection of the "twice born" god.

It is not my intention to recreate an ancient Dionysiac ritual, firstly because we aren't ancient Greeks, and secondly because there are other modern-day practitioners who have reclaimed the

Greco-Roman Pagan path and can present the ancient mystery rituals far better than I ever could. Rather, I'd like the readers (if so inclined) to open themselves up to Dionysian energies—both the light and the dark—and to become inspired by his divine madness.

I suggest you follow Plutarch's lead (up to a point) and gather together a lovely bottle of wine, preferably Greek and red—though Italian will do, some spring water for mixing (to drink straight wine was *de classé* amongst the Greeks), a wide-brimmed bowl or pitcher, a wine cup, grape vine and/or ivy for making a wreath and decorating the altar area, a basket containing ripe fruit— particularly grapes, some additional foodstuffs (see following), and a representation of a phallus.

Now really, did you think I would leave that out? Dionysos energy is all about the erect male phallus as creative principle. If this offends you or you don't have one at the ready (ahem), you could easily fashion a thyrsos staff to serve as the god's symbol. A straight branch or wooden dowel wrapped in ivy and topped with a pinecone is easy enough to put together with a little floral wire and hot glue. If you'd like it to be more authentic, use the wood from a fir tree or a large dried fennel stalk. One priestess I know prefers to use a long hollow stalk of bamboo, which she employs to conduct energy up from the Earth or down from the heavens.

But back to old Plutarch and our ritual supplies. You'll have to do without the sacrificial goat—but a symbol or token of some horned or cloven-hoofed creature would not be amiss: a statue of a satyr, a rattle made of hooves, some faux horns, or even a bit of goat cheese. Personally, I like to use the latter along with some crusty bread for mid-ritual or post-ritual snacking since drinking wine on a totally empty stomach does not sit well with most.

An image or statue of the deity is not required, although I like to have one to help me focus during the ritual. As always, I suggest looking through art books or online for suitable imagery. A foliate or Green Man mask would serve in a pinch, particularly if it has ivy-like leaves in its design. In ancient times a terra-cotta mask was more often than not used to represent the god instead of a formal statue. Large-eyed and bearded, this imposing mask would be set atop a pillar or pole. Branches and vines would then be affixed to mimic a torso of sorts, and then this Dionysian scarecrow was dressed in drapery and animal skins and crowned with ivy. If you wish to go this far in setting up an altar to the god, more power to you!

Other ritual items that you will need are: a censer and storax or a mixture of frankincense and amber resin (pleasing aromatic herbs can be substituted), a rhythmic musical instrument such as a tambourine, drum, rattle, or finger cymbals, a saffron- or burgundy-colored candle, and an ivy plant in a deep pot. Place your altar in the middle of the room and arrange the ritual items to your own satisfaction. This ritual is not about rigid order or following a strict format. That is not the Dionysian perspective. Let yourself be inspired!

However, this *is* a ritual that uses alcohol to commune with the god of wine and ecstasy. A state of intoxication will probably be achieved. It is not meant as an excuse to practice your alcoholic tendencies, but rather to affect an altering of consciousness and shift your perception from the mundane to the sacred, just as one would use chanting, trance, dance/movement, breathing, drumming, meditation and other similar practices. Personally, I think that when you work with Dionysos or Bacchus, it is essential to take in his essence via the fermented grape, since to the ancients he was not merely the god of wine but he *was* wine, much as the consecrated (transfigured) wine in the Catholic Mass *is* the blood of Christ to believers.

However, it is not the intention of the authors to encourage or coerce anyone who does not want to or should not be drinking alcohol to do so. Consequently, if you do not drink, are a member of AA, allergic to alcohol, underage, pregnant, have never drank before, for example, this ritual as it is written is not for you. If you truly desire to connect with Dionysos in a clean and sober manner feel free to adapt my suggestions to meet your own needs. Keep in mind that you must devise an alternate (safe/sane/legal) method of achieving a mildly ecstatic state of mind that fits within the Dionysian perspective.

With this in mind, you should make a few safe/sane provisions. First, don't plan on going out afterwards. Plan on going to bed or spending a quiet evening at home. Have someone else hold your car keys or operate the heavy machinery if necessary. Plan to eat a little something during or after the ritual to help ground yourself. Certainly, this ritual can be performed by two or more people. The larger the group, the bigger the bacchanal-like atmosphere. But consider letting your guests/group spend the night. Although only a relatively small amount of wine will be consumed by participants, remember that not everyone has the same level of tolerance. Be mindful and be careful and obey all laws regarding alcohol and its consumption! 'Nuff said, now back to the preparations.

If you have the option of taking a purifying bath before the ritual by all means do so. Sweeten things by adding some milk and honey to your bath water. If this is not possible I strongly suggest cleansing yourself by washing your hands and face in spring water mixed with a bit of milk and honey.

Both a festive attitude and costume is encouraged when communing with Dionysos. I like to don my "Maenad outfit," which consists of a low-necked, loose-fitting wine colored robe and a trailing wreath of ivy or grapevine worn on my head. You may wish to wear something Greek inspired or to fashion a Roman toga out of a bedsheet. The point is to feel unencumbered and to be able to move easily.

Once the altar is set up and you are purified and dressed appropriately, put on some rhythmic and exotic instrumental music. Greek folk or Middle Eastern belly dance music works well. There is also some wonderful percussive and evocative trance/new age music available. I particularly like the recordings by Gabrielle Roth and the Mirrors for this kind of ritual.

Cast your circle starting in the East, the direction from which Dionysos most often "comes forth." If you wish, shake or beat your chosen instrument in time to the music and proceeding deosil, call the quarters and elements. In addition, invoke the heavens (Olympus) above and the Underworld (Hades) below, as the god is equally at home in both realms. Once sacred space is cast and guarded, stand or kneel before your altar and light the candle and then the incense. You are now ready to call upon Dionysos with an invocation inspired by the ancients:

> *I call upon Dionysos, Divine child of Zeus,*
> *Wild-eyed Roarer, bull-horned and many formed,*
> *Conceived in flame and twice born.*
> *Evohe, Iaachos! Oh, Blessed Lord,*
> *Giver of wine and bringer of divine madness,*
> *I call to you thyrsos-shaking Reveller*
> *Bedecked in ivy and clusters of grapes.*
> *Lead me in thy frenzied dance of life*
> *Preside over this rite of self-discovery.*

Stop at this point and pour the wine and the water into the bowl in a 1:1 ratio, enough for approximately three glasses per person. Ask Dionysos to bless this, his divine gift, as a tool for your enlightenment. Ask that the essence of the god enter into you via this fiery substance. Lift the bowl to your lips and drink with eyes closed, letting your sense of taste and smell take over, savoring its sweetness and tang. As you drink, understand that you are being infused with the essence of a god, that soon you will reach a state of *ekstasis* (standing outside yourself) and *enthusiasmos* (god possession), which will bring with it enlightenment. After each sip praise Dionysos with a cry of *"Evo-heh Ee-yakkos!"*

Do not drink all of the consecrated wine. Some must be reserved for a libation to the god. Be sure to stop or slow down as you begin to feel the effects of this sacred substance. Become aware of the sensations in your body: the warmth in your belly, the rise of your temperature, a sense of energy and delight, or sophoric headiness.

You may be inspired to dance. Make sure space is cleared and crank up the passionate music. Dance freely as if no one were watching. Bang the drum, shake the rattle, sing along, and spin wildly to the rhythm. If you have made a thyrsos, hold it up in your right hand and dance with it. Let the wine and the music fill you with ecstasy until you grow tired. If you are a little dizzy by this point, more the better. Relax. Panting and holding up the grapes, squeeze them between your fingers. Taste them. lick the juice and rub it on your face and arms to cool you. See Dionysos before you in a form both enticing and slightly dangerous, stunningly hand-some as any Greek god, yet as wild-eyed and unpredictable as a panther. He has come to bring you the truth, the truth that lies within yourself when the everyday masks of conformity and ratio-nality are torn away. He confronts you with your irrational, emo-tional self and shows you the wisdom of letting go.

This is the point when truths will come unbidden. If you have not done so, slowly finish the consecrated wine except for the third portion, which you will pour out to Dionysos.

Now what is your heart telling you? What unconscious desires rise to the surface? You may wish to write them down (you should not be so inebriated that you can't write them down). Most impor-tantly focus on how it feels to be free and intoxicated by a god.

When you're through, hold up the remainder of the wine and offer it to the god in thanks for his transformative presence and pour out a libation into the ivy plant or out of doors into the Earth.

Sit or lie down in the aftermath of your experience, but do not allow yourself to fall asleep. If you are drowsy, revive yourself by drinking some water or rinsing your face. Now, pick up your in-strument and release the Quarters starting from the Underworld/heavens and moving around widdershins until you reach the East. There, bid farewell and final thanks to the lord of life, death, rebirth, and illumination. Let the incense burn out, snuff the candles, and feast on the remainder of the food if you so desire.

Correspondences

Symbol: Thyrsos staff, erect phallus, ivy wreath, grapevine, wine, leopard skin, mask.

Color: Burgundy, yellow, green.

Direction: East.

Element: All.

Day/Holiday/Season:
              Traditional Greek Festival dates; Fall, Winter.

Incense/Oil: Storax, frankincense, amber resin.

Associated deities/Mythical creatures:
              Bacchus, Zeus, Semele, Pan, Kybele, Ariadne,
              Persephone, Priapus, Hades, Hermes, Silenus,
              satyrs, nymphs, Maenads, fawns.

The Ritual of the Reaper: Spend a Day With Death

By Lori Nyx

The activities in this ritual and visualization are intended to invoke and inspire power by calling upon this archetype. As I said in the section on the Grim Reaper, we here in the West tend not to be in touch with Death, and learning to be comfortable with him is a great step toward dealing with death in all its forms (even the death of a relationship, job, friendship, for example).

I do not think of my dead relations very much. My Mexican forebears, to the contrary, make a huge deal out of honoring their beloved dead on El Dia de los Muertos. Our Pagan ancestors teach us that the original meaning of Hallows has more to do with placating the souls of the dead rather than handing out Kit Kat Bars. So to get back in touch with Death ourselves, here's how we begin:

Pull the Death card from your tarot deck...which one is it? Triumphing death on the Battle Field? The Reaper? A badly drawn skeleton standing amongst body parts? A darkly shrouded spooky image? Use this image as your starting point and your guide, but give your imagination free reign. The Grim One should certainly appear tall and imposing and somewhat scary to your inner eye. After all, what is mysterious and unknown to us is often scary. Because of my innate sense of the ridiculous, I immediately call up an image of Death from *Monty Python's Meaning of Life*...you know, the fellow who's come about the reaping? Regardless, a good time to contemplate the Reaper is in the waning Seasons, Fall/Winter, around Hallows, the Day of the Dead, All Souls Day or when the moon is in its diminishing or dark phase. Or perhaps when you have just paid your respects at a grave or a funeral or read the obituary column, and thoughts of mortality are preying on your mind. However, I do not mean to suggest that you should ever contemplate Death if you are depressed, in deep mourning, or have even fleeting thoughts of suicide. I believe this kind of meditation works best when you are in a contemplative frame of mind with your emotions on an even keel.

If you do not have a tarot image, find an appropriate image of the Reaper—it is best if it has a border on it and perhaps a setting for the Reaper. You will make this image the focal point of an altar. The altar should be set up in the West and decorated with items that remind you of mortality: a mass card, a memento from a funeral, images of dead relatives, something that reminds you of your ancestors, or even symbolic endings—old divorce papers, dried flowers or leaves...be creative. If it is around the Day of the Dead you might prefer to decorate your altar area in the Latino fashion, with beautiful golden chrysanthemums or calendula, images of your dear departed friends and family, sugar skulls, or sweet bread decorated with bones. Bones are actually a good idea if you have some. (Fake is fine—don't go digging anyone up, please!) Halloween decorations work, too. Your altar may look creepy and out of place particularly if you choose to do this at a time of the year other than Autumn. It doesn't matter; just prepare it as you think Old Boney would like it. All the while, contemplate his image and his lore.

Once the altar is set up it is time to plan your day...wait, didn't I mention that? Today is a day dedicated to Death and his province. Spending a little time with him is the only way you can get to know him. I had originally conceived this ritual as a meditation in sacred space. But it seems to me that we are so cut off from Death in this modern world that it might be necessary to get a little literal. Now wait folks—don't call the cops. I am merely suggesting that before meditating on this archetype you do something experiential. Namely, if possible, go visit a cemetery. When was the last time you tended a loved one's grave? Or lit a candle for that person in his or her preferred holy place of choice? Even if you don't have a loved one interred nearby, go to a local memorial park and just walk there and think for a while about mortality: your own or those around you. As a rule, cemeteries are pretty, park-like places. Try to find an older one with interesting headstones or architecture. Read the epitaphs…if you are lucky enough to be at a very old graveyard, you may find the archaic spelling and poeticism of the words fascinating. Wonder who these people were and what their lives were like prior to their encounter with the Reaper. If you happen to have a plot of your own picked out or a family crypt, then certainly visit that space. Why not? It belongs to you and you plan on resting there one day. Many major cities have cemetery guidebooks that will detail the resting places of the famous; if you live in L.A., San Francisco (more on this in a moment), New York, New Orleans, London, or Paris then you will have no problem finding a guidebook to a cemetery that allows visitors. Why not, for example, visit Holy Cross cemetery in Culver City, California, and visit Bela Lugosi's grave, where he was buried in his Dracula cape? Or drive up the freeway a bit to Westwood, and at the Pierce Brothers cemetery, visit Marilyn Monroe's crypt? The possibilities are endless.

A word about Colma: This is where San Franciscans go when they die. Located a few miles south of San Francisco, it is literally a city of cemeteries. It is worth the trip if you are in the Bay Area, for sure, and an ideal location for this ritual.

If this suggestion creeps you out (why are you reading a book about dark archetypes?) or if you can't get to a cemetery, then perhaps you might want to start with something simpler. Get a newspaper and read the obituary column. This is perhaps something you may want to do anyway as you start your day with Death. For those more stalwart, I might suggest attending a funeral…however, I don't think it's necessary to go *that* far. The idea is to stop ignoring Death altogether and to accept it as a necessary part of life. With this mindset you will be ready to commune with this archetype.

Once you have returned home you might also take the time to look at old photo albums with pictures of dead relatives, friends, and pets if you didn't already do so when constructing your altar. If this makes you too melancholy, don't do it. In fact, if any of these suggestions make you too melancholy, I suggest shelving this ritual for another time when you are feeling more up to it. It is important to remember the good times and happy memories and honor those departed loved ones, not to dwell on your loss or make yourself sad.

If the day is still young, and you are *still* not in the proper mood, I would suggest reading some poetry that deals with death— something gothic, such as Poe. Or read over the previous section of Reaper lore, one of those guidebooks previously mentioned, or a fabulous novel like *The Loved One*. Listen to your favorite Goth CD—aim for melancholic, not demonic. Any sweetly sad music will help set the mood. If you feel nostalgic dig out that old Blue Oyster Cult album and sing along: "Seasons don't fear the Reaper...."

Now you are ready for the visualization. Prerecord the following visualization or have someone read it to you. Do the visualization at dusk. Make sure your altar is suitably decorated; frame your image of the Reaper with lit votive candles—I like those tall white novena candles self-contained in glass; you might prefer an actual Santisima Muerte candle if you can find one—they are common in botanicas. In the traditional Latin Day of the Dead celebrations, the favorite food of the deceased is often placed on the altar. Many Pagans celebrate in a similar way, with a Dumb Supper on Hallows. I suggest that you put a plate of harvested seasonal foods on your altar: something that you like that suggests the Reaper as Harvester yet which contains the seeds of life. Perhaps dried fruit or cake containing nuts or seeds...or last Christmas's fruitcake! Talk about dead!

Now that you are in a suitably morbid mood, center yourself (I doubt you'll need to ground today) and set up sacred and protected space. Dim the lights and light the candles; keep a window open so you can see daylight fade to darkness or if you are on the West Coast, the sunset.

Sit comfortably in front of the altar and focus on the image of the Reaper and as you breathe in and out slowly and rhythmically, see that image (in your mind's eye) become more three-dimensional—life-size. The card becomes a window or an open doorway that you gaze through; then it becomes a landscape with the Reaper, the things around him a solid presence. As you breathe in and out, focus on the slow beating of your heart...can you hear it? If not, imagine you hear a steady heartbeat, or put on a white noise machine that has a heartbeat setting or a tape such as *Heartbeat and Ohm with Subliminals*. This sound will be a warm, reassuring presence throughout your inner journey.

As you gaze on the static form of Death, you realize that the room around you is dissolving and that you are now part of the landscape pictured in your image. Somehow, without even realizing it you have passed over the gate from your world into the realm of Death. You are not frightened; you know you can return to full waking consciousness at any time and that you are not meant to stay with the Reaper. This is only a friendly visit.

Look around you. What is the landscape like? It should at first resemble what is shown in the image you have chosen. Is it bleak and dreary? You notice there is little color, just shades of white, gray, and black with the occasional touch of faded pastel. Before you is the Grim Reaper: incredibly tall and gaunt, the gleam of his death's head half obscured. Take a moment to fully take him in. As you move further into this visualization, he (as well as the setting) may look different from your original image: this is fine, let your inner eye be your guide. If he does not sit astride his mount, then you see behind his great hulking form his pale horse waiting patiently. He holds in his hand that wicked-looking, oversized scythe. What are your impressions of Death? How do you feel in his presence? It occurs to you that he seems to be silently waiting for something. This is a silent place, yet the silence between the two of you is especially palpable. In your confusion you look down and notice that around your feet—in fact, strewn across the grassy ground—are what look to be brittle human bones, and occasional cracked stones carved with lettering. Something that looks like a crown sticks out of the earth near your toe, the gleam of gold still faintly perceptible on its battered surface. You are standing in a graveyard...a very, very old graveyard, and Death awaits you....

Remember, you are here to get to know him, perhaps ask him a question. If you haven't already, take the initiative and greet the Reaper. He answers you quietly, his voice a gravelly whisper in your mind. It is perhaps difficult to tell, but you sense he is pleased that you have come. He lifts one bony hand and points a finger at a tombstone near you. Your curiosity piqued, you examine it, for you get the feeling that there is something he wishes to show you. There is an inscription. It looks vaguely familiar—although you are not really sure if you have read it before or shall in the future. Examine it closely. What does it say? It is important, and you will remember what is written there when you leave this place.

If the message is unclear, you may ask the Reaper to clarify. Be patient; the wisdom will come. You have spent the day meditating on mortality; is there something specific you need to ask him? Or tell him? If so, do so now. He will readily answer you or listen. Don't worry if what you might impart is of a personal nature; Death will keep your secrets. He tells no tales.

When you have finished your conversation with Death, thank him and pay your respects—so to speak—knowing that if you ever wish another audience with him you have only to meditate on his image to "visit" with him again.

After you come out of your meditation and before you close down your sacred space, say a little prayer for or speak a few words in honor of all those who have passed before you, all those who live on in your memory and those you never knew yet somehow touched your life. Remember that you will one day be where they now are, dancing in the wake of the Reaper.

CORRESPONDENCES

Symbol: Scythe, skull, bones, grave, mausoleum, cemetery,
                  coffin, corpse, hourglass, spade, arrow, dark cloak/
                  hood, shroud, death coach or cart, the soul, le
                  danse macabre.

Color: Black, white, gray.

Direction: West.

Element: Earth.

Day/Holiday/Season:
                  Saturday; Hallows, New Year's Eve, February;
                  harvest time, Winter.

Incense/Oil: Myrrh, cypress

Associated deities/Mythological figures:
                  Cronus, Saturn, Charon, Azrael, the Angel of
                  Death, Dis, all psychopomps, Santisima Muerte,
                  L'Ankou.

Hekate: Went Down to the Crossroads

By Lori Nyx

It is tempting to call upon this traditional patroness of Witches
for all sorts of grim and negative magick. Late classical literature
is rife with examples of Hekate-sanctioned necromancy, summon-
ing and removal of ghosts, murder, and horrific transformations
via noxious potions and baleful herbcraft. In ancient days, many a
curse tablet invoked the fearsome power of Hekate to wreak havoc
on one's enemies. By no means has this mysterious and powerful
archetype come down to us as "Little Suzie Sunshine." This is
after all, Hekate—the dark face of the moon, wanderer in the
night, and patron of sorceresses. However, I have decided to forgo
the obvious banishing, retribution, spirit communication, consigning your enemy to Hades, cutting of cords sort of magick in lieu of
something far scarier: making a major life decision. EEEK!

From time to time we are faced with life-altering decisions, exciting new possibilities, or necessary choices as we journey along our respective paths. Sometimes it's easy to make necessary changes, but more often than not we find ourselves tied up in knots over such questions as: Should I stay with the company, look for a better job, or just start my own business? Do I go to the local university or relocate to the Ivy League school back East? Should I finish my graduate work or take this once in a lifetime job opportunity? Should I stay in the Underworld with handsome Hades or return to the land of the living to be with my mother, Demeter? Hey, we've all been there: either frozen on the threshold of the future or tugged in several equally enticing directions. So who better to invoke to help us find our way than Hekate Enodia, she of the crossways—the goddess who waits at the portal of transition and illuminates the path?

The following "Hekaterian" spell was created for those times when we are at a crossroads and can't decide which way to go. It combines the practices of journaling, visualization, and candle divination in sacred space to help one come to a clear and satisfactory decision.

Begin this working three nights prior to the new moon and end it on the night of the new (dark) moon. Using the philosophy of waning moon magick, think of this spell as a "banishing" of your doubts and indecision. With the coming of the new moon, a potent symbol of this dark goddess, you will have planted the seeds for a positive new direction in your life.

Supplies: Three yellow candles of uniform size and circumference. I prefer to use narrow pillar candles about 1 3/4 inches in diameter and 4 inches tall, placed on a flat plate. If these are not available, substitute tapers in three separate but uniform holders. The candles need to be at the same height and their wicks should be evenly trimmed. You will also need 12 inches of black twine or cord; a notebook and pen; Hekate oil (either purchase or steep three strands of saffron in warmed almond oil); charcoal and censer; and a pointed ritual knife or scribing tool. Optional items: candle adhesive, myrrh resin, and a small statuette or image of a dog.

At dusk on the first evening, arrange your altar in front of or near a window that looks out on the sky. Being able to see the waning moon or night sky while you work magick will greatly enhance this experience. If this is just not possible then dim the lights, close your eyes, and imagine the sky overhead or pop outside for those moments when you are required to moon gaze. This ritual space will be set up for four consecutive days, so a quiet location away from daily mundane traffic would be best.

Decorate your altar using colors, objects, symbols, and scents (see Correspondences). A devotional image of the goddess is not required. However, I would suggest placing a small statuette or image of a dog on your altar as a token offering to this dog-loving goddess. Be sure to leave a cleared space in the center of the altar for the candles and notebook.

When it is dark and the moon has risen, set up the sacred space, ground and center. Light a charcoal and cense the area with a few drops of the Hekate oil or myrrh resin. Dim the lights, but do not turn them completely off as you will need to write in a few moments. Stand at the altar, gaze out on the night sky, and invoke the goddess with these words, written in the Orphic style:

> *Hekate of the roads and crossways,*
> *both lovely and terrible, fierce and nurturing,*
> *I invoke you, Daughter of the Starry Sky, Night Queen,*
> *Dog-Loving, Torch-Bearing, Keeper of the Gates.*
> *Mistress of Magick, Dark Moon, Guide of Souls,*
> *I beseech you to come to this holy rite with joyous heart*
> *and to favor me in this my working.*

(Add a few more drops of oil or grains of resin to the charcoal.)

Now, open your notebook and begin the journaling part of this spell. It will be more comfortable for you to sit for this part. Write "Path One" at the top of a blank page. Next describe this path (one of your choices) in detail. Outline the best-case scenario if you were to choose this option but do not embellish the truth.

This spell is designed to help you explore and decide among two or three choices. I find that when presented with opportunities, we usually have more than two, even if we don't at first realize this. Even if it appears that you have an either/or choice, you still have the option of doing neither. To make no immediate change is also a choice. You may also choose to reserve this third path for an unknown opportunity that has yet to present itself. On the first night you will only be dealing with Path One. Once you have written your description/scenario, put the notebook aside and select one of the candles to represent this choice.

Using a ritual knife (if you do not have an athame, then a hatpin or any scribing tool will suffice), inscribe one or two words that best describes this option into the candle. For instance, "move," "new job," "school," or "sell house." Next, dress your candle with Hekate oil, anointing it from the bottom to the top. You will probably have some oil remaining on your fingers; touch this to your third eye and say:

> Hekate, guardian of the crossways.
>
> Attendant at the axis of change.
>
> Guide me through the darkness.
>
> Comfort me in this time of transition.
>
> Allow me to embrace change without fear.
>
> Help me to choose the correct path.

Store the dressed candle and notebook in the center of your altar space.

Now turn off the lights and gaze out into the night sky. If possible, open the window and let the night air in. Breathe deeply and quiet your mind. Meditate on the vastness of the starry sky, the sliver of the waning moon. This is the goddess: remote, vast, and mysterious. Yet, She is also here standing beside you at your own personal crossroads. Do not fret over your impending decision. Know that the goddess will guide you. When you are through communing with the night sky and feel calm and relaxed, silently and respectfully bid Hekate farewell for the night and thank her for her gracious presence. Exit your circle by cutting a door with your ritual knife. You will not be opening the circle until the spell is completed. If possible, go straight to bed.

The following evening re-enter sacred space, ground and center yourself, and repeat the process from the point at which you light the incense and call the goddess. Write a detailed description of "Path Two" on a fresh page in your notebook. Inscribe the second candle with a word meaningful to this choice. Dress the candle and put it and the notebook aside. Anoint your third eye with the oil and repeat the prayer. Meditate on the night sky until you feel deeply calm and centered.

Repeat the process the third night focusing this time on "Path Three," whether that is your life as it is now or a hitherto unknown opportunity. In the case of the latter, write a heading but just leave the page blank. Continue as on the previous nights.

By the evening of the new moon you will have written out an exploration of each possible path. You may already have gained fresh insight by this simple exercise alone.

Reenter your circle, ground and center, and again burn a few drops of oil or resin. Invoke the goddess. Anoint your third eye. Next, arrange your three candles close together to form a triangular wedge. Cluster the pillar candles as close as possible on the plate. If they are not secure, adhere them with a bit of candle adhesive. Place two candles side by side at the back and one in front. Take the length of twine and tie it around the "conjoined" candles at about half way down. If you are using tapers in holders wrap the twine at their bases, using the same triangular formation.

Pick up your notebook and read through all the entries. You may suddenly realize that you already know the correct path. If this is the case, then you do not need to take this working any further. Instead, carefully cut the cord that binds the candles with your athame. Light only the one that symbolizes your choice and allow it to burn down. Turn out the lights, gaze out into the night, and thank the goddess for your newfound clarity. Know that she will protect and guide you on your chosen path as described below. If you are still uncertain of your way, it is time to ask the goddess to point the way via candle divination. Dim the lights. In quick succession, speak the descriptive word for Path One and light that candle, then name Path Two and Path Three and light those candles.

Offer up the prayer to Hekate and focus on the candles' flames. Each is like a torch held by the three form goddess. Each is like a pillar at the crossways—surmounted with a fearsome mask facing different directions. Each is a possible future, waiting for you.

As the candles burn down watch them carefully. Look for any anomaly in their burning. Does one burn much quicker than another? Does one sputter and flare? Does one's flame flicker or smoke? Or perhaps one candle burns tall, bright, and steady. Note which candle—which direction—seems to speak to you, which flame catches and holds your eye. This is the path that the goddess is guiding you toward. This is the torch that leads the way to your future.

Once your choice has been made, cut the black cord and extinguish the two candles that represent your discarded paths. Keep your "True Path" candle lit for as long as possible or until it burns down. Now thank the goddess for her presence. Go to the window, let the night air in, gaze up and say:

> *Hekate of the roads and crossways,*
> *both lovely and terrible, fierce and nurturing,*
> *Thank you for your guidance,*
> *Daughter of the Starry Sky, Night Queen,*
> *With your sanction and protection,*
> *I gladly embrace this path,*
> *Dog-Loving, Torch-Bearing, Keeper of the Gates,*
> *Mistress of Magick, Dark Moon, Guide of Souls,*
> *Thank you for attending this holy rite*
> *And showing me your favor.*

Silently bid farewell to the goddess, close down sacred space, and open the circle. Discard the two "Path Not Taken" candles and their corresponding notebook entries as soon as possible.

CORRESPONDENCES

Symbol: Torch, key, knife/sword, spear, rope/scourge, bowl, pitcher, starry crown, the moon, the crossroads, the Hekateron, gorgoneion, dog, raven.

Color: Black, midnight blue, saffron, gold, white.

Direction: North.

Element: All.

Day/Holiday/Season:
                 Hallows, Aug. 13, Nov. 16, Imbolc; Fall and Winter.

Incense/Oil: Saffron mixed with olive or rose oil.

Associated deities/Mythological figures:
                 Artemis, Selene, Diana, Phoebe, Enodia, Brimo, Iphigea, Perses and Asteria, Nyx and Tartarus, Hermes, Demeter, Persephone, Hades, Cerberus, Gorgons, Eryines, Circe, Medea

Prepare to Unleash Hel, or at Least Her Talisman

By Lori Nyx and Denise Dumars

To make Hel's talisman you will need six inches of silver wire and a suitable length of silver chain. I suggest you raid your jewelry box for an old pendant chain that you no longer have use for—preferably a proper link chain with a working clasp. If too costly, silver-tone metal can be substituted for pure silver; even a large unwound paper clip will do in a pinch. In addition, you will need wire cutters, toothless pliers, and two jump rings. All of the above are readily available at your local lapidary or craft store.

Note: If you are working with recycled materials, purify them first. You may choose to bury them briefly in the ground or in a bowl of salt, rinse them through running water, or smudge the materials with a cleansing herb of your choice. Even newly purchased items can stand a quick cleansing to rid them of other people's psychic residue.

In order to consecrate your talisman you will need some spring water, a small paper or plastic cup, some magickally potent herbs and/or oils (see Correspondences) and access to a freezer. It is also a good idea to make an incense or oil out of these plants to use when invoking the goddess; birch oil is readily available in most aromatherapy shops. I suggest using the ground up bark or dried leaves of one of the trees mixed with the oil, or tincture of one of the plants in a one to one ratio. However, use whatever is most pleasing or available to you.

A potent day to perform any magickal working related to Hel is Saturday, the day dedicated to her father, Loki. Equally appropriate is the evening of the dark moon. For extra oomph, you can be patient and wait to make your talisman on a Saturday that falls on the dark moon.

You are going to construct Hel's talisman in the shape of the previously mentioned Norse rune, Hagalaz (ᚺ). It looks like a stylized letter *H*. When ready to begin, snip the silver wire into three equal parts. One piece will serve as the symbol's slanted crossbar, the others as its vertical sides. With the help of the pliers, wrap one end of the crossbar around a sidepiece about a quarter way from the top. Make sure that the wrapped wire is tight and doesn't slip out of place. Next, take the unwrapped end of the crossbar and wrap that around the remaining sidepiece, about a quarter way from the bottom wire. Trim all the edges to the desired size. File down any sharp edges. I like to loop the ends of the sidepieces with the pliers so that I may easily attach the chain and wear the rune. If you have a soft leather mallet available, you may pound the talisman to flatten and harden the metal. Note: If you are an experienced silversmith or metalworker you can go whole hog and make a much more elaborate amulet.

Once your Hagalaz rune is complete, you will dedicate it to Hel (or charge it/imbue it with her energies) by doing the following: Wrap the rune with the silver chain. As you do so, concentrate on an image of the goddess and say:

Hail Hella!
Great Lady of the foggy halls of Niflheim,
Wise guardian of the dead,
Let Hagalaz be my protector,
My champion, my counsel.
Hail Hella!
Glorious daughter of Loki,
Queen of the world below,
Bestow upon me your grace.
Hail Hella! Hail Hagalaz!

Remember that Hel herself is bound to the Netherworld, waiting (impatiently) for Ragnarok, so she understands fully the essence of bondage and its counterpart, release. Now, take your cup and fill it halfway with some spring water. Add a pinch or two of the herbs and/or a few drops of the scented oil. Place the chain-bound rune into the cup, making sure it is covered at least halfway by the water mixture. The idea is to have the amulet encased in ice. We are creating Niflheim—Hel's domain—in microcosm. Lastly, put the cup in the freezer near the back where it gets nice and misty and leave it there until frozen. If you have the time, leave it there until the following Saturday or the next dark moon.

After a suitable amount of time has elapsed, set up ritual space, not forgetting to ground, center, and protect yourself. Remove the ice cup and place it on your altar flanked by two candles: one black, one white. As the ice slowly melts, visualize that Niflheim itself is thawing and that, in so doing, part of the Hel's essence or power breaks free from her Underworld realm and permeates the amulet. To cement this image you can chant "Heilsa, Heilsa, Heilsa, Heilsa," and focus your will on the talisman or perhaps play "Nithing" from Freya Aswynn's CD of Norse chants.

Before fishing out the rune, anoint your forehead, throat, and wrists with the charged water. Remove the rune and say these words as you unwrap the chain from around it:

What was done
Is now undone.
What was sent
Will now return.
What was closed
Is now open;
What was forbidden
Is now revealed.
Hail Hella!

Dry the rune and the chain with a soft cloth and keep it on your altar until the candles burn down. If you desire, you may want to attach the rune to the chain with jump rings and wear it as a necklace. In this way Hel will be on your side whenever you have need of her. Or you can always keep it in a small gray cloth bag. When not in use I like to keep my ritual jewelry or charm bags on my permanent altar.

There, you have just unleashed a little bit of Hel and invoked the power of the Hagalaz rune: the power to bind and free, to disrupt, protect, and transform. Hail Hel!

Use of the rune Hagalaz in ritual at this time can give one access to the Underworld. As Freya Aswynn tells us, charmed amulets utilizing the Hagalaz rune, when dedicated to Hel, were considered to repel curses; hence, Hel is a goddess of uncrossing and spell-breaking. Hel is also the deity through whom you can access your ancestors, as she is the gatekeeper and the guide to the Underworld.

This amulet serves as a focus. Not only does it reflect the dark aspect of a goddess of death and transformation, but it can also be used to commune with those under Hel's dominion: namely the dead. I am not promoting necromancy here, but I am suggesting that if you do honor the ancestors and desire to communicate with them when the veil is thinnest (conveniently around the time of Hel's holiday, Hallows) you may use this amulet as your conduit for messages or prophesies from the Other Side. The simplest way to do so is as a pendulum. Set up your altar to Hel, light a black and a white candle, and get yourself into a meditative state. You may wish to chant "Hail Hella" or something similar, but do so gently as one would a mantra.

When you feel relaxed and ready to communicate with the dead, rest the elbow of your dominant arm on your altar. Your arm should be bent upwards. Hold the chain of your amulet between your index finger and thumb, and let the Hagalaz rune dangle until it is still. Focus on whom you wish to contact in Hel's realm. A deceased family member? An old friend? Perhaps even the goddess herself? Ask a simple question; one that can be answered with a positive, negative, or neutral answer. Then, with much respect, ask Hel to allow you to speak with the deceased. Ask the pendulum to show you a clear example of a "Yes" motion, "No" motion, and "Neutral" motion. A pendulum usually moves in horizontal lines (side to side or back and forth) or spins clockwise or counter-clockwise. Unless you determine the code for your answers, you won't know whether you and the goddess are on the same page. Be mindful and respectful; don't overtax those on the Other Side, or bother them with trivialities. A few important and sincere questions per dowsing/divination session are best. Once you are finished, thank the spirit for speaking with you and especially thank the goddess. Also ask for her continued protection and for her to close the link between you and the Other Side (better to be safe than sorry).

Another use in which an amulet charged to Hel would come in handy would be for uncrossing or unhexing. Of course, this goddess' energy would work equally well for crossing or hexing, but sweet little me would never suggest that sort of thing: remember, folks, what goes around....

If someone is sending spiteful stuff your way, ask Hel to have it frozen in its tracks and perhaps rerouted to a metaphoric Niflheim, or else reverse its direction and disrupt the life of the perpetrator like a hailstorm on a wheat field.

Correspondences

Symbol: Hail, Hagalaz rune, snow, ice, skull, bones, wolf, serpent.

Color: Black, white, silver, gray.

Direction: West.

Element: Water (frozen), Air.

Day/Holiday/Season: Saturday; Samhain; November; Autumn.

Incense/Oil: Birch, Lady's Mantle, Lily of the Valley.

Associated deities/Mythological figures: Dame/Frau Holle, Holda, Habondia, Loki, Angrboda, Fenris, Jormungand, Thor; Garm.

Sacrifice Your Broken Heart to Kali

By Lori Nyx

Kali is Shakti. Her energy is very sexual, fertile, and nurturing, as well as violent, aggressive and no-nonsense. It should not be surprising that she can be invoked when one needs lovers, sex, fertility, and so forth. A famous Wiccan author once created a spell where one asks Kali to bring them lovers—not the usual thought when working with Kali in a magickal sense. I mean, isn't Kali supposed to be about female empowerment, liberation from ego, and getting back at bad guys? Still, I wonder what sort of lover Ma would send if you asked her. Shoot, I wouldn't turn away the human equivalent of Lord Shiva as a dance partner. I have yet to try the spell myself, but I do congratulate her on her daring. Why not ask the dark goddess for love? Kali, after all, is the great Yogini, the Tantrika, as well as the Death Dealer.

If this archetype is new to you and since this is a book about the darker side of life, you may prefer to play it safe and ask her instead to help with the flipside of love. As you now know, Kali is as much about positive transformation as she is destruction. So,

why not ask her to help you deal with a bad breakup, that unre-
quited longing, those pesky restraining orders…You get the idea.
Nothing derails one's life quite like the lingering pain of an unhappy love affair. Sigh, we've all been there. This is when I usually
call on the Dark Mother to help me make it through the dissolution and disillusion of a relationship.

I have created this spell for those times when your personal
power has been diminished by the loss of a relationship, when
self-love has been replaced by self-loathing, and when the rejection by another sends the demons of regret, despair, and loneli-
ness to possess and overwhelm you—all of that horrible fallout
from when your delicate blossom of a heart has been crushed. In
such dire straights, it's time to call on one big, bad Mama to gobble
up your pain and to help you to process and heal.

For this spell you will need a red altar cloth; a devotional
image or statue of Kali; a black protection candle in a holder; a
full-blown red rose without the stem; a dried red rosebud iIf this
once graced a bouquet from your ex-beloved, all the better); three
rose thorns; chocolates; an offering plate; a fireproof container
filled with sand; charcoal tabs; Kali incense (a commercial blend
or your own mix of camphor, sandalwood, and rose); wooden
matches; a fan or feather for smudging; and lotus or rose oil. Optional: a cushion for kneeling, a trivet, and a mortar and pestle.

This ritual is best performed at night during the waning or new
moon. Set up your altar facing south. Cover it with the red cloth.
Place your rendering of Kali above eye level, but at a point where
you can see it clearly from a kneeling position. Place the offering
plate in front of the goddess. Place the candle on the right side of
the altar. Put the fireproof container to the left and light two charcoal tabs within it. I suggest placing the container on top of a
ceramic trivet and having some extra sand, a metal cover, or another fireproof item nearby, just to be safe. Also make sure that
the room is well-ventilated. You will use the container for both
the incense and for burning your "heart" offering. Periodically
check to see if you need to light more charcoal tabs. Arrange other
supplies nearby.

Light the black protection candle and ask the universe to let no ill will or evil thing enter into your space. Ask to be shielded and protected in your vulnerable emotional state. Next, prepare yourself for the working by grounding and centering. The easiest way to do this is to sit in the lotus position or kneel before the altar; take a few deep pranic breaths, and then chant Kali's mantra, which calls on her as the force of creation, dissolution, and transformation:

Om, Hrim, Shrim, Krim
(OHM, HREEM, SHREEM, KREEM)

Then say: *Divine Mother Kali, I call and bow to you.* Bow before the altar and touch your forehead to the floor. Praise the goddess by saying *Jai Ma! (Jay Mah!)*, which means "victory to the Mother." Light the incense and present it to the goddess by gently smudging her image. Then hold up and silently present the full-blown rose to her and place it on the offering plate.

Gaze upon the rose at the goddess's feet. Allow your mind to wander back in time. Think of your ex-lover. Think back when your relationship was good. Think of all the wonderful things that were shared: the attraction, the courtship, the flirting, that special feeling of connectedness, sexual union—all of the things that you now miss so desperately. Reliving these memories will be bittersweet, so take a few deep breaths to steady yourself if need be.

When you are ready, make the "heart" offering in the following manner: Pick up the dried rosebud and hold it close to your solar plexus. This faded flower represents your heart as it is now—shriveled, shrunken, dead—perhaps before it even had a chance to fully bloom.

Now allow yourself to think of the circumstances in which your heart was broken and the final aching realization that love had soured and cannot or should not be reclaimed. If this rosebud came from your ex-lover, ponder the difference between how you felt upon receiving it and your current circumstances. Focus your pain into the rosebud. Think of the dissolution of the relationship and pierce the bud with one thorn for the past, one for

your present pain, and one for any residual pain that lingers because of this breakup. Do not worry if the flower begins to
crumble—it is the symbolism of piercing that is important. (Optional: you may also pierce your finger and anoint the bud with a
drop of blood. If you happen to be menstruating, that potent
blood may also be used.)

Hold the pierced rose up to your mouth. Breathe on it.
Breathe your hurt into it. Let all of the pain bubble up and spill
into the rose. Cry, rage, or speak out if you wish. Anoint your
"rose-heart" with tears if they flow. When you feel that you have
poured as much emotion into this offering as possible, hold it up
to Kali and say:

> *Om Krim, Kali!*
>
> *Beautiful Dark Mother, I offer you my broken heart*
> *and all of the pain and suffering it causes me,*
>
> *I ask that you purge me of the feelings that threaten to*
> *overwhelm me,*
>
> *Help me to destroy the demons of low self-esteem,*
> *heartache, despair, depression, loneliness and regret, so*
> *that my heart may bloom again.*

Set the rose on the charcoal and pour three drops of the fragrant oil on it. You may need to hold additional matches to it
until it catches fire and burns. Be careful: Have sand or a metal
cover at the ready if the flame gets too high. If you cannot light a
flame at your altar, an alternative method is to crush the rose in a
mortar and pestle, mix it with the oil, and then pour the remains
on the charcoal tab. As it burns, call out triumphantly: *Jai Ma!*
Once the flower is totally consumed, again touch your forehead
to the floor in humility and gratitude.

Next, return your attention to the beautiful full-blown rose.
Pick it up for just a moment. Take some time to admire its beauty.
Smell its heady fragrance. Touch its supple petals. Drink in its
vibrant color. See it now as a symbol of the beauty that rises again
in the wake of destruction. Remember that out of the ever-fertile

womb of Kali, life with all of its attendant pleasures and pains endures. This rose is an offering to the goddess, but it is also a symbol of your heart rising from the ashes to fully live and love again. Lift the rose to your forehead and bow your head, then place it back on the offering plate and say:

> *Om Krim, Kali!*
>
> *Beautiful Dark Mother, I offer you this fragrant and lovely flower.*
>
> *Let it become a symbol of my true heart,*
>
> *a heart that your love, protection, and transformative power makes whole.*

Lastly, it is time for the sweet offering. Kali likes sweets and the sweetness of love must be recalled, especially when we can scarcely remember what that felt like. Place some chocolates on the dish next to the flower and say:

> *Om Krim, Kali!*
>
> *Beautiful Dark Mother, accept this offering of sweetness.*
>
> *May it remind me of the sweetness of truth and love that dwells beneath your fierce exterior.*
>
> *May it banish any bitterness that remains in my heart.*

Eat a piece of the candy, savoring its sweetness.

Now you must thank Kali in your own words. If you find that there is more in your heart that you wish to say to the goddess, take as long as you need. When you are finished, touch your forehead to the floor or bow your head in respect.

It is important to dispose of the ashes of the burned rosebud *as soon as possible.* However, wait until the charcoal and ash cool completely before you do so. Dab the fourth finger of your right hand with a little of the fragrant oil, then pick up some of the cool white ash on your fingertip and anoint your third eye. This will remind you that the bad feelings have been purged in the fire and your heart can now heal and bloom again. Let the protection candle burn as long as you desire.

CORRESPONDENCES

Symbol: Skulls, skull staff, blood, cremation grounds, corpse, ghost, ghouls, severed heads, body parts, sword, cleaver, trident, third eye, triangle/yoni, crescent moon, animal skins (leopard, tiger, elephant).

Color: Red, black, yellow, white.

Direction: All.

Element: All.

Day/Holiday/Season:
Navaratri, Diwali; Autumn.

Incense/Oil: Camphor, sandalwood, patchouli; lotus, rose, musk.

Associated deities/Mythological figures/Saints:
Devi, Shakti, Tara, Parvati, Durga, the Mahavidyas, Shiva; ghosts, ghouls; Sri Ramakrishna.

Lilith: The Rite of Self-Seduction

By Lori Nyx

On a night when the moon is waning, prepare for a visit from Lilith. Open yourself up to sensuality and experience beyond rationality and inhibition. Sometimes she may come unbidden to you, but why not open yourself to her sweet seduction in order to embrace the fiery part of your soul—that part which knows your worth and disregards the constructs of shame and low self-esteem.

Think about why you want Lilith to visit. Is it for a simple release? Or something more esoteric? I have designed the following visualization to aid that part of you that has been rejected, whether by a lover, a family member, a close friend, or societal mores and attitudes. This part of yourself will merit the most from Lilith energy. Lil as seducer will come forth to succor, tantalize, adore, love, embrace, and fulfill your rejected self and in this way, empower and enhance your life.

I don't know about you but I feel naked (pun intended) without setting up an altar to the archetype I wish to invoke. In the case of Lilith, be spontaneous and adventurous. It can be as simple as a fragrant red rose with thorns in a vase or as elaborate as a Victorian bordello in miniature. I set mine up on a night table complete with a sexy image of the goddess, a feather from a wild bird, a candle anointed with cedar or jasmine oil, and a cowrie shell (bottom side up of course!) to represent the yoni. I surround the candle at the cardinal points with four red glass "pebbles." I have a decorative clay oil lamp purchased in Ephesus, Turkey that has a very Lilith-like image stamped on it. I use this as a makeshift holder for stick incense.

After you've set up the shrine, prepare yourself as you would for any night of passion, intimacy, and yes, love. Make up your bed with the softest or silkiest sheets, take a long hot bath or steamy shower, soak or lather yourself with some enticing scent or rub your favorite massage oil into your freshly scrubbed skin. Get a massage, have your hair done, or paint your face—whatever it is that gets you into a relaxed and sensual mood. Be celebratory, lusty, funky, wild, frisky, and unabashed. If you find it soothing, get out the hairbrush and give yourself 100 strokes...grin. Or if you have one of those strictly-for-therapeutic-use back massagers... well, enjoy. Put on your favorite sexy music, dim the lights or light candles. Perhaps you might don something silky or satiny, or do away with clothes all together and enjoy the freedom of nudity. If the music grooves you, dance. Imagine you are dancing for a lover; practice your best striptease. Watch yourself in a mirror or close your eyes and just let yourself go.

Scent is very important. Light a scented candle or incense, or anoint your pulse points and anywhere else with oil of musk, cedar, patchouli, or night-blooming jasmine. Nibble on a chocolate covered strawberry or sip some sweet wine or a refreshing drink. You are nearly ready to invite in Lilith energy. The point is to relax and enjoy your thoughts and your body so that you can fully open yourself up to her lunar fire.

Now it's time to go to bed. Climb in between those fresh sheets; lie back on the soft pillows and breathe deeply and slowly. Be conscious of your body and your breath. Be particularly aware of your sense of touch, the texture of the fabric beneath you, the way it feels against your skin, the way your own skin feels smooth and supple. Now, let the image of Lil in all her decadent, primal splendor emerge. Of course you may substitute Lilith imagery for your most seductive and attractive version of a demon lover, but really now, what are you afraid of? Surely not of a goddess. This is, after all, not a new experience; Lilith energy has often visited you in your dreams or fantasies in some form or another. The only difference this time is that she comes to you bidden. If you prefer not to visualize her consciously, you might instead focus on the intent that she will come to you in dreams tonight. Whatever your pleasure. Just know that this experience is meant to be one of empowerment. If you feel uncomfortable at any time you have the power to stop and abandon the exercise.

She will of course, come—rouged, smelling of cedar, her body decorated with henna and her long, heavy hair curling around her bare shoulders. Her ornaments will tinkle as she approaches your bed; she may be bedecked in the richest fabrics or fur. Perhaps she will appear winged with taloned feet, a strange, primitive conglomerate being as on the Burney Relief. Regardless, she is all attraction, all warmth. Her dark glance burns as it appraises and invites. Her skin is pale as moonlight, yet turns dusky in shadow. Beneath it all she seems very real, very tangible, surprisingly human. All those sensual impressions you have gathered in preparation of her coming seem to emanate from her as she moves over you: her long dark hair, her musky sweet scent, her silky skin like fire against your own. She is not hesitant. Her hands, surprisingly strong, grab hold of you and pull you close. Before you can think or even take in all the impressions and sensations of this very intimate meeting, you feel her lips, tongue, and sharp teeth graze your mouth, your cheek, your jawline, and then finally, her hot breath in your ear. She laughs and it is like no sound you have ever heard; it is like the name of something sacred, unutterable in human speech. And her strange laughter translates into whispered words of lust, love, and acceptance. These words are immediate and specific to you and what they impart is healing. For Lilith can travel into the deepest, most hidden parts of your heart and soul and dissolve every slight, rejection, cruelty and pain inflicted on your fragile self-esteem. For she knows that we all stand equal before God.

From this point the visit may continue, as you will it. In the words of the Great Goddess: "All acts of love and pleasure are my rituals." And this communion with Lilith is meant to be stimulating, pleasurable, and if taken to its logical conclusion...fulfilling.

CORRESPONDENCES

Symbol: Flaming sword, wings, moon, caves, desert, sea.

Color: Red, silver, earth tones.

Direction: East, South.

Element: Fire, Earth.

Day/Holiday/Season:
          Monday; Passover; Summer.

Incense/Oil: Cedar, patchouli; night-blooming jasmine, musk.

Associated deities/Biblical figures:
          Ninlil, Lilitu, Belit, Lamia, Lamashtu, Yahweh,
          Adam, Eve, Samael, Sanvai, Sansanvai and
          Semangelof, the Lilim, Queen of Sheba.

Loki: Hide in Plain Sight, or, The Rite of "Low-Key"

By Denise Dumars

As with Oya, Loki can bring about change, often catastrophic change, but here we are working with him in a subtler, but no less gravely important way. It may seem strange to look to a chaotic god for protection, but that's essentially what we're doing.

One of Loki's best tricks is hiding out by shape-shifting or becoming invisible. While it may not be possible for us mere mortals to literally accomplish these feats, sometimes it's necessary to make oneself less noticeable. Got a boss or a teacher that picks on you all the time? Work as an undercover detective or in covert ops? Have to travel through mean streets to get to work or school? Want to improve your poker face? The Rite of "Low-Key" Loki will help you do all that.

There is evidence that during Pagan times the worshippers of Norse gods sometimes became possessed or "ridden" by the god. In a metaphysical sense, when you perform this rite and use the amulet we are going to make, you are "becoming" Loki. Should you become possessed or "ridden" by Loki during the ceremony of dedicating the runic charm, please write and tell us about your experience!

We are going to make Loki's rune, Dagaz, which means "day." Invisibility and shape-shifting are the properties of this rune when used by the gods. Place the rune in the East or the South when doing the ritual to dedicate this charm, for the Dagaz rune charm will help you appear, well, a little less obvious. As for shape-shifting, there are entire books on that subject, or if you feel the need for a bit of all that, just see the Volos ritual. In fact, you can use the same essential oil blend for both that ritual and this one. Jacob Grimm, after all, equated Volos with Loki.

This ritual will take place in the daytime (that's a *good* thing, for there's less chance of Loki setting things on fire when there are no candles around). The Dagaz rune (ᛞ) that you make for this ritual will act as a charm so that you—and your car, should you wish to include it—become less noticeable.

This is a protection ritual, with the extra-added attraction of making the bearer of this rune less obvious. Let's think about this for a minute. Generally, the police officers chosen as undercover detectives are the most bland, middle-of-the-road-looking people you can imagine. Why? Because they don't want to be noticeable! Those *Miami Vice* guys would *never* have been detectives! But that guy in the polyester sports jacket sitting in the corner booth at Denny's whose face you can't recall just might be one. And that's the point of this ritual, and that's what this runic amulet will do for you. Who was that masked man? I don't know; he wasn't wearing any mask!

A Norse ritual is called a *blot*, their word for "blood," for nearly every Norse ritual honoring the gods included a blood offering. You don't even want to know how they sacrificed to Odin (that'll be discussed in the sequel to *The Dark Archetype*). However, blood is not necessary in this rite, but if you wish to add a bit of your own to the salt water needed to asperge the tree in this ritual, then feel free. Some consider the yew tree to be sacred to Loki, and other trees, including birch, juniper, willow, ash, and spruce are appropriate as well. Since no cults to Loki are described in literature, we do not know for sure what specific correspondences Loki would resonate to, and therefore we have to go with standard Norse practice along with our own modern interpretations, as well as the lore surrounding the Dagaz rune.

This ritual should take place in a natural setting—your backyard, a park, or a forest. Just make sure there are trees around. If you have trees on your property, you might want to dedicate one of them to Loki and asperge it regularly in his name, leaving an offering. If you do this rite in a public place, make sure that you leave a biodegradable offering—Odin's ravens are going to end up eating it, in any case!

Men and women worshipped separately in the Norse culture, it is believed. One of the most well-preserved temples to a Norse deity was one dedicated to Freya. So the directions in this ritual have subtle differences depending on whether it is a woman or man wanting the runic protection. Traditionally, runes are carved into wood and then painted red. Choose one of the types of wood mentioned above or a type of wood that seems right to you from a craft store, or get your own from a fallen branch. You may even dare to get the wood from a living tree, but if you do, you really owe something in return. At the very least, apologize to the tree, pour some water and fertilizer on its roots, and perhaps a little of your blood on the "boo-boo" you left on one of its branches.

However, if it is more practical for you and feels more comfortable—since most of us are used to using stones and crystals in magick—choose a smooth stone or crystal. You might, for example, visit the seashore and ask Loki's son Jormungand to send you a nice tumbled stone. River rocks are appropriate as well, as Loki often hides in a river, disguised as a salmon! Or go to a rock shop and pick a stone or crystal that seems to resonate safety and protection. For a woman, the rune is to be painted on with bright red nail polish. You may outline it in gold if you wish, for extra solar protection. For a man, use model paint in the same colors. Make two amulets and place one in your car, or give one to your partner if you are a law enforcement officer. Better yet, include your partner in the ritual—aw, c'mon, you know there are some closet Odinists in your department! The runic amulet you will make should be kept on your person or kept in your car or office—wherever it is you wish to be less noticeable.

Pork is an appropriate offering to Loki, so leave a McRib sandwich or something similar at the base of the tree where you're having the ritual. Loki would appreciate the humor and the ravens will enjoy it too. Offer mead, beer, red wine, or if you're in a no-alcohol public place offer apple juice; after all, it was Loki who stole Idunn's apples of immortality!

You may make the runic amulet ahead of time or make it during the rite. If you make it ahead of time, you may want to cast a circle and do the rune-making in sacred space. We will not be working with Loki's elements, which are quicksilver (mercury) and lead, as both are toxic, though if you are a law enforcement officer and are doing this ritual in private space, it would not be wrong to place your ammo within the sacred circle. Either way, you will cast a Circle and call the corners this way:

First, ground and center, breathing deeply. Feel a connection between yourself and the World Tree. Feel connected to both the Earth and the heavens, and to all natural spaces and the plants and animals within them. When you feel calm and centered, with the salt water, asperge just a little in a circle around yourself and as much space is needed for the ritual. If you are a man, call Odin in the East for Air; Loki in the South for Fire; Farbauti for Water and Thor for Earth. If you are a woman, call Odin in the East, Loki in the South; Hel in the West; and Skadi in the North. Corners are called in blots by toasting each deity.

Do this ritual any day except Sunday, Monday, or Friday. The Vikings did this sort of magick during the full moon phase of the month.

Dagaz is associated with both midwinter and midsummer. It would also seem especially powerful to do this ritual on Midsummer Day, as this day is considered a "scary" holiday, as it is interpreted in folklore. You may wish to do this ritual in the company of people of your same gender only, unless your partner or other person you wish to give an amulet to is of the opposite sex.

After you have cast the Circle and called the corners, asperge the tree you have chosen to represent Loki with the salt water. Make your rune now or if you've already made it, place it at the base of the tree along with the offering of food and drink. Say these words:

> Loki, master of disguise,
> Loki, you of wit so wise
> Loki, have me fade from watchful eyes!

Explain your personal situation to Loki. If there are specific locations where you wish to fade from view, name them. If you work with or go to school with others who also need this protection, name them too. Be aware that you are not infringing on anyone's free will here; you are merely including them as part of your personal space that needs protecting.

Now you and anyone else participating should close their eyes; imagine a golden light beginning from the top of your head and washing your body, finally ending and dissipating into the earth. Visualize the golden light coming from the abode of the gods. You may draw the light into each of your chakras one at a time if this is part of your practice. This golden light is part of the protection aspect of the rune, which is why you may paint a gold outline around the rune on your charm if you wish. When you feel bathed in golden light and connected to both the heavens and the Earth, you may open your eyes.

Have your partner, or anyone else you have included in the rite, state the words above as well. There is no reason why you can't do this ritual with your coven or other practitioners; it will only increase the power of the magick if you do so. Do the golden light meditation for each person who recites the words. You may also anoint each other with essential oil in the shape of the Dagaz rune. Use a blend of forest oils such as pine, birch, spruce, or fir, or use a strong, sharply scented oil such as clary sage or lemon. You may also anoint yourself every morning by drawing the rune on your chest with essential oil that has been diluted in olive oil. Consider also drawing it on the dashboard of your car.

Don't be afraid if, during the ritual, you feel a presence that is not visible. Norse gods often express their presence in physical ways. You may feel clapped on the shoulder by an unseen hand, or perhaps get a shove from someone who isn't there! Consider any such contact a good—if unnerving—sign.

Keep an eye on anything even remotely combustible during this rite. Don't let anyone smoke, and stay away from barbecue pits if they are present. No candles or incense are required. It's a good idea to bring along Freya Aswynn's CD *Songs of Yggdrasil*, which I believe is still available with her book *Northern Mysteries and Magick*, and play the invocation when you are setting up sacred space.

When you feel you are ready, pour the libation at the root of the tree and leave your offering on the ground next to it. Do not leave anything that is not biodegradable! After the rite, close the Quarters by thanking each of the gods and toasting each again.

This ritual, like all protection spells, needs to be performed periodically in order to retain its potency. For example, if the boss has stayed away from your cubicle for a month and now is suddenly on your case again, recharge the amulet by repeating the ritual. If you have a tree on your own property, consecrate it as Loki's tree and then you will only have to repeat the words above, asperge, and leave an offering to recharge your charm. The Scandinavians believed that the spirit of a god could inhabit a tree, statue, or other sacred object, so if you consecrate your tree to Loki, be assured that you will find him there...whether you want to or not!

It is strongly suggested that you make a charm for your partner if you work in law enforcement or government undercover work. If he or she is not Pagan or does not understand the situation, just tell him or her that it's a good luck charm like Grandma used to make (this works best if your Grandma was Scandinavian, Dutch, or German or if you can convincingly pretend that she was). Obviously if you go to school with or work with someone who is in similar danger—say, taking the bus in a bad part of town to and from work or school—give your friend an amulet too.

While Loki does not mind little white lies (like pretending that your *Strega Nonna* was Swedish), you must not give in to the temptation to use this charm and ritual for unethical or illegal purposes. You don't want to give away your hand at the poker table, but you also don't want to cheat at casino gambling, either. You don't want to try this charm if you're thinking of starting a new career as a cat burglar (Freyja would get you for sure!) or a Peeping Tom. This runic charm should be used for serious purposes only, not to sneak out of class or leave work early! The consequences of messing with Loki can be severe. Be respectful, and be honest with yourself about this spell. Just because it may keep the teacher from picking on you, it won't keep him or her from noticing if you try to copy off of your neighbor's paper during a test!

CORRESPONDENCES

Symbol:　Dagaz rune, ice, fire, volcano, wolf, otter, salmon.

Color:　Black, red, silver, white.

Direction:　East, South.

Element:　Air, Fire.

Day/Holiday/Season:
　　　　Saturday, Fall, Midsummer Day.

Incense/Oil:　Birch, juniper, fir, pine, lemon, clary sage.

Associated deities:
　　　　Hel, Thor, Sigyn, Angrboda, Farbauti, Fenris, Jormungand, Thor, Odin, Hoener, Hod, Skadi.

Lucifer: This Little Light of Mine, I'm Gonna Let It Shine!

By Lori Dyx

The purpose of this working is to help you to embrace your highest aspirations. Everyone has hidden strengths, talents, and desires. But not everyone has the confidence and daring to let themselves shine. In this spell you will reclaim the name and legend of Lucifer as the glorious morning star and embrace your own glorious light, unafraid to show it to the world. It may also be adapted to help you overcome depression and defeatist attitudes after you have "fallen" or failed.

What you'll need: this book or a copy of the below affirmation and a flashlight. Recommended: a star map that will help you determine the position of Venus in relation to your location and time of year. You will also need to find out when the sun will be setting and rising, and if possible, what time Venus will be visible in the night sky. There are on-line local astronomy sites and periodicals where you can find this information.

This spell is to be done outdoors where you can clearly see the night/early morning sky. If you must, you can stargaze off of a balcony or via a window, but it is best done with a clear view of the sky and the horizon. Living by the coast, I do this working on the beach.

Before you begin you must determine how you wish to shine. Start by asking yourself a few questions, such as what is your wildest, craziest dream? What talents and strengths lay hidden or dormant within you? Has all your hard work gone unnoticed? What is it that you have always wanted to achieve but were discouraged from attempting? What makes you think you can't achieve your heart's desire? Who told you that you couldn't do it? Where do you feel you've failed? What have you given up out of fear?

Perhaps you are an actor who's spent the last ten years in food service. Or maybe you quit practicing guitar and singing when your old garage band broke up. Did you have to quit college in your senior year? Has busting your butt at a job where your unique qualities are unappreciated made you miserable? Perhaps it's time to step up and get noticed. What are the heights you aspire too? Whether it's career advancement, a lofty goal, or just being noticed and appreciated for the fabulous person that you truly are, this spell will help you gain or regain the self-confidence to achieve your dream.

Begin the spell by dressing in your most sumptuous outfit. Yes, put on something flashy, something sensual. Think razzle-dazzle. Pile on some jewelry—gold, silver, and precious stones if you have them. Come now, fellas, you must have something in the closet that is a bit Elvis, shall we say? If not, wear something gold, or your best suit. The point is to look maahhvelous, dahling. And don't get all uptight about looking foolish or trailing the hem of your lamé evening gown in the mucky outdoors.

You should start this magickal working at least 15 minutes before the sunset. Go outside and face West. Take a moment to feel the Earth beneath you and the evening air on your skin. If you are at the beach or near a body of water, feel the salt spray or the moisture in the air. Lastly, focus on the fiery sun (not literally; we want you to keep your vision intact!), watching the changing colors of the sky as the sun is on the horizon. While you do this, think of your past failures, untried aspirations or the reasons why you have not achieved your heart's desire. This will probably make you a little sad, frustrated, or upset. That's okay; take hold of all that negative energy and send it into the blazing sun. Let it go down with the sunset, knowing that it will sink somewhere into the sea and be gone.

Next, turn around with star map in hand and locate the Evening Star rising in the sky. Yes, yes, I know Lucifer is supposed to be the Morning Star, but bear with me: They are the *same* celestial body! As the sun sets in the West and the sky darkens, you should be able to see Venus ascendant in the night sky. If you are lucky it will be the first star you see tonight. Perfect for making wishes come true.

As you gaze on the "star," imagine yourself as you always wanted to be—manifesting your heart's desire. See yourself reaching your goal, expressing your talents, and displaying your uniqueness to the world. Don't just desire it: own it as if it already exists. Shut off any negative voices in your head that would dare tell you otherwise. Really concentrate and *see* it. As they say, "if you see it, you will be it". Now take out your flashlight and read the following affirmation out loud. Heck, yell it if you can get away with it!

I am a Bearer of Light, I am the heavenly Star,
I surpass in beauty and brightness all the stars in the sky
It is my right to dream and dare
It is my right to use my gifts and talents
It is my right to aspire to limitless heights
Without Fear of Failure, Without Fear of Falling
Who I am and what I have to show the world is wonderful
and rare
Like Lucifer, I refuse to hide my brilliance
Instead, I take my rightful place and shine.

Take a few deep breaths. Look up at that beautiful star and see yourself in it. Know that you are a being of divine light and breathless beauty, not earthbound, but winged and glorious. Feel unabashed pride in yourself and your talents. You *are* that distant light spiraling in the vast firmament.

Gaze as long as you wish at the star. Then go home and get as much sleep at you can, because next comes the hard part. You have to get up, put on the same outfit and return to this spot before dawn the next morning! Well, we all have to suffer a little for our dreams. For those who are circadianly challenged, make sure you set your alarm clock before you turn in. It will be cold and you will be cranky, but this part is necessary to set the spell and manifest your desire.

As before, note the Earth beneath you, the Air above, Water if it is nearby (or visualize that Element), and then locate the planet Venus once more. This time it is truly representative of Shaher/Helel/Lucifer as the glorious Morning Star, herald of the light. It will soon set, but not before it ushers in the dawning of a new day in your life—a new day in which you are no longer afraid of being noticed or reaching for seemingly impossible dreams. One in which your fears and doubts about yourself have been replaced by unshakable self-esteem, confidence, and effortless skill.

The sky should be lightening somewhat. It may be more difficult to see the stars. That's all right. Know they are always there, imperishable, shimmering. Turn toward the East. Listen to the pre-dawn sounds. Perhaps the larks are starting to sing and small animals are scurrying home to their dens. Take a few deep breaths of the cool, moist air and repeat the affirmation of the previous night. Say it with as much panache and flair as you can muster. Cause the larks to stop warbling in surprise!

Watch in anticipation as first the sky brightens and then turns pink or pale gold. Say good morning to the sun as it slowly rises. See in this sunrise your own ascendance, your own rise to hitherto unreachable heights, your own dazzling light. Smile, hug yourself; you should feel energized and happy. Now, go treat yourself to something luxurious such as a champagne breakfast (or a few more hours rest). After all, you're worth it, Angel!

This working may be repeated anytime you need to feel re-energized or reaffirmed.

Correspondences

Symbol: Star, trident, lightning, angel, devil, apple.

Color: Gold, white, jewel tones.

Direction: East, West.

Element: Air, Fire.

Days/Holidays/Season:
August 1st is the legendary "anniversary" of Satan's Fall according to Rudwin.

Incense/Oil: Cedar.

Associated deities/Biblical figures:
Satan, Iblis, Yahweh, the Bene Ha-Elohim, Shaher, Helel, El, Asherah, Aster, Athtar, cherubim.

Medusa: The Gorgoneion Talisman

By Lori Nyx

The *aegis* was a magickal and protective garment worn by the Greek goddess of wisdom and war, Athena. It is a goatskin shawl with snakes serving as tassels, similar to the one Hephaestus made for Zeus. Initially it served as a kind of cloak of protection on its own. However, the aegis and the goddess who wore it were made invulnerable with the addition of the gorgoneion: the head of the Gorgon Medusa. The marvelous thing about Medusa's head is that it retains the full force of her powers to terrify and petrify— even after her death. According to legend it could move around, its face was expressive, the snakes in its hair could still bristle and strike, its terrible eyes were forever vigilant, and it could still turn those foolish enough to look upon it to stone.

In addition to the aegis, the gorgon's head adorns Athena's shield where it also serves the dual function of prophylactic and terror-inducing talisman. According to one ancient Greek story, a famous warrior was so powerful and threatening to his enemies that just one look at the image on his shield (a gorgoneion) was enough to send his enemies running away in terror. As previously mentioned legendary heroes and common soldiers alike were depicted sporting glaring gorgon faces on their rounded battle shields and military accoutrements. The meaning was clear and literal. Medusa's magic and might shields the wearer from harm.

Although the Greeks in classical times may have lost sight of Medusa as the crone aspect of Athena, they understood the potency of the gorgon's head. Placing this symbol on their shields, temples and household items was certainly more than mere decoration or habit. To many (if not most) the gorgoneion truly functioned to keep evil at bay. When we adopt it for our own protection we are calling upon that same Medusan power: the ancient dark mother as both protector and death dealer. Now don't you feel safe?

I have been lucky enough to find an inexpensive amulet of a gorgon's head made out of pewter. It is about the size of a silver dollar and attached to a cord I can wear around my neck. It is not the face of the semi-beautiful Medusa we are used to seeing via classical Greek art and more recent depictions. Rather, it is the face of an ogre: a grimacing Greek mask with bulging eyes and snake-like hair. I wear this talisman when I need extra protection or when I am engaged in protection rituals.

A similar talisman can be easily made. I suggest looking through some art or mythology books or going online and browsing the ancient art historical sites for images of your own gorgoneion. From this you may trace or make a photocopy onto stiff paper. If you are of an artistic bent, you can always draw, paint, and decorate the image, or perhaps even mold a three- dimensional version out of clay. For ease of wearing, punch or cut a hole at the top to run a jump ring through or attach a pin backing. You may wish to use metallic paints for a faux finish, and I strongly suggest sealing any porous creation with lacquer or fixative.

Although the above talisman is intended for personal protection, the idea is easily expanded. Inspired by the Greek practice of placing the gorgon on the lintels of their temples, I have placed gorgon images around my altar, and over thresholds and on doors to demarcate sacred/secret space. Another idea would be to fashion a gorgon mask that can be worn when working Medusan magick, such as rituals of protection.

On the dark moon, preferably at dawn or dusk—a threshold time pleasing to gorgon guardians everywhere—prepare to consecrate and charge your talisman. Set up your altar and cast sacred space as you usually do. To help with the proper mindset, you can light a protection candle and/or incense. When you are ready to do your magickal workings, place the gorgoneion on the altar and anoint it with protective oil. I suggest making a special oil composed of a mixture of cypress, dragon's blood, and olive oil. If the use of a liquid would damage your talisman, fumigate it with incense made from one or more of these trees.

Anoint the amulet and hold it out before you, and say:

> I call upon the power of the Dark Goddess, Medusa, fierce
> Lady of the wild spaces, Mother of warriors, guardian of
> temples, and Protector in battle. I call upon the might
> and magick of the Ancient One, She who guards the
> Western Shore, Lady of the Beasts, Daughter of the
> Ancient Sea, the Dark face of Bright Athena. I call upon
> you, Dark Goddess, Medusa, Guardian of the Sacred,
> Protector of Secrets, you who inspires awe and terror.
> Ever vigilant you see all that would profane, any who
> intends harm. Your gaze freezes all negativity, neutralizes
> it, and disperses it into the void. You are Great Fear and
> all who do ill shall flee from your deadly glance. I call
> upon you to consecrate this amulet wrought in your image,
> so that it may act as shield and guardian (to whoever
> wears it; of this sacred place, of my home, etc.). May it
> keep all that would do (me, the wearer, this place, etc.)
> harm at bay and allow no trespass of evil or ill intent.

Place the gorgoneion on your altar and stand with palms up,
saying:

> So it is, by my intent and the ancient power of the Dark
> Goddess.

Don the amulet, anoint your forehead with the Gorgon oil,
and say three times:

> I am safe, I am protected, I am guarded by the magick
> and might of Medusa.

Now, do a visualization in sacred space. See the gorgoneion
deflecting any and all negativity away from you; if any are sending
evil your way, it will stop their sending from reaching you. The
petrifying gaze of the gorgon will easily locate the perpetrator or
negative energy and stop the attack. See it doing so in one of
several ways: it may absorb the negativity, swallowing it in its gaping mouth and symbolically devouring it; it can also reverse the

energy, sending it rebounding back at the perpetrator, transforming it to fear and a healthy respect that will send your enemy running for the hills! Imagine that no one can get near you.

Correspondences

Symbol: Gorgoneion, eyes.

Color: Black, green, bronze.

Direction: West.

Element: Water, Earth.

Incense/Oil: Dragon's blood resin; olive, cypress.

Associated deities/Mythical creatures:
Stheno, Euryale, Poseidon, Athena, Metis, the Graeae, Perseus, Chaos, Nyx.

Oya: The Falling (Ivory) Tower

By Denise Dumars

What is the glass ceiling? It is described as an invisible barrier preventing one from moving upward in one's career. Ah, the glass ceiling: Strong enough for a man, but made for a woman!

"Shattering the glass ceiling" is such a well-known phrase that there is even a magazine called _Shatter_ that deals precisely with this issue. Originally geared toward working women, the magazine and its corresponding Website now also take input from and give assistance to men. Welcome to my world, boys! Many over-forty men who expect promotions with their latest job evaluations are finding pink slips instead. Apparently ageism looks down on balding pates from above the barrier as well as sexism.

Oya is not just about breaking glass. She is the tornado that tosses airstreams around for fun, the lightning bolt that strikes the Tower in the tarot deck and sends it crashing down. Can Oya help your career? Does a cow get carried away by a tornado in the movie _Twister_?

Oya has no fear of Wall Street, the military-industrial complex, the old-boy network, or the ivory towers that speak out of one side of the mouth while with the other reinforce such "traditional" notions as classism, ageism, sexism, and racism. If in your world you find that only the rich are getting richer, then you need Oya as your headhunter...okay, in both senses of the word!

This is a ritual in several steps; include them into your life as they are needed. Consider it as updating your job skills! The first thing you will need to do is create an Oya altar. You will also be packing up the altar items and taking them with you if you perform some of the off-site rituals below. The basic materials are an altar cloth (a beach towel will do nicely) in colors of maroon, burnt orange, gold, brown, dark purple, or any combination, an Oya candle encased in glass from a botanica (Our Lady of Candelaria or St. Therese can be substituted, or a candle in one of Oya's colors), and if possible some Oya oil and incense. Substitute Success, Prosperity, or Get-a-Job oil and any of the scents mentioned in the Oya chapter. Add a small whisk and a pewter or colorful plastic chalice. Offerings include red wine or grape juice, eggplant, black-eyed peas, grapes, plums, or starfruit. The last item you will add should change over time. This item is a volume from what I will call the Magickal Management Library.

Here is short list of books you should read in order to make your ascent in the world of work. Some of them are very funny as well as informative. Go to the library and peruse the management and career sections and add to this list as desired.

The Magickal Management Library

Bing, Stanley. *What Would Machiavelli Do?*

Dolnick, Barrie. *The Executive Mystic.*

Goodwin, Marcus. *The Psychic Investor.*

Greene, Robert. *The 48 Laws of Power.*

Hendricks, Gay, and Kay Ludeman. *The Corporate Mystic.*

Johnson, Bob. *Corporate Magick.*

Leeden, Michael Arthur. *Machiavelli on Modern Leadership.*

MacCormack, Mark H. *What They Don't Teach You at Harvard Business School.*

Machiavelli, Niccolo. *The Prince.*

Ringer, Robert J. *Looking Out For No. 1.*

Roberts, Wess. *Leadership Secrets of Attila the Hun.*

Russell, Garner H. *The Effective Entrepreneur: How to Make Bad Guys Finish Last.*

Now comes the ritual, in parts.

WARNING: Oya is all about change: violent change. If you're not ready for drastic change in your life, don't work with Oya. Working with Oya could mean that you might get fired; your office building may burn down; the company may be the victim of a hostile takeover, for example. But there will be reasons for the change. If an Enron-type situation is happening, the Feds could come in and shut the place down and take the crooked management off to jail. Trust me; if the crooks are caught with their hands in the cookie jar then this is a *good* thing. Then you can write a tell-all bestseller about your experience and get interviewed on TV by Larry King. Be prepared. Anything can happen when you're working with Oya.

Now, the working. We will begin with a basic ritual that you can do if you have a simple goal in mind, such as getting up the courage to apply for a different job, or finding a summer job. If you have serious career work to do, consider this Step One. Otherwise, it may be all that you need to affect the changes you wish to happen.

Step One: Set up a temporary altar to Oya at home, preferably in your home office or whatever room you use for study and business-related activities, even if it's just the kitchen table. Anoint her candle with oil and light it. Set out a chalice of red wine and some incense. Light the incense and raise a toast to Oya, saying the following. Some words are in Yoruban; pronounce the vowels as you would in Spanish:

> *Heya! Epaa Heyi! Hekua Oya!*
> *Oya dances and the whirlwind blows*
> *Oya dances and the world changes*
> *Oya dances and all evil is swept away.*
> *Heya! Epaa Heyi! Hekua Oya!*
> *Oya, you are beauty; Oya, you are magick*
> *Oya, you are strength; Oya, you are change.*
> *Heya! Epaa Heyi! Hekua Oya!*
> *Oya swirl your skirts around my world,*
> *Lend me your power, lend me your sword,*
> *For I have a battle to fight. Oya, fight beside me,*
> *Oya, defend me. Oya, [ask for what you need].*

Now, take a drink from the chalice. Meditate a bit on your intention. Know that Oya wants you to be successful—she is not a quitter, and neither should you be. Repeat the lines above when you are through meditating. Then say good-bye to Oya—for now.

> *Hekua, Oya! Omio, Oya!*
> *Oya, brave and beautiful,*
> *Lady of strong magicks,*
> *I bow to you and say farewell*
> *For now. Heya! Epaa Heyi! Hekua, Oya!*

Step Two: Start adding Oya's colors to your wardrobe. Replace that Reagan-red tie with a deep crimson or burnt orange one; they look fabulous with a charcoal-gray pinstripe suit. A blouse in one of Oya's colors works well with a suit. Buy scarves in Oya's colors, too. Read a book from your Magickal Management Library.

Step Three: Try Machiavelli bibliomancy. Bibliomancy is a divining technique that uses sentences from a book—classically, the

Bible—as a divining tool. Think of it as a more intense and accurate form of fortune cookie. Flip through the pages of *The Prince* until you feel you want to stop at one page. Then without looking, place your finger on the page. The sentence or paragraph you've pointed to has a message for you. You can try this before work each morning or as need be.

Step Four: Do your ritual on the beach. Pack up your Oya basket and go to the seashore or the shore of a lake or river. Here in L.A. the strong West wind that blows off the ocean is very pronounced and Oya is in every breath of it, as well as in the hot wind from the East known as the Santa Ana. Assemble your Oya altar. Do the same ritual as in Step One but add the following:

> *Oya of the winds,*
> *She of the rainless storms*
> *She who bends the palm trees*
> *With her swish of perfumed skirts*
> *Blow great change into my life,*
> *Oya's winds! Change me, as I change myself.*
> *Change me, as I change myself.*

Step Five: Now it's time for The Boss Whammy. Yeah, I know it sounds scary, but this *is* Oya, remember? Perform Step One before you leave for work on the day you have an important meeting with the boss or a job interview. While visualizing, see the boss doing what you want him to do: Hire you, give you a promotion or raise, praise you in front of colleagues, whatever. Bring your Oya oil with you and make sure you have some on the palms of your hands when you meet the boss. Shake hands and feel the transfer of power from the boss to yourself. When you get home, offer Oya some nice roast chicken.

Step Six: This is The Cemetery Working, and it is the most intense of the Oya rituals. This working is for the serious careerist only: the person who knows what she wants and wants it so badly that it hurts.

What profession do you want to be a success in? For purposes of this ritual it should be a field you are studying for or are already working in, even if it is only on the periphery of your ultimate goal. This is not a working for the idle dreamer; it is for those who want to sincerely follow through on their plans rather than sitting around Starbucks in Malibu all day waiting to be "discovered."

This takes a bit of background work. You will want to find out where a deceased prominent member of the profession you want to succeed in is buried. This person will be your Ancestor Mentor. Ancestor worship is part of the Yoruba belief system, and the person you choose will be considered your ancestor in the profession you've chosen, as well as your mentor on the astral plane. For example, if you want to succeed in showbiz, well, here in L.A. virtually any cemetery contains celebrities; just check a guidebook such as *Permanent Californians*. If I were to do this ritual, for example, I might choose to do so at the grave of a famous writer; let's say Raymond Chandler, who is buried in Mount Hope Cemetery in San Diego.

Even if you live in a small town without celebrities or have no interest in working in a high-profile field, it is easy to find out where the local land barons and captains of industry make their final resting places. Just go to the local cemetery and look for the largest monument or crypt. Often a groundskeeper will be happy to show you where the "famous people" are buried, even if the office staff disapproves. And if you have an actual departed loved one who excelled in the profession you're interested in, then so much the better—choose him or her.

Spread out your Oya altar for a picnic with the dead on a Saturday near sunset or at least an hour before the cemetery closes, whichever comes first. Bring an appropriate prop for the altar; using my example above, I might bring a copy of *The Big Sleep*. Before the ritual, "commune" with the dead for awhile, reading their names aloud and greeting them and offering any prayers that come to you. I find a mausoleum particularly effective for concentrating energy in this way. Tend a few crypts or graves by retrieving fallen blossoms from flower holders, brushing dirt from gravemarkers, for example. This is to make the Other Side understand that your attention to the dead is respectful and your interest in them sincere; remember that Oya is the guardian of the cemetery and your ritual will backfire on you if you disturb any graves, leave litter lying around, or laugh at the dear departed's "funny" names.

Now go to the grave of the person you wish to be your Ancestor Mentor. Spread out Oya's altar and perform the ritual in Step One. Be sure to take everything with you when you leave except for the Oya candle and a bit of food or drink to share (bring his or her favorite if you can find out what it was—I'll have to check on Chandler's favorite potent potable).

After you have performed the ritual in Step One, think about what you want to say to the departed. Address him or her politely, praising his or her accomplishments. You may ask for career advice to be delivered later in dreams or in subsequent rituals, or just stop and listen with your eyes closed. Ask the deceased to bless your endeavors and then promise to bring honor to your shared profession.

If possible, lie full length beside the grave or if in a crypt or mausoleum press yourself against the wall. Commune with your new Ancestor Mentor for as long as you feel comfortable doing so, or until someone comes along and wants to know what you're doing! (The answer to this is to say that you are visiting someone to pay your respects, which is, after all, true.)

End with a farewell and a thank you to both the departed and to Oya. To reinforce the spell, make a donation to the departed's favorite charity (if you know it) or to a charity associated with your profession.

Correspondences

Symbol: Horsehair flail, sword, machete, knife, multicolored skirts, rainbow, cemetery, lightning bolt, whirlwind, African buffalo.

Color: Crimson, maroon, burnt orange, deep purple, brown, black, white.

Direction: East.

Element: Air, Fire.

Day/Holiday/Season:
> Feb. 2 (Candlemas); Autumn.

Incense/Oil: Mugwort, camphor, cypress, rosewood, mimosa.

Associated deities/Saints:
> Aida-Wedo, Maman Brigitte, Chango, Ogun, Oshun, Yemaya, Osain, Ochosi, Orula, Babalu-Aye, Obatala, Olodumare, Our Lady of Candelaria, Therese the Little Flower, St. Catherine.

Piercing the Veil of Set

By Denise Dumars

This is a guided meditation suitable for individuals or groups; in fact, you may want to do it in a group in case anyone gets "spooked." That's because Set is pretty spooky, and though this is intended to be a perfectly safe working, well, we know how the mind plays tricks on us sometimes. People with psychological problems should not do this meditation.

So who is this for? Well, it's for everyone who loves a secret! It is for those who just can't *not* look when the monster appears on screen, and for those who have ever identified in any way with Pandora.

Just because Set is a creepy guy doesn't mean he doesn't have wisdom to share. In fact, it is through suffering the consequences of our misdeeds that we often learn the most, and Set is certainly no exception. This meditation is based on the little-known story of a veiled Set sitting in the corridors leading to the Underworld. In this story, you have met Anubis and had him take you to the mortuary and prepare you; you've made the 42 negative confessions and Thoth and Ma'at have said "You may now pass Go and collect your $200." Seated in the passage, however, is Set. He is veiled, and if you do not wish to see beneath the veil, then as Dionne Warwick would say, "Walk On By."

It's best to do this meditation in sacred space. Record the visualization ahead of time or have someone read it aloud, perhaps while playing the *Heartbeat* tape mentioned in *Reaper* ritual. I suggest calling the Quarters thusly: East/Air: Thoth; South/Fire: Sekhmet; West/Water: Isis; North/Earth: Anubis. Now begin:

You are walking towards a red door. It is a hot, dry desert day. Take a moment to feel the oppressive heat and the dry desert wind called a *sirocco*. When you reach the red door, open it, and you will see a spiral staircase leading down into the Underworld. We are about to pay Set a visit. Don't be afraid; you will exit this place and come back to the here and now and full waking consciousness after the meditation.

Count down from ten to one, taking a step down with each number. Ten...nine...eight...seven...six...five...four...three...two...one. You are now in an underground passageway. It is dimly lit but you can always see your way. You walk and begin to see that this is an ossuary—a repository for bones. Indeed, the farther you walk, the more the walls appear to be built of human bones and skulls, many of them artfully arranged. You are not claustrophobic, however; there is plenty of fresh air.

You come to a bend in the passageway. The passage now turns a corner and moves to the left. Follow the path. Up ahead you see a candelabra of red candles and know that you are approaching Set on his throne.

As you approach the candles, you see a niche in the wall. Set is seated there on a throne of Egyptian design. He wears the traditional Egyptian kilt. His skin is strangely pale, almost corpse-like. A black veil covers his head. Through the veil you can make out his auburn braids, his oddly shaped head, blending characteristics of an okapi, a donkey, and a jackal. His eyes are closed. A thurible of kyphi incense burns to his left. His right hand rests on a boatman's tiller, symbolizing his current occupation. In his left hand he holds a crook and flail—the phaoronic symbols that he feels are rightly his.

Will you lift the veil of Set? If so, what will you see? What will he tell you? If you do not want to lift the veil at this time, keep on walking. You will eventually come to another staircase, and all you have to do is count from one to ten as you ascend the stairs into the light.

But if you are ready to look behind the veil, do it now! Lift his veil, and behold him, saying, *"Honorable Sutek, I have come in search of truth and knowledge. What secrets will you reveal to me?"* Set opens his eyes. They are oddly goat-like, with green irises. His muzzle is covered with rich, dark auburn hair, and cornrow braids fall down his back. His funny little giraffe-like ears twitch.

"What would you have me reveal?" he asks. "What would you like to see?" Set laughs, a braying sound. "I will show you secrets," he states," But you must realize that these sights are for you alone. You may tell others what you have seen, for each of you will see something different. Just don't expect anyone to believe you." His laughter echoes through the passageway. He stands up, beckoning, and you follow him.

He leads you to another bend in the passageway, and you come upon four doors. Behind one of these doors you will experience Set's message. The first door reveals a theater-like room. If you choose this room, you will view the message Set gives you like a film. The second room, he explains, contains a landscape of your own design, and what you experience within is like a holographic representation of his message. Behind the third door is a classroom. Set is your teacher. Will you sit in on his lecture? Better take notes if you do! The last room is totally empty, and you notice that the walls, floor, and ceiling are all painted red. Set explains that only he can take you to experience this room, and if you enter it with him, you will gain direct experience with his mysteries. This room is not for the squeamish, or for those who do not wish to experience chaotic forces in their lives.

Which room will you choose? Choose wisely, and enter.

Stay as long as you like, until Set has shown or told you all that he has to impart to you today.

When your visit it over, you may thank him. He sits back down, puts the veil over his head, and resumes his pose. Kneel on one leg and place your fist over your heart as a gesture of respect. Then you stand and continue down the corridor until you find the staircase to return to the outside world. Now ascend the staircase, counting from one to ten as you ascend. One, two, three, four, five, six, seven, eight, nine, ten.

Once outside, you take a moment to experience the hot Egyptian sun, the sirocco, and feel how these atmospheric conditions are imbued with Set's essence. Now you may open your eyes.

Nothing is ever exactly what it seems. You are now changed in some way. You are not exactly the same person you were before this meditation. Look for evidence of Set's presence in your everyday life. Do not repeat this meditation until a lunar month has passed. It is best to do this meditation during a waning moon, preferably on a Saturday or a Tuesday.

Which room did you choose? The cineplex, the holodeck, the lecture hall, or Set's bronze-age bachelor pad? What was his secret? If Fig Newtons are fruit and cake, then what's fruitcake? What? What? Sorry, Opus...I think I was possessed by Set the trickster there for a moment...

Correspondences

Symbol: The *was* staff and *djed* pillar; donkey, okapi, jackal, Set beast.

Color: Red, gold.

Direction: South, West.

Element: Fire, Water.

Day/Holiday/Season:
Saturday, Tuesday; July 29 (Set's birthday); Summer.

Incense/Oil: Kyphi, lotus, myrrh.

Associated deities:
Anubis, Nephthys, Osiris, Isis, Horus, Thoth, Re, Sekhmet, Lucifer, Satan, Iblis, Astarte, Anat.

The Ritual of Shiva, Lord of the Lingam: Astral Sex

By Denise Dumars

This ritual is to be performed by consenting adults only. It is based on actual experience of a heterosexual relationship, and is related from the woman's point of view. It can be easily adapted for gay or lesbian couples.

Imagine sex without fear of pregnancy, STDs, AIDS. These are just some of the benefits of astral sex. Sex on the astral plane is without the obvious physical risks of sex, but it is far from being a completely "safe" encounter. One who is experienced in astral projection may find this ritual doable after a few practice runs; for those who have not attempted astral projection or traveling on the astral plane, it is imperative that the basic method of astral projection be studied and practiced first before attempting this ritual.

Besides the benefits already mentioned, astral sex is a wonderful way for a couple to "stay in touch" when they must, through necessity, be apart. It is therefore recommended to keep a relationship strong. And if you're not in a committed relationship, it's a fun way to have casual sex without the usual risks.

The ritual is based on Shiva in his aspect of Lord of the Lingam—a god of sex. We will be working with the seven chakras and crystals. But lest this sound too foo-foo for you, heed this warning: Leaving your body is a dangerous business. You must always stay connected to it during astral travel; ideally, in this ritual you will be experiencing phenomena with both your astral body and your physical body. So be careful. Don't do astral sex with someone you wouldn't have actual sex with, and don't rush headlong into this powerful ritual unless you are sure you can both leave your body and stay in touch with it (pun intended) at the same time.

Shiva's body is often thought of as crystalline. You will need a picture of Shiva for your altar. Find the one that is the most pleasing to you. Preferably get one where he is shown with blue skin, in his purest god-form, rather than the corpse-like whitish complexion he displays in his death-god image. For a woman, the most macho, sexy picture of Shiva available is the best (Shiva is usually, to the Western eye, the most angular and "masculine" looking Hindu god). A man should choose a depiction of Shiva that he can relate to, for he is to "become" Shiva during the ritual, just as the woman becomes his lover, Parvati.

Shiva doesn't ask for much. Burn some sandalwood incense and light an orangish-yellow candle. I like the Island Mango candles from the Yankee Candle Co. for my Shiva altar. You might also want to put a small representation of Kali on the altar—but not a very scary one! A temporary altar can be set up in the bedroom, and the crystals you will need for this ritual should stay on the altar until you are ready to use them. Pass them through the smoke of the incense to clear and consecrate them before you use them for the first time; after that, you may wish to keep them together but not "clear" them each time they are used, for they can then build up sexual energy that will aid the practitioner in subsequent rituals. Always clear and consecrate them, however, if you change astral sex partners.

You will need the following crystals to correspond to seven chakras:

Chakra #1: A red stone such as rhodocrosite, ruby, rhodonite, or garnet.

Chakra #2: An orange stone such as carnelian, coral, fire opal, or orange agate.

Chakra #3: A yellow stone such as topaz, citrine, amber, yellow or sapphire.

Chakra #4: A green stone is traditionally used for the heart chakra, such as aventurine, jade, green tourmaline, emerald, for example. But many like to use pink for the heart; if you wish to, you can use rose quartz, a pink pearl, pink tourmaline, or rhodocrosite.

Chakra #5: A bright blue stone such as turquoise, aquamarine, blue topaz, or sapphire.

Chakra #6: An indigo stone such as lapis lazuli or a very dark sapphire; if these are not available, an amethyst will do.

Chakra #7: A violet stone such as tanzanite, amethyst, or if you've used purple for the sixth chakra, use a clear quartz crystal—preferably a crystal point.

If you wish to draw your beloved closer you may anoint your chakra points with any love-drawing oil; the synthetics are sold in every metaphysical shop or botanica, or you can choose some rose oil or perfume, or Shiva's favorite, sandalwood. But this step may be regarded as optional.

As you prepare for bed, light the candle and incense (you will snuff the candle before actually beginning the ritual). Go through your usual bedtime routine.

You will be nude during this ritual, so if you usually wear sleepwear, plan to put it on afterwards. Kneel before the altar. Prostrate yourself so that your forehead touches the floor. Now sit back up on your heels and face Shiva, and chant his mantra as many times as you wish, but no less than three: *Om Namah Shivaya.* If Kali is present on the altar, you will also want to chant her mantra: *Jai Ma, Jai Jai Ma.*

Chant the mantra until it induces a light hypnotic state. It is at this point that you may anoint your chakras, while still before the altar. Begin with the root chakra, anointing the base of your spine and the lowest edge of your genitals. Then anoint the lower abdomen and genitals, then the stomach, heart, throat, third eye, and finally the crown of your head.

Now the fun begins! Snuff the candle and get into bed. Lie on your back, and place each of the crystals upon the appropriate chakra (the root crystal should be placed on your pubic bone, the crown chakra can rest on the pillow touching the top of your head). Now take three deep pranic breaths while visualizing pure crystalline white light surrounding and protecting you. You should feel slightly buzzed from the chanting and the breathing. Now you are going to take three deep breaths, visualizing each chakra in its clearest colorful form and spinning clockwise. You will begin to feel aroused.

Now visualize your lover. While still visualizing him or her, send your astral form away from your body, while still feeling it connected to you and protected by the white light. See the same thing happening with your lover's astral body. The two of you will meet in what appears to be the black expanse of the universe, unless you have previously agreed upon a particular "background" for this activity.

Draw your lover's astral form toward you. As the two of you meet in the astral realm, simultaneously imagine the two of you meeting in the mundane realm. Feel your lover's body upon or beside yours. When you feel contact has been made, commence with whatever sexual activity you prefer. This can be purely astral or you can simultaneously self-stimulate. When the encounter is over, speak any words of parting that you wish, and draw your astral form back into your body with the cord. Remove the stones to your altar or leave them beside the bed. Now is the time to dress for bed if you feel more comfortable that way. Pleasant dreams, and remember to thank Shiva in the morning.

Correspondences

Symbol: Lingam, trident, crescent moon, snake, tiger skin, skull, jatas (dreadlocks).

Color: Blue, white, black, gray, red.

Direction: All.

Element: All.

Day/Holiday/Season:
          Shiva ratri (usually in March, by lunar calendar).

Incense/Oil: Sandalwood, patchouli, frangipani.

Associated deities:
          Rudra, Pashupati, Bhairava, Sati, Parvati, Kali, Ganga, Ganesha, Vishnu, Brahma.

Tezcatlipoca:
Mirror, Mirror: Divining the Truth

By Denise Dumars

Yeah, yeah, it's everybody's favorite episode of classic *Star Trek*. You know, the one where Kirk and Spock discover a parallel world where all the usual suspects are brutal, evil, and have really cool uniforms. Mr. Spock even has a mustache and goatee so you know he's evil, too. What's the point of this? Well, when we look in the mirror, what do we see? What we want to see, usually. To use an extreme example, studies have shown that anorexia victims still see themselves as fat when they look in the mirror, even if they are near death from starvation.

Be honest with yourself for a moment. What do you see when you read the cards for yourself? When you scry? How do you interpret a reading someone else has done for you? In other words, are you always honest about what you or someone else sees in the cards? Whether we know it or not, we often see what we want to see in the cards, whether we are reading for ourselves or not. It's hard not to lie to ourselves. I've done it innumerable times when reading for myself.

If you have this problem or suspect that you do, and if you feel you want the truth from divination, then you will want to try this method of divination. Tezcatlipoca is often brutally honest, so don't be surprised if you see something you were hoping not to have to face. There is a time and place for divination as with everything else; if you think you hear Jack Nicholson's voice shouting "You can't handle the truth!" in your ear, then save the reading for another time. But I'm willing to bet that you will want to know the truth sooner or later.

The purpose of divination is twofold: First, to clarify the situation, to help explain ourselves and the world around us. Second, it is to make prophesy, to see the future and what it holds in a certain situation or in a more general sense. Tezcatlipoca's dark mirror can be used for either purpose; he used it himself in both ways.

A few simple objects (one of them a bit expensive) are needed to set up your Smoking Mirror: copal incense and charcoal tabs (copal resin is readily available), red candles, a black cloth to cover the mirror when not in use, and a black altar cloth are all you need in addition to your scrying tool. Black scrying mirrors are all the rage now, so you should be able to find one in a catalog such as *AzureGreen* or go to Katlyn Breene's Website to order one of her stunning original creations. If you prefer it to a black scrying mirror, do what Renaissance mathematician, astrologer, and necromancer Dr. John Dee did and buy a black crystal ball. If you look around a lot and price is no object, you may even find a crystal ball or scrying mirror made of the same substance as Tezcatlipoca's: obsidian.

Scrying takes time, practice, and dedication. Since you are investing money in the props, plan to invest time in perfecting your scrying technique. Patience and concentration—as well as courage—are needed. Tarot cards are a piece of cake compared to scrying. At least with cards you have recognizable images, and a book to look them up in. With scrying you're on your own. You'll be working from your own talent and that of Tezcatlipoca's, which you have tapped into. Each time you scry, be sure to thank Tezcatlipoca afterwards. Do not "dismiss" the god.

Set aside time on a regular basis to work with the mirror. Allow yourself an hour at a time to set up, cast a Circle, scry, and power down. To begin, set up your scrying altar as above. If you wish, you may offer Tez a piece of fruit (if you can't find a sapote, then any tropical fruit such as papaya or mango will do) and place his image on the altar. I hear that Marvel Comics has made him a superhero (oy, gevalt!) so if you find that image of him comforting, buy the comic and place it near the mirror. Otherwise, find an authentic artistic rendering—there are innumerable images of Tez from the Aztecs that can be found in virtually any book on Aztec mythology or on the Internet.

If you want to get into the mood more fully, you can put together an outfit to wear while scrying. Maybe something made of Guatemalan cloth, which comes in a variety of beautiful designs and colors. A woman could wear a red skirt and a *huipil*, a traditional Mexican blouse. A man might wear a black *guayabera* and black pants. If you want to go all-out, buy an obsidian knife to use as an athame.

Divine in a darkened room. You may do so in the daytime, but make sure the room can be sufficiently dark so that no bright light is reflecting off the mirror. Nighttime is, of course, more appropriate, but we do what we can!

Some more tips before we begin...Tezcatlipoca can be a little spooky. Do as we gamblers do and don't sit with your back to the door. If being alone with Tez bothers you at all, place another image on your altar that will act as your protector. A picture of someone who is culturally appropriate, such as Frida Kahlo or Che Guevara would be a good choice. And if the red candles bother you, use white. Ground and shield (see "How Is the Dark Archetype Accessed?"). Make sure that the "shield" you set up is porous enough to let in the visions you hope to see in the mirror. In other words, no armor! With your black-handled athame, cast a Circle. Light the incense and the candles. Now focus on the mirror.

There are two ways to invoke Tezcatlipoca before you begin to scry. The first method is to repeat these words. You will need to repeat them each time you scry:

> *Tezcatlipoca, show me truth. Let me see what you see*
> *in the smoky mirror. Allow my gaze to clear the smoke*
> *and see the reality.*

But there is another way to invoke the god. In the story of Snow White, when the queen asks, "Mirror, mirror, on the wall, who's the fairest of them all?" the mirror answers. This means that the mirror is inhabited by a spirit. If you would prefer to invoke the spirit of Tezcatlipoca in your mirror when you scry, say the following:

> *Tezcatlipoca, reside in this mirror. Show me your truth. I*
> *look into your eyes and see reflected my reality. Be here*
> *now!*

Fifteen minutes of scrying is enough to start with. After you have performed the invocation, inhale the heady odor of the copal and look alternately at each candle flame to refresh your eyes. But for the most part, keep your eyes on the mirror for 15 minutes, blinking enough to keep your eyes feeling rested. Make sure that if you wear corrective lenses to keep them on and use eye drops ahead of time if you think you'll need them. After a few minutes of looking at the mirror, the middle of it will start to cloud or look fuzzy. Keep an open mind. Quiet your mental chatter. Try not to have preconceived ideas about what you might see. Try this exercise several times before scrying for any specific purpose. If there is a window nearby, draw the drapes away from it if you can see the stars or the moon, unless you find this too distracting.

If you find yourself unable to see any images after a few practice sessions, try asking Tezcatlipoca directly for wisdom. Say what you're looking for in your own words, in as straightforward a manner as possible. I promise I won't say, "I told you so" if he shows you something you'd rather not see!

Scrying is a skill worth honing. You will find that in the process you are also honing your magickal abilities and your ability to concentrate, which is always a good thing.

In parts of the United States that have large Mexican-American populations, the Day of the Dead is often celebrated by Pagans. Tez can be a great addition to your Dia de los Muertos event; after all, he lives with the Lord and Lady of the Dead most of the time. Have a man who has practiced this technique put on a black cloak and a black floppy hat. After your ritual is over, have him dress in his Tezcatlipoca duds and scry for those assembled.

Correspondences

Symbol:	Obsidian mirror, two reeds, red or black face paint, jaguar, bear, drought, darkness, rattles, flute, obsidian knife.
Color:	Black, red, blue, white.
Direction:	North, East.

Element: Earth, Air.

Day/Holiday/Season:
         May.

Incense/Oil: Copal, tobacco, marijuana.

Associated deities:
         Quetzalcoatl, Xipe Totec, Coatlicue, Obsidian
         Knife Butterfly, Xochiquetzal, Huitzilopchtli,
         Tlaloc, Satan.

Volos: Embracing Your Inner Werewolf

By Denise Dumars

Yes, this references the idea of "embracing your inner child" because your inner child is that wild thing, the werewolf! You will need suitable music such as a recording of wolf calls, Warren Zevon's "Werewolves of London," Duran Duran's "Hungry Like the Wolf," or any good magickal Russian classical music (see Baba Yaga's "Hen Party"), and some good Russian or Polish vodka or, if you prefer, a red ale or dark beer such as Red Wolf lager or Old Rasputin Imperial Russian stout. Unlike many rituals, this one must have alcohol present. If you cannot drink it, you may use spring water or any red juice as the libation, but an alcoholic beverage such as those described above must be offered on the altar. You will need a few slices of Russian rye bread or another "peasant" bread. A suitable offering to Volos would be money donated to or volunteer work done for a wolf rescue group or other threatened species conservation group.

The altar should be prepared with traditional representations of the four Elements. For incense, choose pine or any woodsy incense; better yet, use an aromatherapy oil in a diffuser—pine, fir, cedarwood, birch, or any combination of woodsy scents encourage the feeling of being in a forest and can stand for both Air and Fire. Evergreens, birch twigs, wheat, hops, or ferns (traditional in Eastern European magick) can form the décor. A cup of vodka or ale and a slice of dark bread form the offering and stand for the Elements Water and Earth. Candles can be green and brown to suggest the forest and the soil of Mother Moist Earth, or blue to suggest the waters of the Volga.

Anoint the candles with some of the aromatherapy oil or with Russian amber resin, a scent that calls the ancestors. (Remember, you got your werewolf heritage from somewhere!) You may anoint yourself with Russian amber oil as well, and wear amber jewelry if you wish. On the altar there should be an image of a wolf, whether in the form of a statue, photograph, or artistic rendering. Many Native American groups use wolf imagery as totems; their representations of wolves are very appropriate and evocative. If you have any statues of other Slavic deities then display them as well.

You will need a mirror and a scrying tool. A crystal ball is fine, but a dark scrying mirror (see Tezcatlipoca: Mirror, Mirror) is even more appropriate. The mirror should be placed glass side down or covered (a compact can be used in a pinch; after all, you look in it to assess your looks, which is certainly appropriate to this ritual) until the prescribed moment in the ritual.

Cast the Circle. Elementals will willingly come into this sylvan environment, or if you want to use Slavic deities in the invocations, you can use Dazhbog for Air, Perun for Fire, Rusalka for Water, and Baba Yaga for Earth. Then take a few moments to ground and center, particularly focusing on the "roots" that extend from the bottom of your feet down into the moist Earth. Now you should feel connected to the spirit of the pantheon.

Take a draught from the cup. Close your eyes and look deep within yourself. What makes you angry? In what ways are you unable to vent your anger? Who has misjudged you, or made you feel bad about yourself when deep inside you know they are wrong about you? How have you been made to feel odd, different, or unconventional? Who has said you do not meet their standards of taste, beauty, competence, or wisdom? Who are they to judge? Who has called you "weird," "strange," or criticized your looks?

Now allow yourself to feel what you will feel. Shout if you are angry. Cuss out the person who criticized your outfit or belittled your creativity! Scream, tear at your garments or throw them off, get down on the floor and howl at the moon. Do whatever you can to expunge the negativity that others have put upon you. Take some time to vent the pain, anger, and righteous indignation you feel.

When you feel that you have vented enough, compose yourself and sit before the altar. Now look into the black mirror or the crystal ball. Own your werewolf nature: See the beast that screams when in pain, that snarls when angered, that fights back when attacked. Honor your differences from others. Own your individuality.

The irony is that once you own these things, you are no longer alone. You are part of the pack; wolves, like humans, are social animals. Now you are part of a group who will accept you for who you are, for you are unique, as is each of us. Keep looking into the crystal. *Now* do you see the werewolf? Feel his power. Admire his strength, his beauty. Note his loyalty to his pack, his playfulness. He no longer frightens you, for you are no longer alone, and you no longer buy into society's depiction of him as evil.

Once you feel comfortable in your wolf skin, it is time to return to your human form. Pick up the mirror. Look into it. See your human self; see integrated into your personality all the best qualities of both wolves and humans. Now you are whole. You are who you were meant to be. Now toast yourself with the libation, then toast Volos, and leave the bread and the rest of the drink for him. Open the Circle. Russian teacakes (also called Mexican wedding cookies) and strong tea (such as Russian Caravan) are good for grounding. Repeat the ritual whenever you have had it up to your muzzle in other peoples' attitudes. This ritual is especially recommended for those with low self-esteem; it may be repeated once a month at the full moon for positive reinforcement.

CORRESPONDENCES

Symbol: Wolf, werewolf, dog, stalks of rye or wheat, corn dolly.

Color: Red, brown, gray.

Direction: North.

Element: Earth.

Day/Holiday/Season:
St. Blaise's Day (Feb. 3); Halloween.

Incense/Oil: Birch, pine, fir, Russian amber resin.

Associated deities/Saints:
Weles, Veles, Velnius, Perun, Mokosh, Rusalka, Baba Yaga, Dazhbog, Chernobog, Koschei, Pashupati, Loki; St. Vlas (St. Blaise).

References

Abbatecola, Joni, Ph.D. Personal interview.

Albright, William Powell. *Yahweh and the Gods of Canaan*. New York: Doubleday & Co., 1968.

Andreas, Peter. *Norse Mythology*. New York: The American-Scandinavian Foundation, 1926.

Arcarti, Kristyna. *A Beginner's Guide to Runes*. London: Hodder & Stoughton, 1994.

Aswynn, Freya. *Northern Mysteries & Magick*. St. Paul: Llewellyn, 1998.

Baring, Anne & Jules Cashford. *The Myth of the Goddess: Evolution of an Image*, London: Penguin/Arkana, 1993.

Beck, Stephen, Ph.D. Personal interview.

Begg, Ean. *The Cult of the Black Virgin*. London: Penguin/Arkana, revised 1996.

The Bible: King James Version. Minneapolis: World Wide Publications, 1976.

Brundage, Burr Cartwright. *The Fifth Sun*. Austin Tex.: University of Texas Press, 1979.

Budapest, Zsuzsanna E. *The Grandmother of Time*. San Francisco: Harper & Row, 1989.

Burland, C. A., and Werner Forman. *Feathered Serpent and Smoking Mirror*. New York: G.P. Putnam's Sons, 1975.

Campbell, Joseph. *The Masks of God: Primitive Mythology*. New York: Viking Press, 1959.

Chesterton, Gilbert Keith. "The Black Virgin." Courtesy of Catholic Information Network (CIN) Copyright © 1997 Catholic Information Network (CIN)—14 Apr. 2003. <*http://www.cin.org/blackvir.html*>.

Craze, Richard. *Hell: An Illustrated History of the Netherworld*. Berkeley: Conari Press, 1996.

Cross, Samuel Hazzard, and Olgerd P. Sherbowitz-Wetzor, eds.. *The Russian Primary Chronicle*. Laurentian Text. Cambridge: The Mediaeval Academy of America.

Culbertson, Judi and Tom Randall. *Permanent Californians*. Chelsea, Vt.: Chelsea Green Publishing, 1989.

Dickinson, Emily. *The Poems of Emily Dickinson*. Ralph W. Franklin ed. Cambridge, Mass.: The Belknap Press of Harvard University Press, 1998.

Farnell, Lewis R. *The Cults of the Greek States, Vol. 1*. Oxford: Clarendon Press, 1896.

Forrest, M. Isidora. *Isis Magic: Cultivating a Relationship with the Goddess of 10,000 Names*. St. Paul: Llewellyn Publications, 2001.

George, Demetra. *Mysteries of the Dark Moon: the Healing Power of the Dark Goddess*. San Francisco: Harper, 1992.

Gimbutas, Marija. *The Civilization of the Goddess: The World of Old Europe*, New York: Harper Collins.

Gleason, Judith. *Oya: In Praise of an African Goddess*. San Francisco: HarperSanFrancisco, 1992.

Gonzalez-Wippler, Migene. *Santería: African Magic in Latin America*. Bronx: Original Products, 1987.

Graves, Robert and Raphael Patar. *Hebrew Myths: The Book of Genesis*. New York: Doubleday and Co., 1964.

Gray, Louis Herbert, Ed. *The Mythology of All Races*. 13 vols. Boston: Herbert Jones Co., 1918.

Grimm, Jacob. *Teutonic Mythology*. 4 vols. New York: Dover, 1966.

Gustafson, Fred. *The Black Madonna*. Boston: Sigo Press, 1990.

Harding, Elizabeth U. *Kali: The Black Goddess of Dakshineswar.* York Beach, Maine: Nicolas-Hays, Inc., 1993.

Hart, George. *A Dictionary of Egyptian Gods & Goddesses.* London: Routledge and Kegan Publishing Inc., 1986.

Hawley, John Stratton, and Donna Marie Wulff, Eds. *Devi: Goddesses of India.* Berkeley: University of California Press, 1996.

Hubbs, Joanna. *Mother Russia: the Feminine Myth in Russian Culture.* Bloomington: Indiana University Press, 1988.

Jansen, Eva Rudy. *The Book of Hindu Imagery: Gods, Manifestations and their Meaning.* Havelte, Holland: Binkey Kok Publications BV, 1993.

Johnson, Bob. *Corporate Magick: Mystical Tools for Business Success.* New York: Citadel, 2002.

Johnson, Kenneth. *Slavic Sorcery: Shamanic Journey of Initiation.* St. Paul: Llewellyn Publications, 1998.

Kerényi, Carl. *The Gods of the Greeks.* New York: Thames and Hudson, Ltd., 1951.

Kinsley, David R. *Hindu Goddesses: Visions of the Divine Feminine in the Hindu Religious Tradition.* Berkeley: University of California Press, 1986.

Koltuv, Barbara Black. *The Book of Lilith.* York Beach, Maine: Nicolas-Hays, Inc., 1986.

Larrington, Carolyne, Ed. *The Feminist Companion to Mythology.* London: Pandora, 1992.

Larson, Gerald James, C. Scott Littleton and Jaan Puhvel, Eds. *Myth in Indo-European Antiquity.* Berkeley: University of California Press, 1974.

Le Braz, Anatole. *The Celtic Legend of the Beyond.* Trans. by Derek Bryce. Wales: Llanerch Enterprises, 1986.

Maas. A. J."Lucifer," *The Catholic Encyclopedia,* Volume IX, Online Edition <*http://www.newadvent.org/cathen/ 09410a.htm*>.

Markham, Roberta H., and Peter T. Markman. *The Flayed God: the Mesoamerican Mythological Tradition: Sacred Texts and Images from Pre-Colombian Mexico and Central America.* San Francisco: Harper, 1992.

Marlowe, Christopher. *Dr. Faustus.* New York: Dover Publications, Inc. 1994.

Meeks, Dimitri, and Christine Favard-Meeks. *Daily Life of the Egyptian Gods.* Trans. G. M. Goshgarian. Ithaca: Cornell University Press, 1996.

Monaghan, Pat. *The Book of Goddesses & Heroines.* St. Paul: Llewellyn Publications, 1990.

Mookerjee, Ajit. *Kali, the Feminine Force.* Rochester, Vermont: Destiny Books, 1988.

Moss, Leonard and Stephen Cappannari. "In Quest of the Black Virgin: She Is Black Because She Is Black," in *Mother Worship,* Chapel Hill: University of North Carolina Press, 1982.

Moura, Ann. *Green Witchcraft II.* St. Paul: Llewellyn, 1999.

Norder, Dan. © 1999. *Cronus: Titan, Reaper, Father Time, Crow?* from Mythology Web, "As the Crow Flies," (Sept. 1999), <*http://www.mythology.com/*>.

Osborn, Kevin and Dana L. Burgess. *The Complete Idiot's Guide to Classical Mythology.* New York: Alpha Books, 1998.

Otto, Walter F. *Dionysus, Myth and Cult.* Trans. Robert B. Palmer. Bloomington: Indiana University Press, 1965.

Pereira, Filomena. "Lilith, the Edge of Forever." Thesis D. San Jose State University, 1995.

Richardson, Alan. *Earth God Rising: the Return of the Male Mysteries.* St. Paul: Llewellyn Publications, 1992.

Rudwin, Maximillian. *The Devil in Legend and Literature.* Chicago: The Open Court Publishing Co., 1931.

Russell, Jeffrey Burton. *The Devil: Perceptions of Evil from Antiquity to Primitive Christianity,* Ithaca: Cornell University Press, 1977.

Schefold, Karl. *Myth and Legend in Early Greek Art.* Translated by Audrey Hicks. New York: H. N. Abrams, 1966.

Spence, Lewis. *The Myths of Mexico & Peru.* New York: Farrar & Rinehart.

Suther Judith D. "The Gorgon Medusa," in M. South, ed. *Mythical and Fabulous Creatures: A Source Book and Research Guide.* Connecticut: Greenwood Press: 1987, 164-78.

Teish, Luisah. *Jambalaya.* San Francisco: HarperSanFrancisco, 1985.

TeVelde, H. *Seth, God of Confusion.* Leiden: E. J. Brill, 1967.

Thorsson, Edred. *Runelore.* Weiser: Boston, 1987.

Turville-Petre, E. O. G. *Myth and Religion of the North: The Religion of Ancient Scandinavia.* New York: Holt, Rinehart, & Winston, 1964.

Vaillant, George C. *Aztecs of Mexico.* Garden City, N.Y.: Doubleday, 1962.

Van Scott, Miriam. *The Encyclopedia of Hell.* New York: St. Martin's Press, 1998.

Vega, Marta Moreno. *The Altar of My Soul: The Living Traditions of Santería.* New York: One World, 2000.

Von Rudolff, Robert. *Hekate in Ancient Greek Religion.* Victoria, B. C.: Horned Owl Publishing, 1999.

Walker, Barbara. *The Woman's Encyclopedia of Myths and Secrets.* San Francisco: Harper & Row, 1983.

Warwick, Ioanna-Veronika. Personal interview.

Watterson, Barbara. *Gods of Ancient Egypt.* Phoenix: Sutton Publishing Limited, 1996.

Webb, Don. *The Seven Faces of Darkness: Practical Typhonian Magick.* Smithville, Tex.: Runa Raven Press, 1996.

Wendell, Leilah. *Our Name is Melancholy: The Complete Books of Azrael.* New Orleans: Westgate Press, 1992.

Wilk, Stephen R. *Medusa: Solving the Mystery of the Gorgon.* New York: Oxford University Press, 2000.

Wilkinson, Richard H. *Reading Egyptian Art.* London: Thames and Hudson Ltd., 1992.

Wood, Juliette. *The Celtic Book of Living and Dying.* San Francisco: Chronicle Books, 2000.

Woodward, Jocelyn M. *Perseus: a Study in Greek Art and Legend.* Cambridge: Cambridge University Press, 1937.

Index